Summer's Squall

Praise for *Island of Miracles* by Amy Schisler

"I can already see this book as a movie on the Hallmark Channel."
Blogger and author, Anne Kennedy

"A beautiful account of the love and the healing support of community!"
Christian writer, Chandi Owen

Praise for Award Winning *Whispering Vines* by Amy Schisler

"The heartbreaking, endearing, charming, and romantic scenes will surely inveigle you to keep reading."
Serious Reading Book Review

"Schisler's writing is a verbal masterpiece of art."
Alex Jacobs, Author, The Dreamer

"Amy Schisler's Whispering Vines is well styled, fast paced, and engaging, the perfect recipe for an excellent book."
Judith Reveal, Author, Editor, Reviewer

Praise for Award Winning *Picture Me* by Amy Schisler

"This book kept me turning the pages until the end, great suspense!"
Harps Romance Book Review

"Interesting little mystery!! An awesome story with great characters, so I am giving it a full four fangs!"
Paranormal Romance and Authors that Rock

Praise for *A Place to Call Home* by Amy Schisler

"The action begins on the first page and does not stop until the ending. This debut novel is a novel of hope as well as one of adventure."
Elena Maria Vidal, Reviewer and Author, The Paradise Tree

Also Available by Amy Schisler

Suspense Novels
A Place to Call Home
Picture Me

Contemporary Fiction
Whispering Vines
Island of Miracles

Children's Books
Crabbing With Granddad
The Greatest Gift

Summer's Squall

By Amy Schisler

ISBN: 978-0692946176

Published by:
Chesapeake Sunrise Publishing
Amy Schisler
Bozman, MD
2017

Dear Readers

When you're reading about somewhere you love, it's easy to get lost in the story, allowing the characters and setting to sweep you away to another time or place. The same is true for writing. I derive immense pleasure introducing readers to the places I love most in the world. My family is lucky because we are able to enjoy the waterways of the Chesapeake Bay and Atlantic Ocean near our home in Maryland, and we are able to rejuvenate our minds and souls at our cabin in the majestic Rocky Mountains. Though the two locales are quite different, each holds a special place in our hearts.

In the Southwestern region of Colorado, there is a subdivision called Blue Mesa, high atop a mountain and nestled between the cities of Montrose and Gunnison. Just under an hour from the subdivision is Lake City, the "most remote county in the lower 48," according to the town's official website. But Lake City is more than a small town in a remote area. It's where 372 people, 111 families, call home all year but where thousands of tourists travel for skiing and snowmobiling in the winter and hiking, four-wheeling, and lots of old-fashioned outdoor fun in the summer. It's where nobody can hide from each other but anybody can hide from the outside world. With limited cell service, no fast food or major retail stores, and no stop lights or traffic, our family considers it the perfect place to spend a summer day and the best place in the country to spend the Fourth of July.

While the Lake City in *Summer's Squall,* is the same one in Southwest Colorado, locals and frequent visitors will notice that I have taken the liberty to change some of the names of the businesses and have even given the school a football team (thanks to a fictional decision by Hinsdale and Gunnison Counties to allow boys to attend the school if they live in the proximity and want to play ball). I've also taken liberty with some of the geography and native residents. The descriptions of the city and the surrounding areas, including the mountaintop subdivision, are exactly as described in the book; except they're even more beautiful to the human eye than the reader's mind. All of the characters and the situations they encounter are figments of my imagination.

So, I invite you to come away with me to my favorite small town and some my favorite wilderness areas in the world. I hope that you fall in love with them the way my family did. And maybe, God willing, I will see you there next July. There's no place else I'd rather be.

Thank you, Ken, Rebecca, Katie Ann, and Morgan, my wonderful family, who support my writing, my research. Thank you for understanding my need to be in control that helps me maintain my creative juices, be organized, and meet my deadlines. Thank you, Mom and Dad, Judy and Richard MacWilliams, for your unwavering support. I couldn't do anything that I do without your love and encouragement.

Thank you, Dan and Debbie Froelich and Michelle Zamora, for your friendship and inspiration. The support of my friends and readers makes all the work worth it!

Thank you to my editor, Judy Reveal, and proofreaders, Cheryl Baummer, Cindy Lewis, Anne Novey, Debbie Nisson, and Maureen Parkhurst. A big thanks to my beta readers, Frances Cifuni, Shannon Dolgos, Cindy Lyon, Mary Silfka, and Tammi Warren. I appreciate all your help more than you know.

To the men and women in blue who put their lives on the line every day so that the rest of us may be free from harm. And to the teachers and guidance counselors in schools everywhere who give so much of themselves so that our children may grow and succeed.

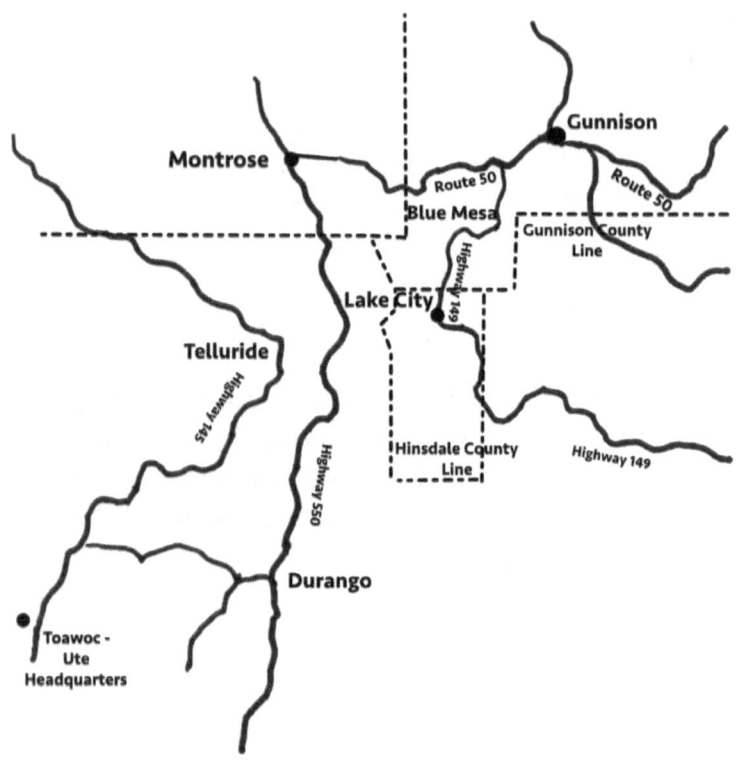

Map of Lake City, Montrose, Gunnison
and surrounding areas.

CHAPTER ONE

"Please, Abe, we need you. Please say you'll come," Megan pleaded over the phone.

"I'll try, Megan, but I can't make any promises. I have a job here and no jurisdiction there. Even if I came, I don't know what good it would do." Abe Lankton could see his boss motioning to him through the glass. "I've got to go. We're going into our morning briefing."

"Please, Abe, I'm begging you."

The pain in his cousin's voice caused a knot to form in the pit of his stomach. How much trouble was this friend in? And what could he do about it? He didn't have any pull in any other part of Maryland, not to mention in Colorado. Nevertheless, he found himself giving in to his cousin, as always.

"I'll see what I can do."

"Thank you, Abe, thank you. I knew I could count on you."

"Don't get your hopes up, Megan. I said I'll try."

"Call me when you arrive at the airport. I'll pick you up."

Abe shook his head as he disconnected the call. There was no reasoning with the girl, never had been.

"Everything okay, Lank?" his superior asked as they walked to the briefing.

"Not really, Sarge. My cousin wants me to head out West to help her with some problem a friend of hers is having. I told her that I don't have jurisdiction there. She just won't listen."

"Trouble with the law?"

"Sounds like it. She was kind of vague. I don't really know what's going on."

"Lank, are you close?" Sergeant McCain tugged at Abe Lankton's sleeve and stopped him at the door.

"Yeah, we grew up together. We've always been there for each other. She was there for me when..." His voice trailed off and he looked away.

"When you got hurt," his sergeant supplied.

"Yeah. She gave up most of her junior year of high school and part of senior year to keep me company and encourage me to move, walk, live." He held back the tears as he thought about the year he spent in bed, believing he'd never walk again and about the part that Megan played in his recovery.

"Then go. You have the time. Take it. Return the favor."

"Sir, with all due respect, I don't know that there's anything I can do to help her."

"And you don't know that there isn't. At the very least, be there for her like she was for you." McCain shook his head. "You work too hard, Lank. If you're going to work your life away, at least spend some of the time helping your family. You don't have anything here so big it can't wait."

Lank gnawed on the inside of his cheek. He knew McCain was right, but the last thing he wanted to do was find out that his cousin was involved with someone who had broken the law or was mixed up in something bad. On the other hand, she wasn't the type to get herself involved in something like that, and she sounded desperate.

"Lank, it's an order," McCain said before heading into the briefing.

"Damn," Lank said under his breath. It looked like he was heading out West, like it or not. He didn't know what was worse, the possibility that he would let Megan down or the inevitability of having to fly.

Lank picked up his bag from the conveyer belt and looked around the small airport in Montrose, Colorado, thanking his lucky stars that he was safely on the ground. He felt out of place in his dress slacks and sports coat. Most of the men wore jeans, boots, and either a baseball cap or a cowboy hat. For a moment, he wondered if he'd accidentally gotten off the plane in Texas, but then he heard a familiar squeal. He braced himself for impact as Megan slammed into him and wrapped her arms around his neck.

"I knew you'd come," she said as she let go and settled back onto the balls of her feet. At just five-foot-two, she had a personality that was larger than life and made her appear much taller in Lank's eyes. She was more than short compared to his six-foot-two frame. She wore hospital-type scrubs, and her dark hair was pulled back in a ponytail. Sunglasses were perched on her head. Lank always thought his cousin looked like a baby doll with her twinkling blue eyes and smooth complexion. She always wore a smile, and just seeing her brightened his day no matter his mood. "How was the flight?" She grabbed her sunglasses as they fell off her head when she looked up at him.

"Don't ask," Lank answered, giving her a look she knew all too well.

"It couldn't have been that bad. You don't look any worse for the wear."

"Yeah, well, my heart still isn't properly seated back in my chest yet."

Megan grabbed his hand. "I'm sorry. I know how much you hate flying. But I'm so grateful that you're here and that you're going to help."

"Don't get your hopes up, Megan. I have no idea what you expect from me. I came only because you asked."

"I know," she said, nodding her head. "It's a long shot, but if there's anything you can do, anything at all, it would mean the world to me."

"I still don't know exactly what it is that you or your friend needs help with."

They walked through the small airport and outside into the bright sunlight. The parking lot was miniscule compared to the one at BWI, but that wasn't surprising. The entire Montrose airport could fit inside just the TSA security area back at the Baltimore airport. Other than the airport, the difference that hit Lank right away was the smell, or lack thereof. The air was crisp and clean like a fall morning after a night of rain. In addition, it was quiet, save for the few cars and trucks on the road passing in front. There were no car horns, police sirens, or people shouting. It was a pleasant change already, or maybe he was just happy to be off the plane.

"I'll explain everything on the ride to the house," Megan said as she opened the back of her Chevy Blazer. "I got it washed just for you." Lank tossed his bag inside and closed the shiny, dark blue door. He joined her inside the SUV and put on his seatbelt.

Megan was quiet as they headed out of town. Lank tried to read her expression, but she stared straight ahead as she drove down the wide street that was flanked on each side by Western wear stores and tourist shops. A restaurant with a buffalo outside drew his attention, as did a blonde-haired beauty rocking cowboy boots and tight jeans as she strolled down the sidewalk.

Once they were outside the city limits, Lank marveled at the mountains on every side and a sky bluer than he had ever seen. He glanced at his phone and noticed that he had no alerts then realized he had no service.

"It won't work outside of town. Not until we get up the mountain," Megan told him.

"How far to your house?"

"About an hour."

"An hour? I thought you said you lived close to the airport."

"I do," she smiled. "An hour is a short drive out here."

Lank watched the scenery roll by. The panorama was a mixture of mountain peaks, running streams, and sprawling hills and meadows of sage dotted with grazing cattle. The road was a loose black ribbon that meandered through a vibrant earth tone terrain that was never flat. It was a far cry from the Baltimore suburbs.

"So, talk," he finally said when it seemed that Megan was not going to say anything.

She raked her bottom lip through her teeth a couple times. Taking a slow breath and then releasing a long exhale, she pursed her lips for a second before beginning. "It started a few weeks ago. At first, Summer thought it was nothing, but then strange things started happening. And now she's scared that she might be in danger."

"Whoa, slow down. First, tell me who Summer is."

"My best friend. She's Johnny's sister. She's the guidance counselor at the school in Lake City and lives alone up on the mountain not far from our place. She bought a piece of land up there and built a cabin that she moved into this past spring. Her parents wanted her to stay in town, but since we're up there, she's not exactly alone. I mean, if we get a lot of snow or lose power or something, she can head to our place. But now that this stuff is happening, she's afraid that her parents are going to freak out. She hasn't told them, of course. They'll want her to sell the house and move back in with them. She's twenty-seven. There's no way that's going to happen."

Lank blinked. Megan always could talk up a storm without ever pausing to take a breath.

"Megan, I still have no idea what you're talking about. Can we start at the beginning?"

"Oh, sorry. Okay," she thought for a moment. Nodding to herself, she continued, "That would be the flowers. A few weeks ago, a FedEx truck left a bouquet of roses for her at school. Dead roses. And I've read enough mysteries and seen enough movies to know that nobody sends dead roses to brighten your day."

"Did she call the police?"

"She did, but they said there wasn't anything they could do. There was no note, and the delivery was sent from a Kinko's in Montrose. There was no name, and no way to trace who sent them. The police said it was probably a prank."

"And she has reason to believe otherwise?"

"Well, no, not at first, but don't you think it's strange? I mean, who does that kind of thing?"

"Megan, please tell me that you called me out here for more than that." Lank shook his head and wondered what the hell was going on. Was this a joke? Had Megan seriously brought him out here for this? He tried not to get angry with her, but he had a bad feeling that this trip was a waste of time and money.

"Of course not. I wouldn't do that." She frowned and cast him a sidelong glance that shook her long, brown ponytail.

"Then I don't see—"

"A few days later, the barking started."

"The barking?"

"Yeah, Cosmo - that's Summer's dog - started waking her up at night with his barking. He's not a barker, so it was strange from the start, but she figured he was hearing coyotes or a bear or a mountain lion, so she didn't worry about it."

"She didn't worry about a bear or a mountain lion?" Lank asked incredulously.

"Yeah, no big deal up here. We've got 'em. We just have to stay out of their way."

"Sounds like a good idea to me." Lank looked out the window, fully expecting to see dangerous predators lurking about. "Go on."

"Okay, so every so often, Cosmo would wake Summer with his emphatic barking. Something very real was out there. It was starting to bother her. I mean, she needs her sleep, right?"

Lank nodded as he watched Megan take a turn at a faster speed than he liked, and he gripped the car door while fighting back nausea. He wasn't any crazier about the idea of slamming into the giant rock face of a mountain than he was about the climb they were making in the vehicle. While enjoying the scenery, it took everything in him to concentrate on Megan and not on the perilous drop on the other side of his window.

"One night, the barking was really bad, and Cosmo kept growling at something in the darkness. In the morning, one of Summer's hummingbird feeders was smashed on the concrete below her deck. Even then, the police said there was no evidence of a crime."

"I hate to say it, but I agree. Her feeder fell and broke. So, what? The dog heard it and barked. I don't see what the big deal is."

"The big deal is that it didn't just fall. There was no wind that night, and those feeders had been up there since she moved in back in April. So, after several weeks, a light breeze causes one to fall from the deck, and it falls so hard that it gets smashed to bits? I don't think so."

"Megan, just how many mystery and suspense novels have you been reading lately? This is ridiculous." Lank's initial attempt at not becoming annoyed was gone, and his annoyance was turning to anger. "You dragged me all the way out here for this? Because you have some kind of desire to be the next Nancy Drew, and since the local Hardy boys won't listen, you figured you'd call me? Jeez, Megan, I've got murders and drug busts and human trafficking to deal with. I can't believe you brought me out here to chase imaginary hummingbird feeder vandals."

Megan turned off the highway and entered an area with dirt roads, open fields, and no trespassing signs. Cows stood in the fields, motionless, watching them as they drove by.

"Dammit, Abe, shut up and let me finish. Crap!" Megan slammed on the brakes. Lank barely had time to brace himself before his head whiplashed toward the dashboard.

"Take it easy, Megan, you're going to get us killed." When he looked up, a very large cow was standing in the middle of the road.

"Move, you stupid cow," Megan yelled at the beast before laying on her horn.

Slowly sauntering out of the way, the cow gave Megan one last look of disdain before moving far enough off the road for her to pass. Lank looked around at the dry fields, not at all what he expected to see. He knew that southern Colorado was arid, but the terrain here was almost like being in a desert except for the mountain vistas all around them. Every now and then, he saw leather-skinned cattlemen tending fences or moving cattle but didn't have time to give them much thought. A sign warned them to stay on the road and not trespass on the reservation. He assumed this was Native American land.

"I hate those cows. They think they own the road." She took a deep breath and blew it out. "Now, where was I?"

"Trying to convince me to investigate a broken bird feeder."

"Oh yeah. So, the police refused to do anything, and Summer was feeling kind of jittery."

"Is this Summer a rational person? Does she tend to come up with crazy, paranoid fairy tales about every aspect of her life?"

"Just listen," Megan said, and Lank detected a level of animosity that he had never before seen in his cousin. "She's not crazy or paranoid. She's a perfectly normal, rational human being. And someone is messing with her. Seriously, I think she's in trouble." The animosity disappeared and was replaced with honest concern.

"Unless there's more, I don't see—"

"There's more," Megan said. "A few nights later, Cosmo starts up again. Now Summer's at her wit's end with her dog, thinking that maybe the police are right, and the dog is just making her jumpy; but in the morning, she opens the door to go to work, and there's a dead mule deer on her doorstep."

"So, there was an animal out there after all," Lank said. "It probably managed to get on the deck somehow, panicked, and knocked down the feeder."

"No," she said emphatically, shaking her head. "The deer wasn't just dead. It had been shot and then put in front of her door."

"Maybe it crawled there and died." Lank was still trying to find a logical explanation, but his instincts were beginning to kick in. There were too many coincidences to just brush off the possibility that something more was happening.

"Nope. Not possible. That's what Summer thought at first, so she called DOW to come up and check it out. That's the Division of Wildlife. They changed their name a couple years ago to something else, but everyone still calls them DOW. Anyway, they told her that the deer had been shot and placed on her property. It's illegal to hunt deer this time of year, and they said that someone probably shot it and then panicked and just looked for a place to dump it."

"Rather than leave it where it was and let the other wild animals eat it and destroy the evidence? How does that make sense?"

"It doesn't, especially when you take into consideration the dead roses and the bird feeder."

"Hold on, she doesn't even know that they're connected," Lank argued even as his mind worked at finding a correlation.

"No, she doesn't," Megan agreed, "and neither do the police, but it's just too many weird things happening to her all at once," she said, as if she'd read his mind. "I don't blame her for freaking out. I'm freaked out by it, too."

"So, what do you want from me?"

"I want you to look into it. Do some of that fancy detective work that you're so famous for back in Maryland."

"First of all, I'm not famous. I didn't break the biggest case in state history, my former boss did."

"But you helped. And you were working with the FBI."

"True, but I was a rookie. I didn't have a clue what I was doing back then."

"And now, you're one of Baltimore's lead detectives. I know about your big promotion. Mom fills me in."

"Okay, but still, this isn't my case. And it's not the kind of stuff I deal with. I wouldn't have any idea where to start."

"That's bull, and you know it. Look, whoever is doing this is escalating, and I'm afraid of what he might do next. If this was happening back home, and you were the cop assigned, it would be the 'kind of stuff you deal with.' Just because it's happening out here doesn't mean you would go about solving it any differently."

She had a point, but it wasn't enough for Lank.

"It's still not my case. The local police aren't going to let some city slicker with no jurisdiction just waltz in and take over."

"So, you don't tell them," Megan said as she pulled into the driveway and put the car in park.

Lank shook his head as he looked out over the hood of the Bronco. The Rockies loomed large ahead of them as dust swirled around outside the vehicle and came to rest on the windshield. The SUV no longer shined, and Lank wondered how often Megan had to wash the vehicle and if it was even worth it.

"Look, Megan, that's not the way I operate. I'm sorry. I feel bad for your friend, but I'm sure the police will figure out what's going on. I'll stay for the weekend, say hi to Johnny, and get the grand tour of your house, maybe see some of the area, but then I need to head back home. I have real cases waiting for me to solve."

"You owe me," Megan said quietly as she stared out the front window.

"What?" Lank said as he blinked in disbelief. Was she really going to go there?

"You owe me," Megan said through clenched teeth. Her knuckles were white as her hands gripped the steering wheel. Lank could feel her anger and her hurt. "I gave up my whole junior year for you and part of senior year. I passed up dates and shopping with my friends so that I could sit at your bedside while you wallowed in self-pity. I baked you cookies and brought you presents that I bought with my own money and spent hours convincing you to not give up. I helped your football coach to drag you out of bed even on the days you were yelling at us to leave you alone. I never turned my back on you. Not once. And I was there on the day you walked across the stage to get your diploma. In fact, after I got mine, I stopped at the edge of the stage to wait for you in case you fell, in case you needed me to help you get back up again. I've been there for you since the day you were born." She turned her gaze to look him in the eye. "You owe me."

Feeling guilty, Lank followed Megan into the cabin. Though made of logs, Lank found it hard to reconcile the house with what he had always pictured as 'Megan's cabin.' Rather than a rustic, mountaintop hunting cabin, it was a large, bright home with expansive windows that ran from the floor to the ceiling, at least twenty feet high. A loft looked down from above what he assumed was the master bedroom, just off the open living room and kitchen. And a staircase near the master bedroom looked to lead to a finished basement. From where he was standing, Lank could see out onto a massive deck with a breathtaking view of a line of snow-capped mountains and endless sky.

"So, she convinced you to come out here after all," Johnny said, coming up behind Lank. Lank tore his eyes away from the view and turned to face Megan's husband.

"She did, but I'm still not sure what I'm supposed to do." Lank crossed the room and shook hands with Johnny. "What, you're not going to stand and give me a hug?"

The joke was old, but Johnny still laughed as he wheeled his chair into the kitchen. "Are you hungry?" Johnny asked. "What am I saying? You're always hungry."

"Little boy's room first?"

"Back around the corner by the front door."

"Thanks," Lank said as he passed by Megan and headed to the bathroom. She was silent when they gathered his things and entered the house, and Lank wondered what kind of plan she was formulating in that never-resting mind of hers.

When Lank returned to the kitchen, he caught Megan and Johnny sharing an intimate kiss, Megan sitting on Johnny's lap, completely ignorant to the fact that he had returned. He cleared his throat.

Without blushing or apologizing, Megan stood and went to the stove. "I've got bacon cooking. Are BLTs still your favorite?"

"They are, thanks." Lank felt guilty after Megan's plea, but he was torn. How could he possibly help?

"Look, Megan, I'm sorry for upsetting you. I'm here until Monday and will hear you out, but I can't promise there's anything I can do to help."

"I understand, but do me a favor." She turned to face him. "Talk to Summer."

Before answering, Lank turned to Johnny.

"What do you think of all this?"

Shrugging, Johnny opened the refrigerator and pulled out two beers, handing one to Lank. "I don't know. I have to admit that it sounds far-fetched to believe that someone is stalking her, but Summer is pretty level-headed. She's not one to make things up or jump to conclusions. She never has been. As her brother, I have to admit that I'm concerned."

Twisting the cap off the beer, Lank took a long swig while he let that sink in. Why had he agreed to come? He had cases back home. He didn't need an imaginary one more than halfway across the country. He looked back at Megan, who had her back to him, as she turned over the bacon. There were few people in this world for whom he would drop everything. His high school football coach was one, his former boss, Jim, was another, along with his mom, and of course, Megan.

Megan had a heart of gold and would do anything for Lank, and her own life was no barrel of fun. After her father's slow death from Parkinson's and Lank's football accident and long road through rehabilitation to recovery, Megan decided to become a physical therapist. She worked at Walter Reed where she met Johnny, a young Iraq War veteran, recovering from a bullet hole in his spine that left him paralyzed from the waist down. By the time Johnny was released, they were engaged, and Megan was moving to Colorado so that Johnny could be near his family. Their wedding was small and private. Lank couldn't even remember who their witnesses were, but Summer might have been one, now that he thought about it. These days, Megan worked mostly with cowboys who were injured on the job or in a rodeo arena.

"Okay, I'll meet Summer, but no promises after that."

"Oh, Abe, I knew you'd come through," Megan said as she threw the spatula on the counter and ran toward Lank. She stretched herself up as tall as she could, threw her arms around him, and pulled him down toward herself in a hug.

"I said, no promises," Lank told her as he tried to escape from her constrictive hold.

"I know," Megan said as she released him and wiped the tears from her eyes. "I'm just so grateful that you're going to listen. Even if you just offer us your thoughts and advice, that's more than we have now."

Lank nodded and looked at Johnny. A grin spread across Johnny's face as he tilted his beer toward Lank. "You're her hero, man. You always were. I knew you'd help."

"We'll see," was all Lank would say. He changed the subject and wondered what he had gotten himself into. "So, when do I get a tour of this house?"

CHAPTER TWO

The wine had been poured, and the elk steaks were just coming off the grill when Lank heard a vehicle pull into the driveway. Concealed by a cloud of dust, the tan-colored Ford pickup truck sat still for a few minutes before Lank, who had walked to the kitchen window, saw the door open. True to her name, the woman who exited the truck was a red-headed beauty with a sun-kissed glow on her cheeks. When she walked into the house without knocking, the smile she gave Megan radiated with warmth.

"As always, you've got perfect timing. Johnny just finished cooking the steaks." Megan took her sister-in-law's hand and led her over to Lank. "Summer, this is my cousin, Abe. Abe, my sister-in-law and best friend, Summer."

"I don't know whether to shake your hand or give you a hug," Summer gushed, her voice as sweet as honey with a slight twang that matched Johnny's. "I can't tell you how much it means to me that you're here."

"First, my friends and colleagues call me Lank. Only my mom and Megan call me Abe." He looked at his cousin and rolled his eyes as she grinned at him. "Second,

I'm not sure I'll be able to help, but I told Megan that I would listen to you and offer advice."

"That's a start," Summer said with a slight lift and release of her shoulders.

Over dinner on the back deck, Lank tried to size up Summer. If she had been in Megan's wedding, he didn't remember her, and that was surprising. She had the type of looks that one didn't easily forget. She wasn't quite as petite as Megan, but she couldn't have been more than five-four. Her eyes were as green as the pine trees that coated the mountain over her shoulder, and her red hair, long and flowing down her back, blew gently around her face in the breeze that curled around the deck as they ate. She wore a mint green shirt and short, white pants. A cross necklace dotted with emeralds, hung just below her throat. Though her voice was low and sweet, she was an animated talker, and he could easily see how she was able to capture and maintain the attention of her students. She was at ease in conversation but not attention seeking. She reminded him of Johnny in her mannerisms and easygoing attitude. Lank tried to observe her with his trained, unbiased eye, searching for anything out of the ordinary that would cause him to doubt her story or her sanity. So far, he detected nothing that was off.

"So, Summer," Lank began noncommittally when they finished dinner and sat sipping the last of their red wine. "Tell me about the things that have taken place that are causing you concern. I've heard Megan's version, but I want to hear yours."

Summer downed the last of her wine and nervously dabbed her mouth with her napkin. Hummingbirds darted to and from the feeder behind her head, and twilight was settling on the mountain beyond, the evening glow giving her an ethereal look as she spoke. "Well, it all started when I received flowers at school." She frowned and looked down at her empty plate. "Though I'm hard pressed to call them flowers."

She related the events pretty much the same as Megan, sometimes looking at him, sometimes looking down and twisting a ring on her right hand, now and then blowing a stray piece of hair from her face as she stared off as if to gather her thoughts or decide how to continue. She spoke calmly and without embellishment, though there was a tremor in her voice at times. She was calm and steady, but Lank detected a bit of humble shyness as she spoke. She'd make a good witness, Lank surmised, and a credible victim.

"Do you have any idea who might send you dead flowers?"

"None," she said as she bit her lips together and hastily shook her head. "It's so bizarre."

"What about the deer? Anyone who might hold a grudge or want to drive home a message or warning?"

Again, she shook her head.

"Megan mentioned that your parents live nearby. You all grew up around here, didn't you?"

"We did. We were born and raised just outside of little old Lake City. Unlike most of my friends and classmates, I had no desire to leave." She looked at her brother. "I think I speak for both Johnny and myself when I say that we've always loved it here, in the mountains, with the snow and fresh air. I went to school in the city and couldn't wait to get back."

"Where did you go?"

"Texas A&M."

"She went on a full scholarship," Megan remarked.

Summer blushed. "That's true. I was lucky, I guess."

"Luck had nothing to do with it," Johnny chimed in. "She's the smartest girl to ever graduate from the Western Slope. Colleges all over the country wanted her."

"I wouldn't say that," Summer said, the blush on her cheeks deepening. It was obvious that she was uncomfortable talking about herself and her achievements. "I worked hard and got noticed by a few schools."

"Yeah, a few Ivy League schools, too, but she didn't want to go too far away or to a college that was too fancy." Lank could see that Johnny was quite proud of his sister and that Summer was embarrassed by his praise.

"Why A&M?" Lank asked, not sure that it mattered as far as the alleged case, but he wanted to get all the info he could about her so that he knew where to start.

"I wanted to have the experience of living in a city, but not too far from home. And many of us Southwestern Coloradans consider ourselves Texans at heart, so it seemed natural for me to go there. Did you know that this area was once part of Texas way back before Texas and Colorado were states? College Station, Texas isn't a big city, by any means. But it's a far cry from Lake City and close enough to Houston to give me a glimpse into city life."

"Did you have a boyfriend?"

"A couple," Summer said quietly, seemingly uncomfortable sharing the private episodes of her past with a stranger.

"I'm not trying to pry, but I need a few more details. Anything serious?"

"Kind of. The first guy was more of a friend. We dated, but we found that we were just better friends than, well, lovers, for lack of a better word." Her blush returned, and Lank felt like a peeping Tom trying to see into the intimate details of her life.

"So, you ended the relationship on good terms?"

"It never really ended. It just…evolved. We dated, but the dates started turning into more of just hanging out together. We never even referred to ourselves as a couple really. We were just always together. He was the first guy I dated, first guy I kissed, and then became my first real friend on campus. One day, in our sophomore year, I noticed how he looked at this girl in a class we had together. It was like he was staring at a piece of artwork. She was the masterpiece that he couldn't take his eyes off of, and I knew. He was no longer mine, not that he ever was." The look in her eyes was one of contentment and genuine fondness, not jealousy or loss. "I pushed him to ask her out, and they've been together ever since. They just celebrated their fifth wedding anniversary and have a second baby on the way." Contrary to the shy girl she was when talking about herself, she came alive when she spoke of her friends, just as she had when talking about her students during dinner. Her eyes sparkled, and her smile was genuine.

"So, you're still in touch?"

"Yes, I still consider Scott one of my very best friends. As well as his wife, Lisa."

"Are they still in Texas?"

She nodded. "In Houston as a matter of fact."

"Okay, so you said a couple of boyfriends. What about the other one?" Lank watched her expression change. The wall went back up as the conversation turned back to her own life and relationship.

"Wyatt and I dated in my senior year. And that time, it was truly a romantic relationship, except that it wasn't very romantic. He was, how do I put it?" She paused and bit her lips. "Selfish? Arrogant? Egomaniacal?

Controlling? Name a negative adjective, and it probably fits him."

"Violent?"

"Okay, maybe not that negative. No, I don't think so. Well, maybe…" Summer nervously fingered her necklace as she thought about it. "On the surface, he seemed normal, popular and intelligent, but underneath, there was this other person. Not psychotic or even neurotic, just someone that I didn't want to be around any longer. Honestly, I think it was insecurity. He was supposed to be this political genius who was going to someday take the world by storm and become the greatest president we've ever had. But the more I got to know him, all I could see was an immature and insecure boy who wasn't ready to be in a relationship or think about anyone other than himself. While always maintaining a nice, happy-go-lucky attitude, he was actually quite manipulative." She stopped suddenly and looked around as if she realized she had said too much.

Lank studied her for a moment. She seemed very uncomfortable being the center of attention, and uneasy, he thought, about having to tell the truth about Wyatt. She was a protector, and even though the man had hurt her, she didn't like revealing his shortcomings. Lank wondered how she could have fallen for a man like that, but it made sense. She would have seen the good in him and would have tried to see it through or even try to change him into a better person.

"How did you become involved?"

"A friend of a friend. I was immediately attracted to him. He was nice-looking, confident, funny and charming, and I was taken in. It wasn't until we'd been dating for a few months that I started to see beneath his cavalier attitude. He would be furious if I did better on my mid-terms than he did, and to be honest, I always did better." The blush on her cheeks returned, and she averted eye contact, again, not wanting to draw attention to herself. "Even though he did well in his classes, I wasn't allowed to get the same grade or higher in any of mine. And they weren't even the same classes. But if my GPA was just a fraction of a point higher than his, he was angry. If I even spoke to another guy, he would sulk about it for days. He had these outrageous outbursts of jealousy both about me and toward me. I was afraid to do well in class, and sometimes," she looked away, "I was afraid of him."

"I'm going to take a guess and say that he and Scott weren't best buddies."

"He hated Scott. And the feeling was mutual. It almost killed our friendship, but thankfully, Scott and Lisa refused to let him push them out of my life. After a while, I realized just how much he was manipulating me, and I got out."

"I imagine it wasn't an easy break-up." Lank nodded his thanks to Megan as she placed a bowl of ice cream in front of him.

"It wasn't. I ended up trying to take out a restraining order on him, though to be honest, I don't think he would have hurt me."

"Why the order then?"

"He made some threats, nothing that was a big deal. He told me not to start dating anyone else and that if I tried to, he'd put an end to it. Meaningless, unspecific things like that. At one point, he told me he'd kill himself if I left him, and that was hard." She briefly looked away as she played with her necklace. "I went to my advisor, and he alerted Wyatt's professors as was protocol. I think it was all a bluff, though. He just didn't like that he couldn't have me," she said quietly.

"And where is he now?"

"I have no idea, but I hardly think he has anything to do with all of this. I really believe that he's harmless. After graduation, he just kind of faded away. As far as I know, he never entered politics. I've never seen or heard from him or about him since I left College Station." Her words confirmed to Lank that she was willing to give people the benefit of the doubt. Admirable, but not always smart.

"Can you give me his full name?" Lank asked as he pulled out his phone and opened his notebook app. "I want to check him out just to make sure."

Summer supplied what little info she had—his name, date of birth, where he grew up. It wasn't much to go on, but in this day and age, it was enough.

"Ever look him up on Facebook?"

Summer's cheeks reddened again as she looked away. "Once or twice. I tried finding out where he was after I got the flowers, but his profile and all his information were private."

"Don't look embarrassed," Megan said. "I would have done the same thing if I'd been in your shoes."

"Me, too," Lank agreed. "Now moving on, is there anyone else you can think of who might have a problem with you? Any other more current boyfriends, teaching associates, or anyone you might have angered or upset in any way?"

"Not really," she said after a moment of thought, and Lank's intuition kicked in. She was hiding something, perhaps protecting someone.

"Are you sure? There isn't anybody who may hold a grudge against you?"

"I don't think so," she said, but the hesitation was still there. "I moved home after graduation, started working the following summer as a classroom teacher, and earned my Master's in guidance online. I have no social life. School keeps me busy. And I volunteer a lot, so I don't really have time to go out or date. I had a bad experience once, so I tend to keep to myself. The little bit of spare time I do have, I spend with Black." She looked away, and Lank knew he was pushing her too hard.

"Black?" he asked, moving on, but making a mental note to come back to her 'bad experience.'

"The real love of her life," Megan said.

"My horse," Summer told him. "Named for the famed Black Stallion, my favorite book series when I was growing up." She blushed again, uncomfortable again with talking about herself.

Lank could picture Summer perched high on a black horse, riding through the mountains with her flaming red hair flowing behind her. The thought made something in his gut twist. He had to clear his throat before speaking.

"Well, I think that's a start, but it's getting cold out here, and I'm dead tired."

"Of course, you are," Megan said, looking at her watch. "It's almost midnight back on the East Coast."

"I'm so sorry to keep you up," Summer apologized. "I'll go and let you get some sleep."

"Don't rush on my account. I can put myself to bed," Lank said, motioning to Summer to stay seated as he stood up. "I really should get some sleep though. It's been a long day and I'm feeling it."

Lank said goodnight and climbed the stairs to the loft. He was suddenly bone tired and couldn't wait to hit the sack. His last thought before going to sleep was that it might be good that he was staying until Monday after all.

∽

Despite being exhausted the night before, Lank was awake at five the next morning, his body clock telling him that he was well overdue for breakfast and should have already been on his way to work. He climbed out of bed, stretched, and made his way down to the main floor to use the bathroom. After brushing his teeth, he sought out the coffee maker. It took more brainpower than he was ready to use, but he figured out the coffee maker and inserted the little pod that would produce his coffee. He had no idea what the difference was between all the little containers in the basket on the counter, but he didn't care as long as he had a cup of black coffee to help him jump start his day.

While the coffee maker was gurgling toward a finished cup of joe, Lank hunted around for something to eat. He found some frozen waffles and stuck them in the toaster. He tasted the coffee and was pleasantly surprised at how good it was. He heard one of the bedroom doors open.

"Do I smell coffee?" Johnny asked as he wheeled himself into the kitchen.

"Want a cup?" Lank asked.

"Sure, thanks. Megan is still sleeping, but I don't sleep much. I heard you come down from the loft and figured I'd see if you needed anything."

"I'm making gourmet waffles. Care to have some?"

"Works for me."

Lank took out two more waffles while he waited for Johnny's coffee to brew. He pointed to the open spaces beneath the cabinets. "Did you and Megan design this kitchen?"

"Yeah, there was a lot of planning that went into the house. I need to be able to access the counters, but that means we have limited cabinet space, so we built the extra pantry there by the fridge. Ordinarily, that would have been extra counter space. Megan was worried that the lower cabinets above the counters would be an issue, but we actually like that we can't store a whole lot on the counters. That Keurig just fits, but the larger, more standard size doesn't, so we have to keep that in mind when shopping for appliances."

"The bathroom doesn't seem like it's big enough for you," Lank commented as he took their waffles out of the toaster.

"It's not, but the master bath is huge and has bars, a spa tub, and other extras that make it work for me."

"What about going downstairs?"

"Now that was a challenge, and an expensive one," Johnny admitted as they made their way to the kitchen table when the waffles were finished toasting. "There's an elevator tucked away in the corner of our bedroom."

"No way," Lank said, almost spitting his coffee across the table. He wiped his chin and looked toward the bedroom door. How had he missed that when Megan showed him around yesterday?

"Yeah. I was okay with a stair lift, but Megan insisted on the elevator. She didn't want me trying to maneuver myself into the lift when she wasn't home. I have to admit that it's a great addition."

"I guess so. It gets you downstairs to that amazing gym."

"Another thing Megan insisted upon. We do a lot of physical training and exercise down there. It's a lot more convenient than going into town. But the thing I love is my office downstairs."

"Agreed. It sure puts my little, glass closet to shame."

Johnny chuckled. "Cyber security is nothing to go cheap on. I needed all state of the art computers, white boards to hash out problems, and space to think."

"And high speed internet. How do you manage that up here?"

"It can be done. You just have to have the right connections." Johnny winked, and Lank laughed.

"I assume you've got those."

"You bet, and speaking of connections, if you need any help running down leads online, just let me know."

"Will do. Thanks. For now, I'm going to call in a favor with my old boss."

"The FBI guy?"

"Yeah, I'm thinking he owes me one."

"After the way you helped him put away the crooked mayor and save his wife and kids, I would guess so."

"Hey, Johnny, I have a question."

"Shoot," Johnny said, taking a drink from his mug.

"What was the 'bad experience' that Summer mentioned last night?"

Johnny took a deep breath and sat back in his chair. "She had a student, Jeremy. He was disturbed, I guess you could say. He confronted her in her office one day. I'm not sure of all the details. She doesn't talk about it much. She said it wasn't a big deal, but his father blamed her for the kid's suicide. I think she blames herself. His death caused her a lot of anguish, and she sort of shut down for a while, but now it's just something she doesn't talk about."

"What about the kid's father? Could he be behind this?"

"Doubtful," Johnny said. "He was a good man. He was pretty shaken, to say the least, when his son died. And Summer was a good target for his anger, but he and his wife moved away soon after. She never heard from him again."

"Should I have Jim check him out?"

"You can, but I just don't see the point. They weren't local and had no ties to the area. Once they were gone, nobody ever heard from them again. Like I said, Summer never talks about it, but I'm sure she's never had any contact with him since then."

"Okay, but I might still have Jim look into him. Can you get me his name?"

"Sure," Johnny nodded. "Hey, I've got the dishes, man. You go ahead and get to work. Unless there's an emergency, my office is closed on Saturdays, so it's all yours."

Lank started to protest but then realized that it was Johnny's house, and he was more than capable of doing the dishes. He headed downstairs and made a point of looking for the elevator. Now that he saw it, he realized that it blended in so well with the décor of the room, it was barely noticeable. Not to mention that it was hidden by the massive gym equipment. He bypassed the machines, vowing to use them later, and made his way to Johnny's office where a work space had been made for Lank and his laptop. Johnny had already hooked it up to Wi-Fi and made sure that Lank had whatever he needed in order to begin his investigation.

Investigation. Lank shook his head. What had he gotten himself into? He told himself that he was going to check out the ex-boyfriend, consider some of the logistics of the incidents, and see if there was anything worth investigating. He still had doubts that he would turn up any kind of conspiracy or stalking or any other real crime, but he might as well put Megan and Summer's minds at ease. He thought about the father of the dead student. Johnny didn't seem to think he was any threat at all, but Lank figured he might as well check him out, too. McCain had given him a long weekend, so there was no harm in staying until Monday and doing a little legwork if it made Megan happy. Beyond that, he'd have to see.

Hating to call Jim concerning business on a weekend, Lank texted his former boss and good friend. Within minutes, his cell phone rang. He briefly explained the situation and listened to Jim's take on the situation.

"I'll make a few calls, rundown the names, and see what I can find out. Let me know if you need anything else," Jim said. Lank could hear giggles coming from Jim's two daughters and wondered how they were doing. The girls had been orphaned, witnessed a murder, ran away from home, and became the target of a hit man, all before being adopted by Jim and Susan.

"Thanks, Jim. I appreciate it. I'll send you all the names and whatever info I have this morning."

"No problem, Lank. Any time."

After ending the call, Lank opened his computer and made some notes, mapped out some possibilities, and did a little research on deer hunting, local florists, and surveillance systems. He wasn't sure how long he'd been working when he heard Megan come up behind him.

"Hey there, you've been at it for a few hours already. How's it going?" She sat down in a soft, comfortable-looking chair where Lank figured she probably spent a lot of time when Johnny was hunkered down here working.

"Good. I've been going over my notes, doing a little research, and seeing what I can figure out. I've got to be honest with you, there's not a whole lot to go on, and I'm still not convinced that anything sinister is actually happening."

"I know, but you're looking into it, and I appreciate that."

Lank's phone buzzed, and a message from Jim popped up on the screen.

It looks like Summer's ex is in the clear. He's working for a state agency in Texas, is married, and has two kids. Same with the suicide victim's father. Nothing there that sets off any alarms. I'll email you everything I found.

"You had him check out Jeremy's dad?" Megan asked.

"I didn't want to leave anything to chance."

"I don't get it, Abe. Summer honestly doesn't have an enemy in the world. Everyone loves her. She was selected to represent Hinsdale County in the Colorado Teacher of the Year Recognition. Her colleagues all look up to her, even though she's young. She'd only been teaching for two years when she was chosen. She's the perfect teacher, friend, confidant, advisor, and now guidance counselor."

"Well, if you're correct, and I'm not saying you are, she's got at least one enemy. Or a jealous rival."

"I just don't understand it. I can't imagine anyone going after Summer for anything."

Lank had to admit that Megan seemed to be right. Before looking into any farther, he had searched for info on Summer Cooper. She was as clean as a whistle. No priors, not even a speeding ticket. He read all the accolades bestowed on her as teacher of the year and was impressed by the praises from her colleagues.

"Hopefully the police are right, and the flowers were just a prank. No matter what you say about the wind, the bird feeder really could have fallen or been knocked over by an animal. From what I saw online, bears can do a heck of a lot of damage, including smashing a bird feeder to bits. And as far as the deer, it's plausible that someone shot it and panicked. Taking each event separately, there really doesn't seem to be cause for alarm."

"But putting them all together?" Megan gave her cousin a hard look.

"Agreed, it does seem beyond mere coincidence, but I'm still not ready to jump to conclusions."

"So, what's next?"

"Do you think Summer still has the flowers?"

"No. They totally freaked her out. She threw them away as soon as the police left."

"The box, too?"

"I think so."

That was going to make it a little harder, but Lank had an idea that he hoped might lead them somewhere.

"How do I get to Summer's from here? You said she lives close by. Or is her house as 'close' as the airport?"

"No, she really does live close," Megan laughed. "Come on, I'll point you in the right direction."

It only took ten minutes for Lank to cross from one side of the mountain subdivision to the other in Megan's Blazer. He was grateful that the terrain was pretty flat at the top of the mountain and that he didn't have to drive any of the sidewinding, switchback roads that he and Megan used on the way up from town. The silver-green sage bushes edged into the graded dirt roads. Small squirrels darted across the road, or started to, only to change their mind and dart back into the rocky embankment. He spotted the cabin and the small, red, fenced-in stable.

As he drove up the lane, he saw Summer standing by the stable, brushing the mane of a tall, black horse. Summer's red hair trailed down her back in a long braid from under a lacy, white cowboy hat, and her jeans hugged her body as they tapered into her boots. As Megan's Blazer approached, with Lank behind the wheel, she turned and smiled radiantly, raising her hand from the horse's shoulder to wave. She was stunning, especially in this mountain paradise with the sun's rays reaching down to kiss her beautiful face and hair. His groin twitched, and he swallowed hard. He was here on business, nothing else, he reminded himself.

Slamming the door, he walked around the Blazer and headed toward the gate. He hesitated when he reached it, unsure as to whether it was safe to enter. Didn't horses rear when startled or something like that? Did they take to strangers? He was willing to wait for Summer to finish rather than take a chance. A golden retriever barked once and then ran over to greet Lank.

"You must be Cosmo," he said as he bent down to pet the friendly dog.

"You're welcome to come in," Summer called. "You can meet Black."

"Thanks, but I'm good here," Lank called back. He straightened up, and Cosmo ran back to Summer, running in circles around her and the horse. "She's, um, taller than I pictured her."

A rich, sexy laugh drifted across the field. "Never seen a real horse before?"

"Not up close," Lank admitted. "I mean, I grew up in rural Maryland, but I never had friends with horses. Back home, only rich people have horses. At least, as far as the people I know."

"Hang on. Let me put these things away."

Lank watched Summer nuzzle against the horse. He wished he could hear the words she murmured against its black coat. As he observed the way she stroked the horse's head and rubbed her face against the smooth, shiny muzzle, Lank suddenly had the strangest desire to be a horse. Summer rubbed the horse's forehead and then walked into the stable with the brush and returned empty-handed. Black seemed content to graze on the silver plants and paid no attention to Summer as she walked by him. Cosmo followed close by her.

"I'm a little dirty. Black and I just got back from a nice ride up onto the BLM."

"The BLM?"

"Sorry, Bureau of Land Management. The feds own most of the land up here. It is all public land open for public use. Black and I like to ride up there looking for wildlife." She led Lank to the house where she stopped on the porch and sat on a bench by the door. Lank watched her take off her boots and found himself mesmerized by her movements. He tried to focus on what she'd been saying.

"Wildlife? Like bears and mountains lions?"

Her laugh washed over him like a cooler of Gatorade after a home victory.

"Maybe, but seeing them is very rare. More like elk or deer and birds." When she opened the door, Lank followed her inside. Cosmo ran into the house with them, took a long drink from his water bowl, and collapsed onto a dog bed. Lank was happy to see that Summer seemed more at ease with him this morning, or perhaps she was just more at ease on her own home turf, talking about horses and wildlife.

The layout of Summer's house was different from Megan and Johnny's. It was open, but there didn't seem to be a bedroom on the main floor. Instead, a long L-shaped balcony ran above two sides of the room, and, from what he could tell, there were at least two rooms up there, and probably a bathroom. Summer also had a wall of windows looking out at the mountains, and Lank was drawn to them.

"Those are Redcloud Peak and Sunshine Peak," Summer said, coming up behind him. "They're the same mountains you see from Megan's, but a slightly different view. I think they are the most beautiful mountains in the San Juan's"

"I thought we were in the Rockies," Lank said as he stared at the massive, snow-covered peaks.

"We are, but we're in the San Juan range. This is the southern-most part of the Rockies. The terrain is different out here, dryer, dustier, but still with majestic snow-topped mountains of rock and lots of beautiful flora and fauna."

"Speaking of flora and fauna, what are those silver bushes that I see everywhere?"

"Sage, same as the herb."

"Sage, like in the old folksong?"

"The very same. It's wonderfully aromatic and tasty and grows wild here in the San Juan's."

"I'll say. It's everywhere."

"And the deer and elk eat it. It's what makes them taste so good."

"I have to agree; those steaks we ate last night were better than any game I've ever had."

"Yep, sage. And Johnny's culinary skills."

"Is there anything that man can't do?" Lank regretted the words before he finished saying them. "I mean,"

"I know what you mean. He's pretty amazing despite the chair."

They stood for another minute taking in the splendid scene before Summer turned toward Lank. "I know you didn't come here for a lesson in the local plants or to talk about Johnny's amazing skills. What's up?"

Surprised by her straight-forwardness, Lank realized that Summer was unassertive but had no problem cutting to the chase. He filled her in on Wyatt and told her that he didn't think her ex or Jeremy's father could be counted as suspects. Then he asked about the flower box.

"I'm sorry," she said, shaking her head. "I just wanted to get rid of the whole thing. It was creepy and upsetting, and I didn't want to look at it for another second." She played with the emerald-encrusted cross that she wore around her neck, the same one he had noticed her fingering the previous night.

"It's fine. I just wish I had the box to be able to show to the local florists. Somebody might've been able to identify it."

"I can identify it, but that won't help."

"Why?"

"Because I already tried what you're thinking. I went to all the local shops in Lake City, Montrose, and Gunnison. I even drove all the way to Crested Butte. None of the florists had any kind of boxes like the one that the flowers were in. I can't even tell you for sure that it was a florist box. He could have bought the flowers, waited until they were dead, and then sent them in some other kind of box. I mean, that's what I would have done."

"Me, too," Lank said. He took a deep breath and puffed it out of his cheeks in a long exhale. Where to go from here, he wondered.

"Look," Summer said, "I know that Megan had you come all this way on a whim, and I really appreciate it. I don't want you to feel like you have to waste your time on this. The police found nothing, and it's not like I'm in any danger. Honestly, I think I freaked out because of, well, I don't know. I guess I freaked out over nothing. I mean, nobody has tried to hurt me, and I have Cosmo here to protect me."

At the sound of his name, the dog lifted his head, and his tail began to beat against the wood floor.

"Yeah, he seems like a real attack dog." Lank smiled at the dog, but once again, his instinct told him that Summer was holding something back.

Summer smiled. "Seriously, what I'm trying to say is that you don't need to stick around here trying to solve a puzzle that's missing way too many pieces that may not even go together. I know that you have a life back in Maryland, a job, probably a wife or girlfriend. I don't want to keep you here unnecessarily. This whole crazy thing blew into my life like a squall moving across the mountain. If I'm lucky, it will blow out just as quickly."

Lank looked at Summer long and hard. Here was his out. She was telling him that she didn't need his help and that he could go home. But the look in her eyes said otherwise. She was scared, even if for no good reason. She didn't want the attention and didn't want to ask for help, but she was afraid. If Lank left now, that look would haunt him all the way back to Maryland.

"The truth is, Summer, it's not looking good as far as finding answers, but I don't mind trying. I'm here until Monday, so I'll see what I can dig up, and then you can go from there. You can take whatever I might find to the police, and if I find nothing, then maybe you can sleep a little easier at night."

"Are you sure?"

"Positive," Lank answered even though a voice in the back of his head was telling him that he should just say goodbye and take the first plane back to civilization. He was certain there was more going on than she was saying, and he didn't think he was going to like the picture if and when he solved the puzzle.

CHAPTER THREE

About a dozen cows and calves stood along the road, as Johnny and Lank headed to Montrose. One very large cow stood motionless in the middle of the road watching the approaching Blazer, forcing Johnny to come to a complete stop. After about 10 seconds, the standoff ended with the cow turning its giant mass and running down the road, still blocking the way for Johnny to drive by. After about 75 yards of following the cow as it lumbered down the road, it finally veered off into the sage, and Johnny could pass. Lank thought, *that cow must be exhausted.*

Lank looked around. They were on the same road Megan had taken when she picked him up from the airport in her just-washed SUV.

"What's the deal with this land and all these cows running around? And why all the 'no trespassing' signs?"

"It's private land operated by the Utes," Johnny answered.

"Utes?"

"Ute Indians. The Utes have vast land holdings in this area that they either own, work, or both. A few of them live here year-round, but mostly they tend cattle here during certain months. Most of them live farther south where the tribal headquarters is. The county roads have right-of-way grants through this land, but it's private property on both sides, and the Utes don't like people using it like it's public land."

"When you say public land, do you mean the area where Summer rides her horse?"

"Yeah, and the subdivision where we live are the lots that were divided up. It was all theirs at one time, so to speak anyway. The Utes don't believe in land ownership by individuals. They believed that the land owned them, not the other way around. In the 1700s, gold and silver were discovered in this area, and the Utes were forced off their lands in favor of the almighty dollar. The government tricked them into giving up both their land and the rights to the minerals. It wasn't until 2009 that some of the rights and lands were returned, but by then, most of the land was privately owned by US citizens. Some of these reservations didn't even have water rights until the late 20th Century. This land, though, has been Ute land for as long as I can remember."

Lank watched a group of young children kicking a ball in front of a group of small dwellings set back from the road. The kids stopped and watched the car go by, and Lank felt like an interloper.

"Now, alcoholism is a major problem," Johnny continued. "And many of the families live in poverty."

For the rest of the drive to Montrose, Lank thought about the children they passed. He had seen poverty in the Baltimore slums, and he had seen hopelessness, but he had never felt responsible for it. Somehow, even though he had nothing to do with the plight of Native Americans, he felt a profound sadness that his antipathy was part of the problem. He had grown up in a nice, two-bedroom house in a quiet suburb, gone to a good school, and even after suffering from a life-threatening accident that left him unable to walk for the better part of a year, he was able to find meaningful work. And he had never given a second thought to those people who had none of that through no fault of their own. He might never be able to watch an old Western movie the same way again.

"I can't believe she agreed to let you install a security system at her house," Johnny said to Lank as they perused the home security section at the Home Depot.

"Yeah. I told her that even if there isn't someone stalking her, as a single, young woman, living alone on the top of a mountain, she should have a better system than a barking dog."

"I don't know how you convinced her. She wouldn't listen to me or our parents."

"I'm a cop. It's my area of expertise."

"I guess so. I'm just glad she said yes."

The men looked at some of the systems that Lank's research recommended and chose the one that they thought would work best for Summer's needs and lifestyle.

On the way back to the subdivision, Lank tried to think of other angles he could pursue. "Johnny, do you know if the police looked at any surveillance videos from the flower delivery? Were they able to identify the person who delivered the roses?"

Johnny shook his head. "No video. This isn't Baltimore. We don't have crime like that around here. Our community is pretty safe and the school doesn't have surveillance cameras."

Lank couldn't imagine a school without a video camera following the moves of everyone who entered the main office. Heck, most of the schools he dealt with had metal detectors and armed guards. Then a thought hit him.

"Even after Columbine?"

Johnny nodded slowly. "That was certainly a tragedy for Coloradans, but Littleton, where Columbine is located, is a suburb of Denver. It's a whole different way of life on the Western Slope. That might as well be another state."

Lank understood that. They were a five-hour drive southwest of Denver, on a good day, and across the Rockies. He guessed it was like comparing Baltimore or DC with the rural Eastern Shore or the far Western range of Maryland's Allegheny mountains.

"What about a visitor's log?"

"No luck there either," Johnny told him. "The flowers just appeared in the office with a note that they were for Summer."

"Damn, no wonder the local police didn't do much. There's really nothing to go on."

"Nothing at all," Johnny agreed. "Except my sister's word that someone is stalking her. For what it's worth, Lank, I believe her."

Johnny's opinion and his resolute tone reaffirmed Lank's inkling that maybe there was something going on after all. Still, he wasn't ready to admit that it was more than a prank or even Summer's imagination.

"I know she's your sister, but what makes you think this isn't all in her head?"

"I don't know. Just a gut feeling. Summer isn't about attention. She was right about being a small-town girl, having no social life, working and volunteering all the time. She has plenty of friends, but none that she actually *does* anything with other than Megan. Not even friends from high school. Unless she's at school or volunteering at the church, she'd rather be alone and read or ride her horse. She would never cry wolf or involve the police or anyone else," he looked pointedly at Lank, "unless she really felt threatened."

Lank didn't answer. He let Johnny's words sink in as he watched the semi-paralyzed man drive the customized SUV that had been adapted to his needs. It had certainly crossed his mind that Summer was crying wolf. Her story, while plausible, wasn't credible. There just wasn't enough to convince him, or evidently the local police, that she was in any danger. On the other hand, at dinner the previous night, Lank watched her hand shake as she took a sip of her wine, heard the tremor in her voice when she described finding the deer, and then saw the same look of fear earlier that day when she told him to go home. Either she was a helluva good liar, good enough to fool her own brother, or she really believed she was in danger.

"Here's the thing, Johnny," Lank said as he admired the way Johnny handled the vehicle on the mountain roads, "I want to believe her. I do. She seems genuinely worried, and I know you believe that she wouldn't lie, but I just can't see a pattern here. The things that she's alleging were done —and I only mean that in a legal sense —I'm not saying she actually is lying, but these things that happened, they just seem like random events."

"Dead roses being delivered anonymously to the school where she works? How is that random?" Johnny's voice rose, and Lank knew he was pushing the boundaries with Summer's brother.

"I'm not saying that's random. In fact, I agree that someone wanted to scare her, or at least play a prank on her, but the other instances just don't seem to have any connection to that."

"Yet we're still installing this system, for which we just paid a pretty hefty sum, at her house. Why?"

"If it gives her some peace of mind and makes her feel as if the worst is over, then it's worth it. Right?"

"I guess so," Johnny said after a minute of thought. He didn't sound convinced, which made sense because Lank wasn't sure he was convinced himself. Summer was right. The whole thing was like a puzzle with missing pieces and no guarantee that the pieces fit together.

ॐ

"So that's it?" Summer asked.

"That's it," Johnny replied. "It's wireless, will call you and me if it's triggered, can be set using your phone, and won't go off every time Cosmo moves."

"It sounds complicated." Summer frowned as she looked at the monitor installed by her front door.

"It's not," Lank assured her from the open door of the back deck where he had just finished installing a motion sensor light. He had also installed them on the other three sides of the house along with a security camera at the front door.

"Don't you guys think this is overkill? The system, the lights, *and* the camera?" Summer asked, but Lank didn't think her tone matched her words. He detected some relief on her part. Or was it resignation? Did the system make her feel more secure, or was she worried it would dispel her claims that someone was stalking her?

"That depends upon how safe you want to be, or feel. I assume you *want* to catch this guy," Lank said matter-of-factly, challenging her with his gaze. Summer shot him a look of contempt but ignored the challenge.

"The camera feed goes directly to your laptop," Johnny told her, still concentrating on the equipment and oblivious to the exchange. "It's set to save the feed but erase it in 24 hour segments every 72 hours, so if something happens one day or night, you can access it for a few days. If something does happen, and let's hope it doesn't, but if it does, you can save a select time-period in a separate file that won't erase."

"Again, it sounds complicated."

"Well, it's the only solution," Johnny snapped at his sister. He took a deep breath and closed his eyes before leveling his gaze on her. "Look, we're just trying to help. You're the one who's afraid that someone might be stalking you."

"Oh, so now I'm the only one who's afraid 'someone might be stalking me'? I thought you, of all people, believed me."

"I do believe you." Johnny sounded defeated. "And I'm trying to do whatever I can to make sure that you not only *feel* safe but *are* safe."

An only child, Lank watched the exchange with interest from his vantage point on the back deck. He still wasn't sure how he felt about Summer. There was something about her that caught him off guard, and he didn't like the conflicting feelings he had about her and her situation.

"I know, and I'm sorry," Summer said to Johnny as Lank continued to observe their interaction. "It's just that, now that you guys have installed all these gadgets, I feel like I'm on an episode of Big Brother. I can either live being paranoid that I'm about to be attacked or paranoid that everything I do is being recorded."

"I can promise you that isn't the case," Lank told her, coming into the room and closing the door behind him. "It's only recording activity at your front and basement doors. There isn't any sound being recorded, so feel free to blast your music, dance in your underwear, and sing at the top of your lungs. Your secrets will still be safe."

"Apparently, you already know all my secrets." She immediately grimaced and turned bright red.

Though he was sure she hadn't intended to, Summer's remark stirred a reaction in him that caught Lank off guard. He swallowed before responding, and Lank could tell that she wished she could take back the words. She was trying to be light-hearted, but hearing the words out loud, he knew by her blush that she regretted them.

"I'll be sure to call before I stop by next time," he said, trying to keep things light. Lank grinned as her face turned to an even deeper shade of red.

Still oblivious to the sparks that were flying between Lank and Summer, Johnny bent down to pack up his tool kit.

"Can you give me a hand with this, Lank?"

"No problem," Lank said, rushing over to pick up the box, grateful for the distraction from Summer's green eyes, fiery red hair, well-toned body, and conflicting messages.

"I guess we're done here. If I don't see you tomorrow, Summer, it was nice meeting you." He awkwardly reached to shake her hand with the tool kit between them. When they touched, Lank couldn't help but think of a line from his mother's favorite movie, "It was like… magic."

The town of Lake City was hopping that afternoon as Lank walked around and took in the sights. Megan and Johnny had gone to the Saturday evening Mass in town, apparently the only Mass option in this remote area. The three of them planned to meet afterward for dinner.

Lank did not grow up as a member of any church but remembered his mother going to a nondenominational church regularly after his accident. He had thought about going once he could walk, just to thank the man upstairs, but somehow, it never happened. He didn't remember Megan being particularly religious, but evidently, that changed after she married Johnny.

Once he had taken in the entire town—the walk from one end to the other didn't take more than twenty minutes—Lank headed over to the school to have a look around. Johnny was right. To Lank's trained eye, there was no security of any kind in or around the building, no cameras, metal detectors, or alarms. He'd had a hard time believing that when Johnny told him, but now he conceded that this place really was quite different from the world he was used to. Lank stood outside one of the classrooms and peered through the window, wondering where Summer's office was.

"Mind if I ask what you're up to, boy?"

Turning around slowly, with his hands up, Lank faced an older gentleman in a sheriff's department uniform.

"Pardon me, sir, I'm just visiting a friend who works here and thought I'd take a peek."

"You feeling guilty or something?" The man gestured to Lank's raised arms.

"No, sir, but I'm a police officer in Baltimore City. I know what the sound of an officer's command sounds like."

"At ease, son. Do you have ID on you?"

"Yes, sir. Do you mind if I reach into my back pocket to retrieve it?"

"Go ahead. You don't look like a hardened criminal to me."

Lank wondered about the level of trust that the officer was putting in him as he reached in his back pocket for his identification. He handed his driver's license and police ID to the man, who, now that Lank had gotten a better look at him, appeared to be the town sheriff.

"So, Officer Lankton, what's a police detective from," he glanced back down at the ID, "Baltimore, Maryland, doing here in Lake City, Colorado, peeking into the school classrooms?"

"Actually, sir," Lank said as he took back his cards, "I'm a friend of Summer Cooper, her sister-in-law's cousin to be exact. She asked me to come out and…" Now this was going to be tricky, he thought. He didn't want to insult the local law enforcement. "She wanted me to help her install a surveillance system at her house."

"She needed you to come all the way out here just for that?"

"Well, to be honest, sir, she wanted my opinion about the incidents she has experienced, the roses and the deer." He didn't want to mention the bird feeder as it didn't seem as compelling as the other things. "It isn't that she doesn't have confidence in your department, sir. She just wanted a second opinion."

The Sheriff eyed him suspiciously. "Her brother's a fancy cyber security investigator, am I right?"

"Yes, sir. He and I have been looking into this together."

"Uh-huh," he said. "Because you don't think we did enough?"

"No, sir, that's not it at all. To be honest, I'm not even sure that there's anything to look into, but I promised my cousin that I'd do whatever I could to help Summer feel safe."

Lank was sure that he was going to be run out of town and told to never come back. He stood his ground, holding his eye contact steady, and waited for his judgment to be handed down, but the Sheriff reached for Lank's hand.

"Sheriff McCoy, pleased to meet you, Detective Lankton. Let's say you and I have a chat about these incidents, as you called them, and see if we can come up with some explanations. To be honest with you, our police force is a little short-staffed." He walked toward a bench near the playground, and Lank followed.

"How many deputies are there here in town?"

"You're looking at the whole sheriff's department," the older man replied as he took a seat. "And I plan on retiring at the end of the year, so there will be a new sheriff in town, quite literally. I'd like to go out with a clean slate. We had a deputy, but he moved over the winter. Said he needed a warmer year-round climate. I guess the next sheriff will take care of replacing him. Most of the law enforcement around here is done by the DOW as it involves searching for lost hikers, monitoring hunters, and the like."

"So, you were the person who talked to Summer about the flowers," Lank stated.

"Yes, I was. I admit that it seemed strange, even threatening, but there didn't seem to be anywhere to go with it. There was no note, no suspects, and no way to tell where they came from. I was baffled, to be honest, but I couldn't really say that a crime had been committed."

"I felt the same way, sir, and would have handled it exactly the way you did." The older man nodded. "What about the deer? Did you investigate that as well?"

"No, that was the Gunnison County Sheriff's Department. I'm strictly Hinsdale County. But seeing as this is a pretty small town, word gets around. They came down and asked me about a possible connection to the flowers, but I couldn't legitimately give them one."

"Unfortunately, neither could Summer."

"No, and I felt really bad about that. I wanted to do something to help that gal. She was really upset, but there just wasn't enough to go on."

"I understand, sir. I feel the same way."

Lank told the sheriff about Summer's ex-boyfriend, Wyatt, and about the surveillance system he and Johnny had installed. He asked about the situation with Jeremy, but the sheriff looked puzzled.

"I heard rumors that the kid was sweet on her, but that was it. This is the first time I ever heard about him attacking her. For a small town, it's strange that I wouldn't have known or at least heard something, but it was never reported. The dad tried to make a fuss for a bit about her being the cause of his death, but nothing came of it. Shortly thereafter, he and his wife moved away."

Lank nodded. "I guess she's right that it wasn't as big a deal as it seems."

"It would seem so," the sheriff said.

The two sat and talked for forty-five minutes until Lank's phone buzzed.

"Where are you?" Megan asked. "We've been at the restaurant for over fifteen minutes."

"Sorry, Meg, I'm on my way."

"I'll let you get to your dinner," Sheriff McCoy told Lank. "Let me know if you need anything or if there's any more trouble."

Shaking hands, the two men parted, and Lank made the short walk through the town to Packer's Steakhouse, said to have the best buffalo burgers in the area. Every person he passed smiled and said hello, children ran free without overprotective parents hovering nearby, and tourists wandered from shop to shop seemingly without a care in the world. Lank felt as if he had gone back in time.

When he arrived at Packer's Steakhouse, he was surprised to see Summer and her parents seated at a table with Megan and Johnny. Megan tilted her beer toward him with a smile before taking a drink.

"Sorry, guys, I ran into Sheriff McCoy, and we had ourselves a nice chat." He took a seat and motioned to the waitress to bring him a beer after shaking hands and re-introducing himself to Summer and Johnny's parents, Steve and Monica Cooper. He hadn't seen them since Megan's wedding.

"Uh-oh. Was it one of those chats that ended with the suggestion that you take the first ride out of town?" Megan asked.

"No, he's cool with me being here. He actually feels really bad about not being able to do more to, ah," He glanced toward Summer's parents and cast a look at Megan asking for help.

"It's okay," Summer told him. "I told them. I went over before Mass and filled them in." She blushed as she looked away from her parents' concerned but scolding looks.

"She should have told us sooner," Steve said.

"I know, Dad. I'm sorry." She looked back at Lank. "So, he does believe me?"

"I don't think it's a matter of believing or not believing you, Summer. I think it's a matter of not having enough information to do anything. And to be honest, I hope we don't get enough information because that means that whoever did these things isn't done yet."

A heavy silence fell over the table as they nursed their drinks. After ordering their meals, they fell into a light conversation until dinner arrived. They held hands while they said grace, which was new to Lank. Praying at all was something he rarely, if ever, did. Over the meal, they talked about Lank's mother and his aunt, Megan's mother. They made comparisons about the weather there versus in Maryland, and about some of Lank's more interesting cases. They all made a point of skirting around the one topic on everyone's mind – Summer's stalker.

At one point, Lank asked Summer a question that had been nagging him for a couple days. "Summer, yesterday you said something about this situation blowing into your life like a squall on the mountain. What was that supposed to mean?"

"Do you know what a squall is?" Summer asked.

"Well, sure, kind of. It's a storm or something, right?"

Johnny answered, "It's a storm all right. Accompanied by a sudden, violent, wind. And there's thunder, lightning, and rain or even snow. They can be deadly if you're caught in one on top of a mountain, and they come in fast and without warning."

Lank nodded. He agreed with Summer. It sure seemed that the last few days had been an ominous squall that had blown in over Summer's peaceful life.

CHAPTER FOUR

Sunday was quiet on the mountain, and Lank enjoyed the peacefulness as he and Megan spent the day hiking the government land near Summer's cabin. Dinner consisted of elk again, but Lank didn't complain. He knew he would miss the wholesome goodness of the elk and the buffalo meat once he got home. He drifted off to sleep easily that night, but the sound of voices during the night woke Lank from a dead sleep. An image of Meg Ryan taking Tom Hanks' hand, at the top of the Empire State Building, lingered from his dream, only Meg had long, flowing red hair. He reached for his phone and saw that it was 1:03am. He heard the bedroom door open below him and detected both footsteps and the unmistakable sound of wheels rolling on the hardwood floor. He hastily threw off the covers, jumped from the bed, and headed to the railing that separated the loft from the rest of the house.

"What's going on?" he called down.

"Get dressed. And hurry. Summer's alarm went off and woke me. I called her, and she's a bit freaked out."

"Did she see or hear anyone?"

"I don't think so, but she asked us to come over."

In a flash, they dressed and dashed over to Summer's house. There were no lights from any other vehicle to be seen anywhere on the mountain. They were on Summer's doorstep in less than fifteen minutes from the time of the alarm. Summer opened the door, already dressed in jeans, a sweatshirt, and tennis shoes, with her hair pulled behind her head. The scent of a fresh pot of coffee wafted out from within the house.

"Cosmo heard something and started growling, then the alarm started going off. That's when I noticed that the lights were on and the alarm had been triggered."

They followed her into the house where she already had three cups of coffee sitting on the counter. A fourth cup was in her hands, and Lank noticed that it shook a bit as she took a sip.

"Could it have been an animal?" Megan asked.

"Not likely," Johnny said. "The alarm would only trigger if someone was trying to open a door or window."

The coffee in Summer's mug splashed over the rim, and Lank reached to take it out of her hands. She let him take it and lead her to the couch with his free hand.

"Do you remember hearing anything at all when Cosmo woke you?" he asked as he set the mug on the table in front of her.

Summer shook her head. "I don't. It didn't register at first. I wasn't fully awake, and then the alarm sounded."

"It was the basement door," Johnny said. "The console indicates that someone tried to open it."

"Megan, sit here with Summer," Lank said as he stood up and gave his cousin his seat. "I'll go check it out."

He was back in minutes. "I don't see anything. No 'gifts' this time. He didn't try to force the door and probably ran as soon as the alarm sounded. It's too dark to tell for sure, but I think there are footprints in the dirt by the patio."

The patio was just a cement pad under the deck where Summer stored a snowmobile covered with a heavy-duty tarp.

"Should we call the police?" Megan asked.

"It wouldn't hurt to have it on record," Lank said. "And maybe they can get an impression of the shoe print. I don't know if that works out here with all this dirt and the steady breeze. It's not like the moist soil or the mud that we deal with back east. Dry dirt doesn't tend to stay in one place for very long."

"Did you get a picture of it?" Johnny asked.

"Yeah, but like I said, it's dark out there. Even with the light on, it's not very good quality."

As they waited for the Gunnison County Sheriff to arrive, Lank tried to think of some reason why this was happening. What had Summer done, or not done, and to whom? What would cause a person to act this way or come all the way out here to terrorize someone? Was it someone just trying to scare her, and if so, why? That was the key word that kept coming back to him—why? There had to be a reason, an explanation for whatever message he was trying to send her. And was it even a 'him' who was doing this? Why not another woman? Someone who was jealous of her or thought of her as a threat?

"Summer, we've been concentrating on the possibility of this person being a man, which makes a certain amount of sense because of the props that were used—flowers and the dead deer. But what about a woman? Is there someone who would see you as a threat or an enemy? A jealous girlfriend or a former friend?"

"I can't think of anybody. I never date, haven't since Wyatt and I broke up before graduation. That was five years ago. I grew up with the guys around here, and there's zero interest on my part or theirs. And while I don't actively socialize with too many people, I wouldn't call anyone a 'former' friend. The only person I can think of who has ever held a grudge against me is Jeremy's dad, Nathan Cranford."

"Summer, I need to know what happened with you and Jeremy."

All eyes turned to Summer as they waited for her to speak. She looked up and moved her gaze from one person to the other.

"I really don't think it's him. It's too crazy." She reached for her necklace and turned it over and back with her fingers.

"That's not what he asked," Johnny said to his sister. "You've never told any of us what really happened between you two. Maybe it's time you leveled with us."

She sighed and rolled her head back against the couch. "I just don't think he would do something like this. When he attacked me…"

"Nathan Cranford attacked you?" Lank asked, wondering why nobody had mentioned this.

"No, no," Summer backtracked, holding her hands up in protest. "Mr. Cranford didn't attack me. I didn't mean that. It was more like a confrontation. When he confronted me, it was out of grief. I know that his anger wasn't really directed at me." Once again, Lank thought he detected something amiss, but he listened as Summer continued.

"Jeremy was a child with issues," Megan explained. "Everyone knew it. He had severe learning and behavioral problems and acted out in some pretty aggressive ways. He was always in trouble and tended to make some destructive choices."

"He was a young boy when I first started working with him, only fourteen at the time. I tried to reach him," Summer took over the narrative. "I thought that if I paid him some extra attention, treated him like he was special, that he would improve, but it only made it worse."

"Jeremy thought he was in love with you," Johnny interjected. "Isn't that right?"

"Yes. I didn't realize it at first. I really thought I was getting through to him. He stopped skipping school, started paying attention in class, and even began making friends. At the end of the year, he was promoted from the eighth to ninth grade, and I moved from the classroom to the guidance office. I thought he was doing just fine. He came by my office every morning to say hello, and now and then he brought me gifts—wildflowers he picked on the way to school, a cookie that his mom baked, a chocolate bar. I thought he was just being kind. Sometimes, when I left school at the end of the day, he would be waiting for me by my car to tell me about his day. And then one day, he started acting up again. I saw it as a cry for attention and suggested that he start coming in every day at a certain time for some counseling. After the first few visits, I knew that I'd made a mistake.

Summer stopped talking and reached for her coffee cup. Lank knew it was cold, but Summer took a long drink before putting it back down and continuing, seeming not to notice the bitterness that coffee took on once it was cold.

"Jeremy was older than the other ninth graders. He had started school a year later and was already taller and stronger than his classmates. One afternoon, he stopped by just as I was leaving. It was a Friday, and I was there late, long after everyone else was gone. He closed the door to the office and told me that he had been doing a lot of thinking, and it was time to take our relationship to the next step.

"There was something different about him. I could feel it in the air. I knew I was in trouble, and not just in a teacher / student relationship kind of way. I feared that he was going to do something, hurt me in some way. For the first time ever, I knew that I was going to be a victim. I had this feeling that he was going to kill me. It was his stance, the way he looked at me, and that he locked the door. Then, he took out a knife," she said quietly as she looked away. A tear ran down her cheek. "He was a kid, but he was strong, and he'd been violent in the past. I knew he would and could…" The words trailed off as she stared into the empty air.

Lank eased himself into the chair that sat across from the couch. Every nerve in his body tingled. He clenched his jaw and felt the heat rising through him. He dreaded hearing the rest.

"I tried to talk to him, tried to reason with him, but he wasn't listening. He took a step closer to me and shoved the chair to the side, essentially blocking my only escape. I was trapped between the desk and the bookshelf. He was so close." She closed her eyes and continued as if reliving that moment.

"He pushed his body up against mine and looked down at me. He put his hands on the bookshelf, pinning me under him with the knife still clasped in his right hand. The knife was so close to my face, I could see the glint of the blade out of the corner of my eye. I told him that he needed to back up, that he was invading my personal space. He understood these words. It was something we had talked about in reference to other students when he got in trouble for bothering them. I reminded him that I was his teacher and that he would be in a lot of trouble if he hurt me. He didn't budge.

"Next, I pleaded with him. I tried every tactic, but nothing was working. Then he bent down to kiss me, and I screamed. It caught him off guard, and he took a step back. I pushed him away and tried to run past him, but he grabbed me and pushed me onto the desk, putting the knife to my throat. I knew it might cost me my life, but I refused to go without a fight. I kneed him, and he backed up again and then lunged at me and pinned me to the desk again. That's when Mr. Fields, the custodian, unlocked the door and ran in. He pulled Jeremy off me and restrained him on the floor."

Summer looked around the room. When her gaze fell on Johnny, her eyes pleaded with him for understanding. Her brother's jaw was tense, and his eyes were alight with fury.

"You never told me this. You never told anyone," Johnny said, looking incredulously at his sister. He sounded torn between anger and pain. "Why the hell didn't you tell someone?"

"He was just a boy," she pleaded with her brother for understanding. "Yes, he was almost sixteen and certainly almost a man in stature, but mentally he was still a boy. He was living in a confused and delusional world without any true understanding of what was real and what was made up in his head. I told Mr. Fields to let him go. Mr. Fields was very angry with me, but he did as I asked, and Jeremy ran off. Mr. Fields insisted on taking me to the hospital to be checked out. On the way, I promised that I would speak with the principal and that we would have a meeting with Jeremy's parents. The meeting never took place."

She stopped talking and shook her head. With trembling hands, she picked up the coffee again and drank it so quickly that Lank doubted she even tasted it. Tears filled her eyes.

"Jeremy killed himself that weekend," Johnny told Lank. His tone was filled with disgust, rather than pity, for the boy. "He used his father's hunting rifle. He left a note that read, 'Tell Ms. Cooper that I love her and I'm sorry.' Is that why you never told? Were you afraid of people thinking it was your fault?"

"Maybe," Summer hesitated. "I was in shock, I guess. When I walked into the funeral home, Mr. Cranford looked at me with such hatred, it gave me chills. He left his wife's side and practically ran across the room until his face was as close to mine as Jeremy's had been that other day. He kept his voice calm and spoke in a hushed tone. He told me that I was not welcome there. Rather than cause him any more pain, I left. He tried to have me fired, but Mr. Fields defended me, saying he had seen Jeremy confront me. He never told anyone what really happened," she said quietly. "I was forced to take a leave of absence, but after a few weeks, I was allowed to return. I've done my best to forget about it, but now, I don't know what to think."

"How long ago was this?" Lank asked.

"Two years ago. It started the year I was Teacher of the Year and went into my first year as a guidance counselor. Mr. and Mrs. Cranford moved away, so I really hadn't thought of him as a possibility until now."

"Why now? Why would he come back and start terrorizing you now?"

"I don't know," she told Lank, shaking her head. "I know it doesn't make any sense that he would suddenly start terrorizing me after all this time. I just don't know who else it could be."

They heard the police SUV turn into the driveway. Its headlights cast an eerie glow across the yard. Megan got up to let the Gunnison County Sheriff and his deputy into the house.

By the time they inspected the scene, and Summer had rehashed the entire story, the sky over the mountains was beginning to turn purple. The police left, and Summer, wrapped in a blanket, went out onto the back deck. She stood by the railing, seemingly oblivious to the cold, morning air. Lank, with his third cup of coffee in hand, watched her from the doorway. He silently stood behind her, his gaze taking in her silhouette against the backdrop of the coming dawn. He was mesmerized as the purple horizon gave way to pink. The trees, mountains, and clouds were dark silhouettes against the sky, and Lank marveled at how different the scene looked compared to the first time he saw it. Gone were the green trees, the blue sky, and the white mountain peaks. Everything was black against a backdrop of purple, pink, and now orange. As he watched, the low-hanging clouds took on a purple hue, and a striking line of dark pink separated the clouds from the glowing horizon that matched the color of Summer's hair, now becoming visible in the glow of the first light of the day. When the yellow beams began to rise from behind the black shapes, Lank held his breath. Never before had he witnessed such a beautiful sight, and it struck him that it wasn't just the dawn that awed him with its breath-taking splendor.

"Did you talk to your boss?" Johnny asked as Lank appeared in the office doorway.

"Yeah, and to Jim. I'm clear for the rest of the week. Jim did some checking into Nathan Cranford. He and his wife moved to Montana after Jeremy's death. Jim's checking into his whereabouts over the last month. Have you heard from Megan?"

"Not yet. I hope she and Summer are still sleeping. I had a hard time getting back to sleep once you and I got back. I have a feeling they did, too."

"I know what you mean. I tossed and turned quite a bit. Too much on my mind. And too much coffee, I'm sure." Lank took a seat in Megan's cushioned chair. "What are you working on?"

"Nothing overly exciting. I'm representing a financial firm that suspects a foreign entity is trying to hack into its system."

"So, what's your role when something like that happens?"

"I check out the integrity of their network, their firewall, and their online databases. Then I ensure the security and stability of any backdoors they may have, run analytics on their systems and the possibility of being able to break their codes, stuff like that."

"And you can do all that from this office?"

"Sure, I can do it anywhere that I have a computer and a secure Internet connection."

"And how often do you find holes in someone's security?"

"All the time. Even the firms or corporations with the tightest security can have a flaw in their system."

"That's kind of scary," Lank said.

"You have no idea," Johnny answered.

The sound of the front door closing and footsteps overhead had Lank on his feet and Johnny unlocking the brake on his chair. They were upstairs by the time Megan took off her shoes and grabbed a glass from a kitchen cabinet.

"Hey there, Babe," she said as she bent down and gave Johnny a kiss. "Did you get some sleep?"

"After a while. How about you?"

"Same. Summer's still pretty shaken, but she's getting ready to take Black out for a ride, so that should help settle her nerves. The principal gave her the day off. She would have let her have the whole week, but Summer insisted that she would keep working through the end of the semester."

"How much longer until school is out?" Lank asked.

"The school year is over at the end of this week," Megan answered. "Then she has another week to go before she starts a lighter schedule of two days per week. To be honest, I think that's going to make it harder on her. I may cut back my hours at the clinic and try to spend more time with her. Most of my PT patients are at the point of being able to work without me most days, and Summer needs to be kept busy."

"I agree," Johnny said. "I don't want her spending too much time alone. It's bad on her nerves, not to mention the danger she might be in."

Megan took a long drink of her iced tea and then frowned. "Here's what I don't get," she said, leaning back against the counter. "What was he or she trying to do? As far as we know, he hasn't made any attempt to get into the house before, and he didn't leave anything behind."

"That's not quite accurate," Lank said as he turned a chair around and sat down backwards with his arms hanging over the back of the chair. "We don't know that he hasn't tried to get in, or that he hasn't actually made it inside. Summer didn't have any type of security until yesterday. And we can't say that he always leaves something behind. If he or she is the same person who broke the bird feeder, nothing was left behind."

"True, but I don't get what he was trying to do last night."

"None of us do," Johnny answered. "He seemed to know about the camera at the front door because he went to the back this time, and he didn't run away when the lights came on. He had a purpose, and only the alarm made him change his mind."

"And we don't really know if it's a man," Lank added.

"How could he have known that you installed a camera out front? You just did that on Saturday?"

"Maybe he was watching us," Lank said, and he noticed Megan shake as if a chill ran down her spine. "Or maybe he went up there Saturday evening when we were out or Sunday when Summer was riding. He could have spotted it during the day. It's not like we hid it. It had to be in the right spot to see the door. And hiding it wasn't an issue since it seems he only comes at night."

"But that's changed if he was there to notice it during daylight hours," Megan said.

"Right now, it's all speculation," Lank told her. "We really know little more than we knew on Friday."

"So, what's next?" Megan asked.

"I'm waiting for some info from Jim. As soon as I hear from him, we'll figure out where to go from here. In the meantime, I'm thinking about staying at Summer's tonight. Not in the house, maybe on the deck. I need to be able to be outside if the lights go on so that I can get to the guy in a hurry."

"He won't be back tonight," Megan said.

"How do you know?" Lank asked.

"Because he only comes on Sunday nights."

Lank and Johnny looked at each other and then back at Megan. "How do you know?" Lank asked.

"The feeder was broken on a Sunday night, and the deer appeared on a Monday morning. Even the flowers were delivered on a Monday."

"Why didn't you tell me this before?"

"I didn't realize it until just now. It didn't seem important before, but there does seem to be a pattern."

"There sure as hell does," said Lank as he stood from the chair and headed for the stairs.

"Where's he going?" Megan asked Johnny.

"My guess is to call Jim." He reached for his wife and pulled her onto his lap. "Good going, Babe. You might just have given us our first break."

CHAPTER FIVE

"So, he's not the stalker either," Summer put her head in her hand, elbow on her desk, and closed her eyes.

"I'm sorry, but Nathan Cranford's alibis check out for every single date in question." Lank stood in the guidance office and watched Summer, knowing that he was ruining her Tuesday but not seeing any sense in putting off delivering the news. "And the shoe prints were a bust. Nothing special or identifiable about them."

"Great. Just what I wanted to hear." She closed her eyes and took a deep breath, then opened her eyes and stared straight ahead at her computer monitor, not seeing the screen at all. "If it's not Mr. Cranford, then who's doing this? Why is someone trying to scare me? Or worse?" she asked, the pleading in her voice breaking his heart. Her eyes were moist when she looked up at Lank, but she held back the tears.

She's one tough woman, he thought.

"I wish I knew why this was happening." Lank felt helpless standing there, but he didn't know what he could possibly do to help.

Summer slowly nodded, holding his gaze. A bolt of electricity slammed into Lank's chest and went straight to his heart. He couldn't move, could barely breathe. Something primal rose in him, the instinct to protect Summer at all costs, to shield her with his own body, to take her in his arms and….

What was wrong with him? He knew better than to have thoughts like that about someone involved in a case. He cleared his throat.

"I'm sorry, Summer. Sorry that I can't give you answers."

Summer nodded. "It's okay. Thanks for coming," she said as she turned back to her computer monitor, a tremor in her voice. "I guess I should focus on getting things settled around here before summer. I have schedules to complete and transcripts to send. And with the seniors gone, the juniors think they can get away with anything." She gave him a weak smile. "They're keeping me on my toes."

"I'll go," Lank said, but he hesitated. "Summer, I'm heading back to Megan's, but I can come by later, maybe bring dinner, if you want to talk or don't want to be alone. I'm also happy to stay the night. I told Johnny it might be best if I did."

"Thanks, Lank. I really appreciate you and Megan looking after me, but I think I need to be alone tonight. Please tell everyone that I'll be fine on my own."

"Are you sure?"

"Yes, I'm sure. But thanks."

Lank nodded and went to the door. Before opening it, he looked back at Summer once more. She kept her head down, and Lank wondered if she was really reading the document in front of her, lost in thoughts about her situation, or just avoiding looking at him.

❧

The call came long before nightfall. It was barely five in the evening when Megan answered her phone. Lank listened as she quickly hit the speaker button on her cell and stood, looking horrified at her cousin. Summer's screams echoed through the house.

"It's still in the barn. Please, Megan, tell them to hurry!" Summer pleaded.

"I'm taking your car," Lank barked at Megan. "You come with Johnny. No offense, but it will take too long to wait for him."

Lank headed toward the door but turned back. "Megan, I need a gun."

"You didn't bring one?" she asked, her eyes wide.

"I never thought I'd need one. I won't make that mistake again."

Without delay, she ran into the bedroom and returned just seconds later with a shotgun and a box of shells. "This isn't a service revolver. Do you know how to load it?"

"That might be the dumbest question you've ever asked me," he said as he grabbed the gun and ran from the house.

He whipped around the winding turns on two wheels and said his first prayer in many years. *Please, God, let me get there in time.*

He threw the Blazer into park as he cut the engine, grabbed the gun, and leapt onto the dirt driveway. Dust swirled around him as he threw open the gate and ran through the field. A hysterical Summer met him halfway.

"Black is still in there. I was too afraid to go to him."

"Where is it?"

"I don't know. At first, I only heard it, but then, I saw it slither under one of the stalls. And I saw the tail, so I know I'm not mistaken."

A tight knot formed in Lank's chest. He'd dealt with Copperheads, but Rattlers were a different breed. He had no idea how fast they were or how far they could strike. He suddenly regretted not waiting for Johnny, but what good would that have done? Johnny could only do so much.

Pushing the door open, Lank looked into the barn. The horse whinnied, and even Lank could tell that he was nervous and upset. Did that mean that the snake was in his stall? With his heart pounding, Lank stepped inside the barn. He could no longer hear Summer crying and hoped that she had the sense to stay outside.

When Black's whinnies stopped, the barn became unnervingly quiet. Lank thought he could hear his own heart beating as he tiptoed farther inside. Then another sound broke the silence. It was a rattling sound, and though he had never heard it in real life, the sound sent chills through him. On trembling legs, Lank went further in toward the sound. Black began blowing air through his nostrils and pawing his hoof at the ground.

A pitchfork stood near the first stall, and Lank reached for it while trying to hold the gun steady. It was impossible to handle the weapon with one hand, and he longed for his own pistol, mentally scolding himself for leaving it locked up in his locker back in Maryland. He would never again leave home without it.

Trying to balance both the gun and the pitchfork, he held the tool out in front of him and pried open the stall door. He didn't realize he was holding his breath until he let it out at the sight of the empty stall. He let go of the door, and it slammed shut, causing Black to again become agitated.

Listening for the rattling, Lank tried to figure out how close it was to the horse or to him. Something wet ran into his eye, and he realized that he was soaked in sweat. The barn seemed stifling, even though he knew that it was only in the 70s that afternoon, and there was no humidity here like there was back East.

Using the pitchfork, Lank opened the next stall and once again breathed a sigh of relief. He knew that his luck was running out, though, and that he would soon be face to face with a poisonous snake poised to strike. He listened for it, but the barn had gone silent again. All of his senses were heightened. He could smell the hay in the barn and the scent of nervous musk that Black emitted. The hair on his arms stood, and his stomach turned in knots. The air was heavy with anticipation and fear, both Black's and his own.

Lank turned around to inspect the area behind him, afraid that the snake was on the move, and unsure of where it would go. He was about to turn back around and continue his search when he heard a loud hissing sound behind him. He closed his eyes and prepared himself for the strike that was to come.

The strike was louder and more powerful than Lank could have ever imagined. When he spun around, he saw the snake flying into the air from the impact of the shot. With disbelief, he looked at the back of the barn where Summer stood in the open doorway. She was shaking, but somehow she must have managed to hold steady long enough to hit the snake before it made its deadly strike. Dropping the tool, Lank ran to her and put his arms around her to steady her just as Johnny's SUV pulled up behind the Blazer. Black cried from his stall as the truck's tires skidded to a halt.

"I did it," she whispered. "I actually shot it."

"Thank God you did," Lank laughed with relief.

"Are you okay?" she asked.

"I'm fine," Lank said, though he trembled with relief, as did Summer.

"Oh God. What if I had missed and hit you?"

"You didn't," Lank told her, wiping the stray hairs from her face. "That's all that matters."

"What happened?" Megan yelled as she ran over to Lank and Summer. Lank dropped his arms and hoped that Summer had stopped trembling enough to support herself.

"I was outside feeling helpless, and then, oh God, I'm going to be sick," Summer said, as she put her hand to her mouth and sank to her knees. Lank walked toward Johnny and left Megan with Summer. Lank assumed Summer would want some privacy, and he wasn't feeling too great himself. It was all he could do not to drop to his knees and heave into the pasture as Summer was doing.

After a few minutes, Megan helped Summer to her feet, and the women made their way to the back of the truck where Lank sat on the bumper. Megan eased Summer down beside him.

"How did that thing get into my barn?" Summer asked, looking around.

"How did you shoot *that thing* and not me?" Lank asked with a nervous chuckle.

"I have no idea," Summer said honestly. "I decided that I wasn't going to just stand there and do nothing, so I ran inside and got my gun. When I got back, it was quiet, and I was afraid I might be too late. I went around back because, well, I don't even know why. I just had this feeling that I should go around back. And when I looked in the door, I saw the rattler slither up behind Lank. It coiled and hissed, and I shot." She looked up. "I shot, and then I had this horrible feeling that I hadn't aimed right, that I missed and shot…"

"You didn't miss. Your aim was perfect." Lank put his finger below her chin and lifted her eyes to meet his. "You saved my life. I came here to save yours, and you saved mine."

Johnny wheeled away and went into the barn. They could hear him talking, in soothing tones, to Black.

"How about we check on that horse of yours?" Megan said, holding her hand out to Summer to help her up.

While Summer and Megan checked out Black, Lank and Johnny looked at the rattler that lay in pieces on the dirt floor.

"What do you think?" Johnny asked in a hushed tone.

"I think I'm a lucky man that your sister owns and knows how to use a gun."

Johnny called the police, but the Gunnison County Sheriff's office referred the call to the DOW, as was the protocol when dealing with any wildlife on the mountain. After the officer left, the four of them sat down at Summer's kitchen table. Lank watched Summer as she picked up the cross from her chest and unconsciously raised it to her mouth. She gently bit the tiny ring that held the cross to the chain as she gazed out the window toward the barn.

"So, it wasn't another warning, or worse," Megan said.

"Hard to say," Lank told her. "You heard him say that rattlers aren't common up here on this particular mountain, but they're definitely in Montrose. It's not out of the realm of possibility that one could find its way up here, though it would be pretty unusual. But, according to DOW, catching and relocating a live rattler without getting bitten is nearly impossible."

"This is just bewildering," Megan said. "As if Summer didn't have enough to deal with already." She reached across the table and put her hand over Summer's.

"I'm just grateful that we're all okay and that Black wasn't harmed." Summer looked appreciatively at Lank.

"I am, too," Lank said, "The officer doesn't think this is related to what's going on, but he did admit that it's quite a coincidence, especially with no reports of rattlers being spotted anywhere else in Gunnison County and our elevation."

"What do you think?" Megan asked. "Do you think this was attempted murder?"

Lank shook his head.

"I don't know. This is way out of my area of expertise, but he did say that rattlers don't tend to wander above 9,000 feet."

"We're over ten," Megan said. "Shouldn't that be cause enough to think that someone put it there?"

"Maybe," Lank said noncommittally. He wasn't sure what to think, but there was no sense getting the rest of them riled up about it. "But you'd have to be crazy to catch a rattlesnake. And if the DOW doesn't think there's cause for concern, then I don't think Summer should worry." Lank noticed Johnny's questioning gaze and shot him a quick look, hoping to convey that he didn't think they should push the issue at the moment.

"I can't think about the possibility that somebody..." Summer shook her head. "Nope, I'm not going to go there." She sat up suddenly and looked at Megan. "Hey, let's go out. Please. I need to get away from here for a while, and since I've been told to take leave for a few weeks, I don't have to worry about getting up in the morning."

"Go out?" Megan asked incredulously. "Why don't we just go to our place? I can cook. You've had quite a traumatic day."

"Oh gosh, I wasn't thinking. I might be off, but you have to be at the clinic in the morning, and Johnny has to work. Never mind. We don't have to go out. It's just that," She looked around. "I don't know. I think I just need to get out of here and regroup."

"I'm not going anywhere in the morning," Lank offered. "Where do you want to go?"

"There's a new restaurant over in Gunnison that I've been dying to try."

Johnny and Megan exchanged looks. "Summer, I think it might be best if you take it easy tonight. Get some rest, and then come to the house. Megan and I can cook."

"No, Johnny, I need this. I need to get out of here. I can't explain it. I just have to go somewhere. But there's one condition." She looked at Lank. "We are *not* going to talk about any of this. Not one word. Understood?"

"Understood," he agreed reluctantly. "I'll go back to Megan's and change. But I don't have a car of my own. Do you mind picking me up in about an hour? I can drive from there if you want."

"That would be perfect," she said with a smile.

Lank's heart tugged at the sight of her happiness, but a voice in the back of his head sent him a warning. Something just didn't feel right about this.

"How's your meal?" Summer asked once Lank had taken a few bites.

"It's pretty good," he said. "Yours?"

"Really good. I like to think of myself as a ribs connoisseur, and these stack up pretty well against some of my favorite recipes." Licking her fingers, she felt Lank's gaze on her. She felt the heat rise to her cheeks and quickly took her fingers from her mouth, reaching for the little package of wet towelettes the waitress had left on the table.

They had said very little before dinner arrived. Summer and Lank both spent a good deal of time perusing the menu and remarking on the choices without making any real conversation. Summer felt awkward being alone with this virtual stranger, and she wondered if she had made a mistake in suggesting they go out. Once dinner arrived, she was relieved that they had reason not to talk.

"Tell me about your work," Lank said, breaking into her thoughts.

So much for not talking, she thought.

Lank wiped a spot of barbecue sauce from his chin with his napkin and reached for his beer, taking a long drink as he watched her.

Summer felt uncomfortable under his scrutinizing gaze, and she wondered what he thought of her. A little voice told her not to think about that. He was Megan's cousin. He had come all the way out here as a favor to Megan. Summer knew very little about him, and she wasn't interested in knowing more. Still, she couldn't help but wonder what he was thinking. His greyish-blue eyes gave nothing away, yet she still felt unsettled sitting across from him. While she, in no way, considered this a date, there was something intimate in sharing a meal in a darkened corner of a new restaurant.

"Well," Summer said, realizing she hadn't responded to his question. She swallowed and shifted in her seat. "It keeps me on my toes." She smiled and tried to concentrate, but her mind kept drifting back to the word, 'date.'

"It's a small school, so I get to know all of my students on a more personal level than most guidance counselors."

A scene from the past trespassed on her thoughts, and she momentarily lost track of what she was saying.

"I mean, I really get to know them as people."

Lank nodded. "That must be nice. I had a few hundred kids just in my graduating class."

"I can't even imagine that," Summer said. "Did you even know everyone in your class?"

He shook his head. "Not really. In a school that big, you tend to stay within your friend group. Most people gravitate toward others with one shared interest or another—sports teams, music, art, drugs." He shrugged.

"And your group was?"

"The football team, mostly. Until I got hurt my junior year. After that, my friend group consisted of just Megan and me."

"Didn't your team support you, visit you, let you know they cared?" She couldn't fathom a community that didn't support each other in a time of need.

"Some did. Others didn't. After a while, most of them went back to life as usual."

"Were you off the team?"

"Oh, yeah, I was off the team. I was lucky to be alive," he said, finishing his beer and motioning to the waitress to bring another.

"I had no idea," Summer said. "I mean, I knew that you had to go to rehab, and that's what made Megan go into that line of work, but I never realized it was that bad."

"It was," was all he said. "But back to you. How much interaction do you have with the kids?"

Summer found herself relaxing as she spoke about the students, their quests to find the right colleges, and the thrill she got when she heard success stories from graduates who excelled in college and beyond. Lank was easy to talk to and didn't push her to reveal anything personal. She appreciated that. She could talk all night about 'her kids,' as she thought of the students, but she found it difficult to talk about herself.

By the time they finished dinner, Summer was yawning but not from the company. She was surprised to find that she actually enjoyed spending time with Lank. Pushing away the thought, she reminded herself that she was in no position to look at Lank as anything other than Megan's cousin and a police officer there to help.

"Dinner was really good, Lank, thank you. I didn't expect you to pay." Summer said as they walked back to the truck.

"I was happy to pay, but you seem to be getting tired. I guess everything that happened today is catching up with you."

Summer sighed. "I guess it is. I am tired, but I'm not sure how I'll sleep tonight. I thought that going out would take my mind off things, but it's no use. Now that it's time to head back, I'm starting to think about all that's happened—this guy being at my house, trying to get in the basement, maybe not for the first time, the rattler in my barn. What next?" She looked hopelessly at Lank. "I'm just so sick of this. I want my life back." She kicked at the dirt as they stood at the rear of the vehicle. "In spite of everything going on, I've always felt safe at home. Today changed that, and it wasn't even the stalker, or whoever he is. It was nature. Something I couldn't stop or do anything about. It's all really starting to get to me."

Lank was always good at reading people, and he could tell it was hard for Summer to admit her fears to him. For some reason, she had built a high, dense wall around herself, and she didn't like letting anyone in. Instead of responding, he just let her say what she needed to say.

The sun was almost behind the mountains, and twilight's glow encircled them as Lank watched Summer wrestle with her feelings. Her hair waved in the breeze, and her eyes clouded over with anger. It was then that Lank realized just how much he was attracted to her. He pushed the thought aside and tried to focus on what she was saying.

"I hate this feeling of helplessness, of dependency. I can't stand relying on others. It makes me feel whiny and inadequate. I just want to be left alone." She turned away, her jaw set, and her eyes closed. "And now, I have to worry about whether I have a rattler's nest by the barn or that this guy is somehow a snake charmer. I'm sorry. I'm just rambling on and on." She turned her gaze toward Lank, a defeated look in her eyes. "I'm afraid," she said quietly. "I'm afraid that next time something happens, I won't be able to get away. What's going to be next?"

Lank gently took hold of her arms and felt her go stiff. The hairs stood on the back of his neck as he realized that his touch frightened her. Why? He wondered if it had to do with what was going on, or if the confrontation with that kid, Jeremy, had had more of an impact on her than she let on. Or was it something else? She was such a mystery to him.

Letting go of her arms, Lank looked into her eyes. "I won't let anything happen to you. And you're not helpless. From what I can see, you're one of the strongest women I've ever met. That snake seems to be a fluke. And we're going to get this guy, and your life will return to normal. But for now, it's okay to be angry, and it's okay to be afraid. In fact, that's better than wallowing in self-pity. It means that you're not going to take this lying down, and he needs to know that. It might cause him to ramp up his game which will mean that he's going to make a mistake. He's going to screw up, and we're going to catch him."

She swallowed and turned her gaze back to him, meeting his blue eyes with her green, as bright as the glistening back of a tree frog in the bright summer sunlight during the day, and as dark as the Colorado pines at night. When their eyes met, the world stood still, and the ground seemed to fall out from under him. He took a step back, swallowing hard.

"It's getting late. We should go," Lank said.

Summer stared at him and swallowed, an unreadable expression in her eyes. After what seemed like an eternity, she slowly nodded.

"Yeah, we should go," she said quietly, but neither moved until a family emerged from the restaurant and broke the stillness of the evening. Lank walked around to the passenger side door and opened it for Summer. She climbed in without looking at him or saying a word.

On the hour-long ride back up the mountain, the air inside the truck was heavy with things left unsaid and an underlying current of attraction that Lank tried to ignore.

"Nothing?" Lank repeated, his brain a jumble of thoughts and disappointment.

"Nothing," the DOW officer confirmed. "Like I said, we've had no other reports of snakes in the area, but I have no reason to believe that someone put it there. She's damned lucky that the rattler didn't bite her, or the horse, or both."

"What about the possibility that somebody bought the snake online and did put it there?" It was a stretch, but Lank was pursuing every possibility.

"It's possible," the officer conceded, "but not likely. It's an expensive proposition, and illegal here in Colorado."

"Illegal, but not impossible," Lank pushed.

"Well, no, not impossible. But that's a hell of a way to get someone's attention. One wrong move, and the perp becomes the victim."

"True," Lank agreed, "but still possible."

"Yeah, it's possible," the officer sighed in agreement. "But trying to prove it would be damned difficult."

Lank agreed. He was certain even Jim would have a hard time proving that one. From what Lank had discovered through his research, buying poisonous snakes online was a booming business, and one that operated right on the line between legal and black market.

"I just thought maybe there was a chance…" Lank sat in the chair on the back deck and looked up at the snow-capped peaks.

"I'm inclined to believe it was a coincidence. I mean, stranger things have happened. I wish I could help you out, but there's not much more we can do."

"Okay, thanks for keeping me in the loop."

Disconnecting the call, Lank stared at the mountains and tried to reconcile what they knew with what they didn't.

It had been two days since he had seen Summer. Megan spoke with her several times a day, and they texted often. Johnny was in touch with his sister as well. But she hadn't been to the house, and Lank hadn't attempted to reach her. He knew that she was trying to go on as normal, riding her horse, tending her garden, and running errands. She had remote access to the school's network and could work on the schedules for the next year.

Lank, on the other hand, felt like a latch-key kid during summer vacation. He was bored and restless. He could go out if he wanted, but where would he go? Megan and Johnny both had jobs, and he had a growing desire to say the heck with all of this and go back home.

Why not? He once again asked himself the question that had been nagging him since he arrived.

What was he sticking around for? They had nothing but dead ends, and around every turn, a roadblock was staring him in the face. There had been no incidents since the weekend, unless the snake was in fact part of the game, and all he was doing was wasting his leave by sitting in a chair on Megan's back deck. It was time to go home.

He turned his gaze to his phone and stared at the blank screen. He needed to call Summer and give her the news. He needed to let this go and get back to Baltimore. He needed to stop allowing his attraction to get in the way of going back east. Why was he putting off the inevitable? There was no reason for him to stay here. Sure, he was attracted to Summer, but Lank had found himself attracted to many good-looking women in his life. Summer hadn't given him any signs that she was attracted to him, and he sure as hell wasn't going to stay here in the mountains for no good reason. He unlocked the phone and made the call.

"Hey, Lank," she said when she picked up. "How have you been?" Her casual tone caught him off guard, but what had he been expecting? Maybe she could return to life as normal just as he was going to do.

"I'm fine, Summer, but I wanted to see you...about the incidents. Can I come by?" Where had that come from? He hadn't intended to see her. He only needed to tell her that he was leaving, and that could be done over the phone.

A few seconds passed before she answered. "Sure, I'm home."

"Okay, I'll be there in about fifteen minutes."

After hanging up, Lank realized there was a problem with his snap decision to see Summer. Megan was at the clinic, and he had no idea how to drive Johnny's modified vehicle. He called her back.

"I don't have a way to get there."

Summer laughed, and Lank felt like he'd been punched. Just the sound of her laughter knocked the air out of him.

"I'll come to you. Is Johnny there?"

"He is. How about I meet you out front, and we go back to your place. I'd like to talk to you in private."

Another silent moment passed between them, and Lank again asked himself what had gotten into him. He should just say goodbye and be done with it. Finally, Summer spoke.

"Lank, is everything okay?"

"Sure. I just have some questions for you, and I want you to physically walk me through some things again." There was no case, no need for questions or walk-throughs, but his mouth seemed to be working without consultation of his brain.

"Oh, okay," she hesitated. "I'll be there soon." She disconnected without saying anything else.

He stood and walked around the deck, trying to gather his thoughts. He was going to question her one more time and look at the situation objectively like he had in the beginning, before he got to know her, before he heard her laugh, before he watched her smile, eat, and tuck that lose strand of red hair behind her ear. And then he was going to tell her goodbye. But something told him that telling her goodbye was going to be the hard part.

Oh man, he thought as he dragged his hand down his face. *I'm in more trouble than I thought.*

The ride back to Summer's cabin was tenser than the ride home from the restaurant. Lank felt restless and claustrophobic. He noticed Summer glancing at him frequently, but he kept his gaze ahead and made no attempt to speak. Partly because he had no idea what he was going to say to her or ask her, and partly because he was wrestling with his own feelings about this virtual stranger.

When Summer put the truck into park, she looked over at him. "Where do you want to talk?"

"Let's go to the barn," Lank said as he reached for the door handle without looking at her. The barn seemed safer than the house, though he couldn't say why, especially considering recent events. He still needed to figure out what he was going to say, why he was here to begin with.

They walked in silence, Summer opening the gate, and Lank waiting for her to close it behind them so that she could lead the way. He could hear Cosmo whining in the house and understood how he felt being trapped inside.

"Tell me again exactly what happened, from the minute you closed the gate and headed to the barn."

"Okay," she took a deep breath and began. "But why?"

"I just want to make sure we didn't miss anything," Lank told her. The truth was, he just wanted to spend time with her, to hear her talk, to put off saying goodbye.

She looked at him with suspicion, but she talked as they walked. "I could hear Black as soon as I walked out of the house, and I knew he was agitated. Something was off."

"Why didn't you call me or Johnny at that moment?" Lank interrupted. "Why go alone?"

"Lots of things can make a horse restless. I guess I wasn't thinking that it might be related to something minor. Black could have been sick, or some other animal could have been in there. It never occurred to me that it could be a rattler. I've certainly never heard of one being up this high. We don't have rattlesnakes in the high country, so it's the last thing I would've expected to find."

That was exactly what the DOW officer said and Lank's research had confirmed.

"And you weren't worried that it might be the guy who has been bothering you, hiding in the barn?"

"Maybe a little, but no, I was more concerned about making sure Black was okay."

And that's what had been bothering Lank. Why wasn't she worried that it could have been someone waiting for her? Why wasn't she taking more precautions?

She stopped talking and looked around the barn. "I got to the door, and Black started whinnying pretty loudly. I think he was trying to warn me."

Lank didn't question her. He'd heard stories of dogs and cats doing some pretty amazing things to help or alert their masters. Why not a horse?

"When I walked in, everything seemed okay. I didn't hear or see the rattler and really didn't think about one being in here at all. I couldn't figure out what was wrong."

"You told the police that you went right to Black. Is that true?"

Summer nodded. "Yes, I went to see what was wrong with him."

"Okay, go on."

"I looked around but didn't see anything out of the ordinary." She began to walk toward Black's stall, reenacting the scene. "I started to go to Black, and that's when I heard the rattle. Black started braying, and I wanted to let him out, but I wasn't sure where the snake was. I didn't want it to suddenly strike either of us, and I was also a little bit afraid that if I let Black out and he got spooked that he might kick me. So, I ran out of the barn and called Megan."

"You had your phone with you?"

"I did. It was in my pocket."

"And you hadn't seen the snake yet at that time?"

She shook her head. "No, not yet."

Lank nodded. "One more question. Can I get a drink?"

Summer smiled. "Sure. Come on back to the house."

Lank walked to the house and wondered for the hundredth time that day what the hell he was doing. He was just putting off the inevitable.

❦

"I'm sorry to see you go," Summer said after Lank told her that he was heading home.

He studied her and tried to find some hint that she felt something for him; that she wanted him to stay. Her expression was unreadable once again, and Lank realized how good she was at masking whatever feelings she may have had for him, if she had any at all.

"I wish I could do more," Lank said. "I'm sorry."

"I understand," she said. "It was a long shot anyway. I really appreciate you coming out here."

"It's strange," Lank began.

"What is?"

He shook his head. "The method of stalking, the lack of communication, the random series of events. There's no pattern, no rhyme or reason."

"Which is exactly why there's nothing to go on," Summer sighed.

"None of it makes sense," Lank said. "It's almost as if…" He stopped and looked away, unwilling to voice his thoughts.

"As if I'm making it up," Summer finished the thought for him.

Lank was surprised that she knew what he was thinking and at her frankness.

"Yeah." He shook his head. "I'm sorry, Summer. I don't want to make accusations. I really want to believe you, but the cop in me can't help but consider all the angles."

She raised her eyes without moving her head. "Gee, thanks for your vote of confidence."

"Look, I'm not saying you aren't telling the truth. I'm just saying that—" The buzzing of Lank's phone made them both jump.

"Excuse me," he said as he looked at the screen. Summer motioned for him to go ahead.

"Hello, Lankton here." Their eyes met as he listened to the call. "Sorry, boss. Yeah, I'll take the case. I'll be back in the office tomorrow."

Lank ended the call and looked at Summer.

"So, that's it," Summer said. "You ride in on your white horse, decide I'm just some crazy, attention-seeking maniac, so you just say goodbye and head home."

"First, I never said that. And second, what else am I supposed to do, Summer? I don't have any reason to stay. Do I?" He leveled his gaze on her, waiting for her to answer.

They stared each other down for a moment, but Summer never let her wall down. She held his gaze without taking the bait.

"I guess not," she told him in an even tone. "You're right. It's time for you to leave."

"I think that's a good idea," Lank said as he stood, downed the rest of his tea, and headed toward the front door.

"Aren't you going to tell me not to leave town?" Summer said coldly. He turned back to face her. "Isn't that what you're supposed to say to a suspect?"

"I'm not accusing you of anything, Summer," Lank said, his tone evenly measured. Why was she angry all of a sudden? He had simply told her the truth. Even she admitted that nothing added up. She had to see the absurdity of the whole thing.

She stood and looked at him, her jaw set and her eyes shooting daggers.

"But you don't believe me, either," she challenged.

"It's not that I don't want to believe you. I don't know what to believe."

"You son of a…" She shook her head. "I thought you came out here to help me."

"I did, but there's nothing more I can do. I've looked at every angle, analyzed every possibility. You said yourself that it's time for me to leave."

"Yes, but I'd rather you leave without thinking I'm crazy or a criminal."

"Summer, I can't pull clues out of the air or decide you're telling the truth just because," he stopped and looked away.

"Just because, what?" she demanded, taking a step toward him and placing her hands on her hips. When he turned back, her green eyes were filled with such intensity that he couldn't look away.

"Let's not go there, Summer. We just agreed that it's time for me to go home."

"You're right," she said, her voice low and challenging, and…sexy. "Just go home. I never asked you to come here to begin with."

Lank held her gaze a moment longer as he fought an inner battle between his mind and his body. Heat and desire radiated from Summer, and Lank heard himself make a low, instinctual noise akin to a growl. Without thinking, he grabbed Summer and pulled her to him. His mouth crushed hers, and her mouth opened to his. Her hands went to the back of his neck, and he enfolded her into his embrace, kissing her mouth, her chin, the hollow of her throat, until she groaned with the same primal urge that he felt himself.

Suddenly, Summer's eyes opened, and she pushed him away. She stood, staring at him, her eyes wide and filled with passion. As if waking from a dream, she suddenly looked panicked and wrapped her arms around her chest, her hand going to her mouth to cover it, her eyes closing.

"Oh God, I, Lank," she shook her head and turned away. "I don't know why I did that. I, I don't know what to say. Please, you need to go."

"Is that what you really want, Summer?" Lank said quietly, coming up behind her.

Without turning around, Summer shook her head. But she didn't change her mind.

"Yes," she said quietly. "I want you to go."

"I'm sorry, Summer," Lank said as he turned to leave. He glanced back once more, but Summer refused to face him. He hurried from the house and started to walk down the driveway before he realized he didn't have a car. He stopped, closed his eyes, and shook his head, resigning himself to a long, lonely walk back to Megan's.

Darn, what have I done?

Summer closed her eyes and took a deep breath before sinking into the same chair that, moments before, Lank had been occupying. She ran the chain of her necklace back and forth across her chin as she tried to think. She could still feel his arms around her, and it felt both good and terrifying at the same time.

Summer was confused, to say the least. There was something about that man that got to her. She had no idea what had provoked her into challenging Lank. It was not her nature to behave like that, even if she was attracted to him. Which she wasn't, she assured herself. Anyway, even if she was, how could she trust her feelings when she didn't know if any attraction to him was real or just a result of her needing help and him wanting to help her?

From the moment Megan suggested she call her cousin, Summer knew it was a bad idea. She had read the articles about Lank's heroics, heard all Megan's stories about him. She knew he was a smart, upstanding, honorable man. She knew that he would do everything in his power to 'save' her because that's what he and Megan did. They saved people. Megan saved Lank and then she saved Johnny. And Lank was a cop, the original superhero, saving lives every day.

What could she do to prove to Lank and everyone else that someone was after her? And how could she trust her feelings about him? Not that it mattered. It was too late. He was leaving, and it was probably for the best. She was not looking for a relationship, not now, not ever.

CHAPTER SIX

Johnny's laid-back attitude was nonexistent when his truck pulled up beside Lank. "Get in," he snapped without looking away from the road.

Without a word, Lank opened the door and climbed into the SUV. After a few minutes, he spoke.

"Look, Johnny, I-"

"Save it. I don't want to hear it. You can tell Megan when she gets home. Then you can pack up and leave."

"That was the plan," Lank said. There was no use saying more. Summer was Johnny's sister, and Lank understood his protectiveness toward her.

They drove in silence. Megan's car was still missing when they pulled into the driveway. Lank went straight to the loft and began throwing his clothes into his bag. When he finished, he went on the back deck, a beer in hand, and stared off into the distance, losing himself in the immense, mountain-lined sky.

By the time he finished his second beer, he heard Megan's Blazer pull up to the house. He remained in the chair on the back deck and listened as she slammed the door and went into the house. Her footsteps faded as she walked downstairs. From beneath the house, he could hear her and Johnny arguing, but he couldn't make out what they were saying. He sat and waited.

"So, you're just giving up and going home?" she said when she walked out onto the deck. Lank turned and saw her, hands on hips, head cocked to one side. It was the same look she had given him every time he found himself wallowing in pity and pain, vowing to never do physical therapy again.

"I don't really have a choice, Megan. Johnny wants me out, I have a new case waiting for me at home—at my real job, and there's nothing more I can do out here." He turned back to the landscape and heard her let out a breath.

Megan walked over to the railing and stood between Lank and the view. "What happened? All Summer told Johnny was that you don't believe her and that you're questioning everything she's told us. She's upset, and he's pretty ticked."

"That's not quite true, Meg," Lank said, not meeting her gaze. "There's no rhyme or reason to any of it. There are no suspects. There are no logical connections between any of the things that have happened. Even Summer knows that the whole thing seems crazy. There's no reason for me to stay." He looked at his cousin while she took it all in.

Megan grabbed a chair and pulled it over near his. "Really? You can't think of a single reason worth staying?" Megan looked at Lank, and he knew that she saw deep into his soul. She could always read him. But this time, he wasn't going to give in to her. He had given Summer a chance to express her feelings. She had responded to his kiss, with as much passion even, and then she had thrown him out.

"Megan, I don't know what you are imagining or where you're going with that, but no, I don't have a reason to stay."

Megan looked at him for a moment and then seemed to change tactics. "What about what's happening to Summer? What do you think, honestly, your gut instinct?"

"The hell if I know." He propped his elbow on the arm of the chair, cupped his forehead, and slowly shook his head. He blew out a breath of air and looked back at Megan. "Honest to God, Meg, I want to believe and help her, but the whole thing just feels like a wild goose chase."

"Could someone be gaslighting her? You know, like in that old Hitchcock movie where Charles Boyer tries to make Ingrid Bergman think she's crazy?"

"Do you know how inconceivable that is? That might happen in books and movies, but it doesn't happen this way in real life, not without an intimate and personal motive. And if that's the case here, what's the motive? Why would someone be doing that? What sense would that make?"

"I don't know. Some twisted form of revenge?"

"For what? Seriously? Is there anyone or anything you can point to that would allow that to make sense? Other than the two people we have already ruled out?"

Megan was silent. Finally, she shook her head. "No, I can't. I wish I could." She picked off a piece of lint that was stuck to her medical scrubs and watched it float away in the breeze after she released it. "I don't know what to tell you. Summer's my best friend and Johnny's sister. I've known her for three years. I know it's not a lifetime, but we do everything together. I know her as well as I know you. At least I thought I did," she added, looking away. Lank didn't know if she was questioning her relationship with Summer or with him. He sighed.

"Look, maybe it's me. Maybe I've become jaded and am creating a suspect out of a victim. Who knows. What I do know is that it's time to go. I'm not helping here, and I may be just getting in the way. McCain called this morning, and he's got a case waiting for me. It's best if I go back home and get back to my own job."

"I'm really sorry I dragged you out here." She tried to smile. "But it was great spending time with you again."

"Yeah, that was nice. Maybe the next time we see each other, it will be under better circumstances."

"I hope so."

They stood and hugged. "I'm gonna miss you," Megan said into Lank's chest, and he felt her trembling.

"Hey," he pulled back and forced her to look up at him. "Are you crying?"

"Maybe," she said with a weak smile and a tear on her cheek. "But I'll be fine. I just hate to say goodbye."

"It's not goodbye. It's just, see you later," Lank said, repeating an old phrase Megan used to say to him. It made her laugh, and she gave him another tight hug.

"So, have you called the airport?"

"I checked online. There's a flight to Denver this evening. Then I can get a red eye tonight or take an early flight in the morning. I'll see how I feel when I get to the airport."

"Okay, I'll give you a ride." She reluctantly let him go and headed inside.

Lank looked straight out the windshield and avoided turning to see the drop-off on the side of the road.

"Thanks for the ride, Meg. I know it's a pain after you've been working all day."

"It's fine. I just wish you were leaving under better circumstances."

"Yeah, me, too." Lank looked out the window. He was going to miss those snowy mountain peaks and the beautiful sunrises and sunsets. There was nothing that compared to this back home, not even the Western Maryland mountains. Of course, he was not going to miss peering out over the treacherous drop as it flew by when they rode on the mountainside. He was looking forward to driving on flat roads.

"What the…" Megan said, an underlying tone of panic in her voice.

"What's wrong?" Lank asked.

"There's something wrong with my brakes. They don't seem to be working right."

Lank swallowed hard and looked at the winding road ahead.

"What do you mean, they don't seem to be working?" His heart began to beat faster, and cold sweat broke out on his forehead.

"I mean, they're not working!" Megan's voice rose as she pumped the brake.

Lank looked out his window and saw that they were perilously close to the edge of the road, and there was no shoulder, only a long drop off the twisting, mountain road. They were coming up on a turn, and his heartbeat quickened. He started to feel a panic attack coming on as Megan took a turn at death-defying speed.

"Abe, I can't slow us down! I don't know what to do," Megan called as she gripped the wheel.

The turn ahead loomed closer as the SUV continued to increase in speed.

"Abe, what do I do?" Megan screamed as Lank tried to figure out what to do. His thoughts were muddied, and he was afraid he might vomit.

"You've got to slow down, Meg. You're going to hit the turn too fast," he yelled as his breathing accelerated at the same pace as the car.

"I can't," she screamed as the turn loomed ever closer. "They're gone. The brakes are totally gone!"

"We're going to go over," Lank yelled, feeling panic firmly take hold and seeing his life flash before his eyes.

"Hold on," Megan yelled as she yanked the wheel and careened around the turn. Lank was sure their back tires hit air as they made the turn. His heart was in his throat along with his dinner.

"I have to get off this road." Megan's voice was shrill as she looked back and forth from side to side.

Another car was coming at them, and Lank feared that Megan was going to lose control and kill them all.

"Megan, you've got to find a way to stop the car!"

The Blazer flew down the mountain. Lank's heart felt like it was going to burst from his chest, and he fought to not get sick. He looked around in terror as they neared another treacherous turn.

"There!" Lank yelled, pointing to where the mountain began to level out, and a grassy field lay to the left below a short, rocky drop. "Turn there. Now!"

Megan yanked the wheel as hard as she could just as the other car passed them. The Blazer hit the rocky ledge hard, and Megan and Lank both pitched forward as the truck's front tires landed in the grass. It spun around in a circle, tearing up sagebrush and throwing dirt everywhere. A loud crunching sound and a spine-tingling screech emanated from under the SUV as the vehicle stopped just inches from a large body of water nestled between the road and the rocky face of another mountain.

The other car's brake lights illuminated, and it slowed to turn around. Lank hoped they would call for help as he was in no condition to do anything. He fumbled with his seatbelt, pushed open the car door, and barely exited the vehicle before getting sick.

"What the hell just happened?" Megan said, through ragged breaths, as she made her way to Lank's side of the vehicle, holding onto the SUV for support. "My brakes were just fine when we left the house."

"I have no idea," Lank said, his breathing ragged, his head spinning, and his heart still banging out a rhythm of fear.

Megan's hands shook as she sat in the back of the police cruiser, holding a thermos of coffee. While she was in a state of shock, Lank was back to rational thinking and back to discerning the situation based on his police training.

The County Sheriff told him that the preliminary report would say brake failure, but Lank had a feeling there was more to it than that. His police instincts had kicked in, and he had a heightened awareness of something sinister at play.

Megan's father-in-law, after a call from Johnny, arrived on the scene and was relieved that Megan was unharmed.

"Can we take Megan home?" Steve Cooper asked, his arm curled protectively around his daughter-in-law.

"Sure, she's had a rough night," the officer said.

Lank watched Megan as she shakily came to her feet. Johnny was supervising as the Blazer was lifted onto the bed of a tow truck. He had already agreed to let his parents drive Megan back to the house while he stayed with Lank to get the full assessment of the scene. Lank wanted to go with her and be there for her, like she had always been there for him, but he knew that he would need all the details when he talked to his aunt the next day so that he could assure her that Megan was all right. He was glad that she was close to Steve and Monica. There was no doubt that they would take care of her just like they loved and took care of Summer.

The sheriff stood with Lank and watched as the tow truck hauled the Blazer away. The front bumper and hood were damaged, both front tires had blown on impact, a back tire had blown in the spinout, and the chassis was damaged by the large rock that they ran over as they spun through the dirt. They surmised that the rock had saved them from plunging into the reservoir.

"What do you think?" Johnny asked Lank.

"Hell if I know," Lank answered.

"Do you think this was just an accident, a brake failure?"

"No," Lank said, shaking his head. "Have I got any proof? No. Does my gut say that someone tampered with Megan's brakes? Hell, yes."

"Why?" Johnny asked, his voice full of anguish. "Why go after Megan?"

"I'm not sure," Lank said. "Maybe the target wasn't Megan." He turned to look at Johnny. "Maybe the target was me."

CHAPTER SEVEN

Unable to sleep most of the night, Lank found himself standing by the railing on the back deck when the sun rose shortly after five-thirty the next morning. With his coffee in hand, he watched the sky once again change from a glowing landscape of silhouettes to a canvas of pink, red, orange, and yellow. Every morning, the sunrise was slightly different, depending upon the clouds, the presence of mist, or whatever other atmospheric variations combined to influence the hues.

He sipped his black coffee and thought about the events of the past day. He felt like he was on a roller coaster, moving at full speed, twisting and turning, going up and down hills, and roaring through dark tunnels. And that was all in one day. Was Summer crazy, or was Megan right, and someone was manipulating her into thinking she's crazy? Was she truly in danger, and was she somehow endangering the rest of them? Were his feelings for her real or part of the ride? He closed his eyes and shook his head. He just didn't know.

"Mind if I join you?" Johnny asked from the doorway.

"Come on out. It's your deck." Lank said without turning around.

"Lank, I want to apologize."

"No, Johnny, I'm the one who owes you an apology." Lank turned to face the man whom he had come to regard as a good friend. "I'm sorry for what happened yesterday with Summer."

"She's pretty upset about it," Johnny said.

"I know, and I feel bad. I lost control. I was frustrated and angry, and I should never have grabbed her like that, or forced myself on her by kissing her—"

"What did you say?" Johnny asked, and Lank saw the shock register on his face. "You kissed Summer?"

Lank felt the heat rise from his neck up to his forehead. "I thought that was why…"

"Why I wanted you gone?" Johnny wheeled closer to Lank. "I wanted you gone because you accused her of lying, of being crazy. How the hell did you go from that to kissing her? Or was it the other way around? When she didn't return your feelings, you turned on her and accused her of making it up?" His voice rose as he spoke.

"No, Johnny, it wasn't like that," Lank defended himself. "And for the record, she kissed me back. In fact, she made no secret of the fact that she liked kissing me."

"Oh, is that a fact?" Johnny yelled, his voice echoing across the mountain.

"Boys, knock it off," Megan called from the doorway. "What the heck is going on out here?"

"Did you know?" Johnny whipped his head around to face his wife.

"That they kissed? No, not until now." She looked at her cousin. "Care to explain?"

"I don't have to explain anything. I'm an adult. Summer's an adult. And maybe I read things wrong, but from what I recall, she responded to my kiss in the affirmative."

"The hell she did," Johnny's spat. "My sister's not like that."

"Knock it off. My goodness, you're like two children fighting over your toys. Don't you think we've got enough upsetting things going on? My nerves are frazzled, and the last thing I need is you two fighting." Megan walked onto the deck and stood between them. "Now, get in here where it's warm, and let's have Lank tell us what happened. Then you can ask Summer for her side if you want to. But I don't want any arguing. I can't take it."

Lank looked at Megan. There were dark circles under her eyes, and she was pale. He thought he heard someone getting sick when he woke up, and he realized just how hard she was taking this. She had to be scared to death. He winced at his own thoughts. They had almost died, he and Megan. It was enough to make him sick again as well.

He dragged his hand down his face and took a deep breath before following Megan into the log house. He sat at the kitchen table across from where Johnny usually sat in his chair. Once they were facing each other, eye to eye, Megan began.

"So, what did you leave out, Abe? There's obviously more to the story than either you or Summer told us."

"Are you sure you want to do this, babe?" Johnny asked as he cupped his hand over hers.

"No, I'm not sure of anything right now." A tear escaped as she swallowed and blinked. "But I can't take you two at each other's throats, and I can't keep thinking about last night. So, talk." She looked at Lank, and his heart ached with love for his cousin. If this was what she wanted, he would oblige.

"I got a call from the Gunnison County Sherriff yesterday morning. He told me that he is dropping the investigation. He doesn't believe anyone purposely put the snake in the barn, and there isn't enough evidence that anyone is trying to harm Summer." Johnny started to say something, but Lank raised his hand. "Hear me out. Maybe someone is trying to scare her. I'm not saying they're not, especially after last night." He looked at Megan. "Sorry to bring it up, but my instincts are telling me that there's more to our accident than faulty brakes. Anyway, there hasn't been anything concrete; so, unless something turns up once the car is inspected, he's putting the case on the back burner if not closing it altogether."

"Do you think Summer is crazy or that she's lying? That she's making this whole thing up? To do what? Draw attention to herself? Do you really think that?" Johnny looked at Lank expectantly.

"I'm not saying she's doing that, but I am saying that I wouldn't be properly doing the job you all asked me to do if I didn't look at every possibility, every angle. I can't prove Summer didn't do it unless I also look at the possibility that she did."

"I'm not buying it," Johnny said, crossing his arms over his chest. "Why would she do something like that? She's not crazy." Johnny was adamant.

"I don't know. I just don't have another plausible explanation at the moment." Though he wasn't going to voice it, Lank still had his doubts about Summer's state of mind. He planned to keep an open mind and a closer eye on his cousin's sister-in-law.

"Summer was with me last night. She came over after you left. She was here the entire time." Johnny said.

"I know. And just so you know, I don't think she tried to kill us. With all that I've learned about Summer, I don't think she knows how to tamper with brakes so that they work fine until they're needed most." Though he couldn't rule out the possibility that she was involved, or that she hadn't hired someone to mess with the brakes.

"But you think that somebody did do something to the brakes. You don't think they were faulty," Megan said. She looked pointedly at Lank.

"I don't know what to think, but I don't like the timing."

"But you were leaving," Megan said, "so why risk it?"

"Only you, Johnny, and Summer knew I was leaving," Lank said, the implication hanging between them.

As he thought about what he had just said, it occurred to Lank that it made no sense for Summer to tamper with the brakes, knowing he was leaving. Nor would she have had time. If, in fact, someone had done something to Megan's car, it had to have been while Megan was at work. Was he barking up the wrong tree? Could Megan have been the target? No, he felt sure that whoever did this knew that Lank had been using Megan's vehicle whenever she wasn't working. They knew it would get her home but would give out if he used it that night, as he had been doing, to go to Summer's at night to check on her.

"Before we get too far into last night's events," Johnny said, breaking into Lank's thoughts, "let's get back to your fight with Summer. You're still leaving out one important thing." He leveled his gaze on Lank.

"The kiss," Lank supplied. Johnny nodded. "Summer was angry. She said I didn't believe her and that I was accusing her of being crazy or wanting attention or whatever. I tried to tell her that I hadn't drawn any conclusions yet, but that I was leaving unless she could give me a reason to stay. She told me to leave. And I was leaving, but then," he looked away, finished the last of his coffee, and turned back to Johnny.

"I said too much. I told her that I couldn't just take her at her word because," Again, he looked away.

"Because what?" Johnny demanded in a calm and cool but forceful voice.

"That's all I said. Summer assumed the rest, that I was attracted to her. She wasn't wrong, but I wasn't going to admit it. I was prepared to walk away, but then she walked over to me. She challenged me to continue, but I refused. She didn't back down, and then," Lank slammed the mug on the table, stood, and walked to the back door, running his hand over his head. "I grabbed her and kissed her. And she responded. Boy, did she respond."

Megan laid her hand on Johnny's arm and squeezed it to signal him not to say or do anything. Lank looked at them.

"As soon as we realized what was going on, we stopped. I let her go, she pushed me away, and I left. We both felt bad, were both confused. That was obvious. I just thought it was best if I got out of there. When you picked me up and told me I had to leave, I figured she told you what happened."

"She didn't tell me that," Johnny conceded.

"Well, now you know," Lank said. "I'm attracted to your sister, and I accused her of not being honest with me, and I made both of you hate me. So, what now?"

Silence filled the space between them as they looked at each other in the glow of the bright morning sunlight.

"Breakfast," Johnny said. "We eat breakfast, and then we talk to Summer and the mechanic, and figure out where we go from here. But I think it would be best not to mention this conversation to Summer."

"Agreed. I'll be back as soon I call McCain and tell him what happened. I think I'll also call Jim. I have something I want him to check on," Lank said, pulling his cell from his pocket. He walked toward the back deck where he would get the best reception.

"And no more kissing," Johnny called to Lank, but that was a promise Lank wasn't sure he could make, no matter how much he questioned things about Summer. His body and his mind seemed to be at battle, and he wasn't sure which one was going to win.

❧

"Hey," Summer said when Lank sauntered into the barn.

"Hey, yourself." He walked over to where she was leading Black out of his stall, instinctively scanning the floor with his eyes and listening for rattling with his ears. He suppressed a shiver.

"Johnny says you're not leaving. Is that true?"

Lank leaned against one of the stalls.

"It looks that way," he said, crossing his arms over his chest as he watched her. "Johnny and I have come to an understanding of sorts, and I'd like to see what the mechanic says about Megan's car."

Summer eyed Lank with curiosity but was silent as she moved past him to take a saddle off the wall and put it on Black before looking at him again.

"Is Megan okay? I mean, mentally, emotionally?"

"Yeah," he said with a sigh. "She's doing okay. She's pretty tough. But it was a helluva night."

"I'm sure. And I feel terrible about it. Johnny said it's possible that someone tried to warn you to stop helping me. Is that really what you think?"

He shrugged. "Right now, it's as plausible as anything."

She nodded and bit her lips together as she went back to concentrating on Black. He watched her adjust the saddle and pull the stirrups, making sure that everything was just right.

"I owe you an apology. For several things," he said after a few minutes of silence. He had decided that it was better to work with Summer. He would either find her stalker or expose her for the liar or insane person she is.

"I accept," she offered, without waiting for him to elaborate, "If you'll accept mine. I pushed you," she said, looking over at him while still making final adjustments to Black's bridle. "Instead of trying to help you find answers, I got defensive. And then," she looked away, "the way I behaved was totally inappropriate. I know you're trying to help me, and I put you in an uncomfortable situation."

"It didn't feel uncomfortable to me," he said in a low, husky voice. Mentally he kicked himself. Once again, his mouth was working without the permission of his brain. She seemed to have a way of making that happen.

Summer's hand froze on Black's bridle. She lifted her eyes to meet his. "So," she said quietly before darting her tongue out to lick her lips, a move which made Lank's heart skip a beat. "Where do we go from here?"

"I'm not sure," he said honestly, holding her gaze. "It seems that we are at an impasse when it comes to trust, and that's not a good place to be for solving a case or giving into attraction."

"No, it's not," she said quietly, her eyes focused on Lank's.

"So, the real question is what do we do about it? The trust issue?"

"Well. You could start by telling me that you finally believe me when I say that I didn't do these things myself nor am I working with someone who is. And that I'm not crazy." She held his gaze, never breaking eye contact, imploring him to believe her while at the same time, standing her ground.

"One thing I'm pretty sure of is that you didn't tamper with Megan's brakes."

Summer looked at him with shock and horror. "Was that even a possibility in your mind? I would never, ever hurt Megan or do anything that might remotely cause her harm. And that includes causing something to happen to you."

Lank nodded, "I know. I've given that a lot of thought since last night. You wouldn't hurt Megan, and you wouldn't have had time or opportunity to mess with her car."

"That's not exactly an admission that you believe I wasn't involved," she said defensively, turning back to the horse, her shoulders slumping in defeat.

"Summer," Lank pushed himself away from the stall and reached for her arms, gently turning her back toward him. "I'm trying to be honest with you. I'm at a loss for understanding what's happening here, and we don't seem to be getting any closer to answers."

"Are you talking about the stalker or about us?" Though there was a catch in her voice, and her eyes pleaded with him for the right answer, he just didn't know what the right answer was.

"Is there an us? Outside of us working as a team to solve this?" He gave her a hard look.

She took a deep breath. "I don't know, I mean," she sighed. "No, there's no us. It's a confusing time for me. I know I sent you mixed signals," she said, avoiding looking him in the eye, "and I'm sorry. I'm a mess right now, and I don't know what I was thinking, what I was doing….." She tugged away, and Lank realized he was still holding onto her arms.

Letting go, he suddenly felt naked and exposed. He took a step back and crossed his arms over his chest again. "I'm sorry," he said, not sure why he was apologizing.

She swallowed and nodded slowly. "Look, I don't want you to get the wrong idea. I'm not looking for an 'us' with you or anyone. I have no idea why I acted the way I did. I just want you to trust me." She took a deep breath and wiped her brow before looking at Lank. "You know that I hate this. I've always been independent, fighting my shyness to prove that I could be successful and make it on my own without always hiding behind others. I spent my whole childhood trying to overcome my shyness and the stigma of being too smart and then most of my adulthood trying to convince people that I can use my brains as a teacher, that I'm not 'wasting my talent.' This makes me feel like a failure, like I can't take care of myself, like every decision I've ever made should be called into question."

"I think you did a pretty good job of taking care of yourself and me when you blew away that rattler."

A grin slowly spread across her face. "Yeah, I guess I did okay in that situation at least."

"So, back to the matter at hand. What can we do to gain each other's trust back?"

"Jeez, you mean saving your life wasn't good enough? You're a hard man to please." She gave him a weak smile, shook her head, and turned her attention back to Black, who was making signs of becoming restless. Lank watched her rub the horse's nose and whisper to him in a soft, soothing voice. She had no idea what little she would have to do to please him at that moment. He gave a quick shake of his head to clear his thoughts.

"How about another dinner? Tonight. And this time, we will talk about what has been going on with the creep, and you'll hear me out on the things that are bothering me. We'll talk through everything we know and try to find something we can work with."

Summer placed her foot in the stirrup and mounted the horse. From high above Lank, she looked down with a tentative smile.

"I can live with that, but you have to do something for me. We can do dinner tonight, but I'd like to drive separately. I have something I need to do first. Also, I want you to meet me here tomorrow morning at eight a.m. Wear jeans and boots if you have them. I'm going to teach you what it means to put your complete trust in someone. Deal?"

Lank thought about it and then nodded. "Deal," he answered, and then observed as she turned the giant animal and rode out of the barn. He took off his baseball hat and scratched the back of his head as his eyes followed her to the back door of the barn. He watched her as she rode to the end of the paddock, climbed down to unhitch the gate, remounted, and took off into the trees that rose along the mountainside.

"Damn," he said to himself. "What am I getting myself into?"

The house was quiet as Lank sat in Johnny's office staring at the text from Jim.

Got a guy working on the online black-market angle. He's good. If there's anything there, he'll find it, but it's a long shot at best. This angle just doesn't make sense to me.

Lank typed a quick reply of thanks and took a deep breath. Was it possible that the rattler had been bought illegally and put in Summer's barn? Or that someone caught it in a neighboring county and relocated it to Summer's? He had dismissed both possibilities until after the incident with the car. Whoever was after them wasn't above attempted murder. But handling a poisonous snake? Lank shook his head. He couldn't imagine it himself, but who knew whom or what they were dealing with.

Deciding not to bring it up to anyone else, he resigned himself to keeping his suspicions under wraps until he heard back from Jim. In the meantime, he would check in with the mechanic about the car. Maybe they'd get lucky and get some kind of break. Unfortunately, his gut told him that things wouldn't happen that quickly or easily.

The restaurant was crowded, but it was a Saturday night at the beginning of June in Lake City, and the tourists were flocking to the quaint little town in the Southwestern Rockies. Summer had texted and asked him to meet her at the steakhouse where they had all eaten on the weekend he first arrived. Lank sipped his beer and tried to appear nonchalant as he watched the door for Summer to arrive. Mass ended an hour earlier, but Summer had her errand to run before dinner. When she finally walked in, she did not disappoint. She was wearing a pair of tight jeans and red cowboy boots. Her red t-shirt set off the fire in her hair and was perfectly offset by the white denim jacket she wore over it. She spotted Lank and made her way to the table.

"You have a head start on me," she said as she sat down across from him.

"I just started," he said, motioning to the waitress to bring a bottle for Summer.

"What are Megan and Johnny doing tonight? They left in a hurry after Mass."

"Making a romantic dinner for two. They told me not to hurry back. I think I'm interfering with their love life."

"Um, yuck, that's my brother you're talking about." She smiled, thanked the waitress, and took a sip of the locally brewed ale.

"Hey, I didn't even know that they, that he, oh whatever, never mind." Lank felt his cheeks grow warmer. He looked away but was drawn back by Summer's rich laughter.

"Again, yuck." She took a swig of her beer.

"Are y'all ready to order?" the waitress asked, and Lank couldn't have been more grateful for the timing.

"You just got here," Lank said to Summer. "Do you need more time?"

"No, I'm good," she said. "I'm getting my favorite thing on the menu."

After ordering buffalo burgers with fries, they settled comfortably into conversation. Lank's plan was to keep Summer totally at ease, assess her mannerisms, and get to know her better. He needed to figure out whether she was capable of masterminding this whole operation or if she seemed to have a screw loose. He needed to make small talk but also get her to open up, maybe catch her off-guard.

"Question for you," he said.

"Okay," she said before taking a sip of her beer.

"Your necklace," he gestured to her throat, and she absent-mindedly reached for the emerald-dotted cross.

"It's the only one I've ever seen you wear, and you play with it when you're nervous. What's its story?"

Summer dropped the cross and looked down at the pendant that hung around her neck.

"I do?" She looked up at him. "Play with it when I'm nervous?"

"You do," Lank nodded. He took a drink and pointed the bottle at the cross. "Tell me about it."

"It was a gift," Summer said. "From my grandfather."

"Go on," Lank said after it appeared that she wasn't going to elaborate. "Tell me more."

Summer looked uncomfortable talking about her personal life, but she took a deep breath and continued.

"He died when I was just eighteen, but before that, he was the most important person in the world to me. I loved him fiercely and spent as much time with him as I could. He taught me to ride," she said with a sad smile. "When I turned eighteen, he gave me this and said, 'Never forget that the true cross held treasure worth more than these gems. Lean on it when troubles come your way.' I've never forgotten those words." She looked away, and a tear formed in her eye, but she blinked it away. "He died two months later. Cancer. He never even told us he had it."

She looked back at Lank and attempted to smile.

"Thanks," he said, and he meant it. "Thanks for sharing that with me. "

"I'm trying to remember his words these days, I mean, with everything going on. I feel like I'm barely holding onto my sanity, but then I remember my grandfather's favorite Bible verse, 'I can do all things through God who strengthens me.' It has become my mantra."

It was a verse with which Lank was familiar. His mother quoted it often when he was fighting his way back after the accident. It was something he had honestly never understood, the ability to believe everything was going to be okay just because one believed in God.

He motioned for another beer and changed the subject. "Tell me about learning to ride a horse and what else you did around here for fun when you were a kid."

At first, Summer had to be coaxed to open up, but after a few questions about her childhood, she began to relax. Lank learned that his upbringing in the Baltimore suburbs was worlds apart from Summer's childhood in the shadow of the Rockies. While he played street hockey and video games with the boys in his neighborhood, and then went on, before the accident, to play football for his high school, Summer spent her days climbing mountains, hiking, and riding a horse. Lank's house was locked at all times, while Summer's family never owned a house key. Social activities back east consisted of parties and day trips to the beach. Out west, Summer spent a great deal of time at rodeos and livestock shows.

"Were you ever bored?" Lank asked.

"I was going to ask you the same thing," Summer said. "How could I possibly be bored? In the summer, there's fishing and hiking and summiting the mountains. In the winter, we ski and snowmobile and ice skate. And I can ride a horse all year." Lank smiled as he watched her. For the first time since they met, she seemed to be totally at ease, and he enjoyed the animated way she talked about life in the mountains.

"But what about all the snow? Can't the winters be brutal?"

"Yeah, I guess so, but you'll never in your life see anything more beautiful than a landscape covered with several feet of fresh snow, with the sun rising over the mountain, casting its golden light on the white powder." She closed her eyes, and Lank watched her as she envisioned her own picture of paradise. He was captivated by her, that was certain, whether he fully trusted her or not.

"Here y'all go. Watch the plates. They're hot." The waitress slid the dishes in front of them.

"You're really going to eat all of that? It's the biggest burger I've ever seen," Lank said as Summer put just a dab each of ketchup and mustard on her buffalo burger.

"Prepare to be amazed," she said with a smile. "But do you mind if we say grace first?"

It was something Lank was getting used to. Megan and Johnny never began a meal without thanking God for the food. What he hadn't gotten used to was holding hands while saying it. He'd never been a touchy-feely guy, but now, as Summer reached for his hands, he felt a lump in his throat.

The now familiar words of the mealtime blessing were just background noise to the beating of his heart as he held her hands. He closed his eyes and tried to concentrate on the prayer, but all he could think about was how good her hands felt in his. When she was done, Lank looked up and met her eyes. A shy smile played on her lips and she reached for the enormous burger and lifted it to her mouth. Lank's own mouth began to water, and he knew it wasn't on account of the food.

Shaking off his feelings, Lank squirted ketchup on his burger and asked Summer more questions about her childhood. When they were finished eating, and had exhausted most other subjects, Lank brought up the investigation.

"I talked to the mechanic earlier, and the sheriff." He finished off his beer and motioned to the waitress. "Two coffees, please."

"Oh, decaf for me, please," Summer added. "I don't know how you drink so much coffee and still sleep at night."

"It comes with the job," Lank told her. "Anyway, we were right. It appears that Megan's brake line was tampered with. It was cut just enough for her to make it home and then for the brakes to go out completely the next time it was driven down the mountain."

"Oh, my God," Summer said quietly, closing her eyes and taking a deep breath through her nose, exhaling it the same way.

"Yeah, that was Megan's reaction, too." They sat in silence for a moment, both lost in their own thoughts about the implication, about the possibility that Megan might have been hurt, or worse, about the boldness this guy was beginning to show.

"What I don't understand is, what is the point to all of this?" Summer said, pausing to smile at the waitress who delivered their coffees. "Is he trying to scare us, taunt us, or actually hurt us? And why go after Megan?"

"The only thing I can figure is that somewhere, somehow, we got too close, and he's now trying to tie up the loose ends. He had no idea that I was heading home, but he must have known that I've been using Megan's car when she's not working. He's trying to stop me from getting too close. The ironic thing is that we have no idea where it is that we might be close. Until now."

"What do you mean?" Summer asked.

"We now know that this guy knew what he was doing. He knows about cars and how they work. That gives us a solid lead."

"I hadn't thought about that," Summer said.

"It's not much, but if I do come up with a list of suspects, it gives us something to go on."

"Knowing that he really knew what he was doing makes me even more grateful that you and Megan weren't hurt. And, though I hate that her car is totaled, at least it wasn't Johnny's."

"I agree. Hopefully this gives us something to go on, though."

"Good because despite all that fancy equipment you installed, we've got nothing on film of him being at the house."

"This guy obviously gets off on scaring you. It's only a matter of time before he slips up, and we get something on film or catch him in the act. I find it hard to believe that he doesn't sit nearby and wait for your reaction after he does something. He wants to see how you react, know that he has scared you. It's part of the game. If he can't watch and be entertained, then what good does it do to play?" Lank knew that his assessment applied to both an unknown stalker and to Summer, and he wondered again if she played a part in the whole thing, but it seemed less and less likely the more he got to know her and the more ramped up this guy was getting.

Summer put down her coffee. "I hardly think this is a game," she said.

"Not to you, it's not, but to him, yeah, I think it is. I just don't know how far he's going to take it."

"Well, he's already tried to kill you and Megan. He might even have been there the day the snake was in the barn. He probably took some strange delight in watching me almost get killed and go into a full-out panic."

"I agree," Lank said. "He seems to like it when you're upset or not in control."

Lank stared at his coffee for a few moments, lost in thought. Was this about control? It usually was where stalkers were concerned. Or when someone on the edge feels the need to take control of her life. He shook the thought away.

"So, what's his end game?" he asked, looking at Summer. Was this guy going to try to kill Summer, as most of these cases ended, or did Summer have some twisted ending of her own in mind?

Summer shrugged. "I have no idea. That's what we brought you out here to find out."

Lank nodded and watched Summer, her red hair glowing in the candlelight. He knew they expected him to find something, to solve this puzzle they were living, but Lank was deeply afraid that he was in over his head. In more ways than one.

CHAPTER EIGHT

"What do you mean their stories don't match?" Lank was in Megan's rental car the next morning, on his way to Summer's, when Jim called.

"Everything seems to be getting pretty out of control there, with the snake and the brake job. I decided to go over my notes again, and things just weren't adding up. It was bothering me, so I contacted Wyatt Ewing." Jim relayed his findings to Lank. "He says that things were the other way around with him and Summer. He claims that she was needy, always in trouble, always needing him to bail her out of something. He said that she wouldn't have passed half her classes without his help and that her only connection to any type of social life was through him. In fact, he said that he broke it off with her after she went hysterical on him for talking to some girl at a party. He said she's crazy, maybe bipolar."

"Could he be lying? Holding a grudge and still wanting to make her life hell?"

"I don't know, Lank. He told me that the best thing he ever did was get her out of his life and that he would prefer I not call again. He said he had enough of her drama back in college."

The picture he painted didn't square with the one that Summer held to. It also didn't correlate to the Summer he had gotten to know. She was intelligent, confident, and didn't seem the jealous, possessive type. Of course, his judgment might still be a bit clouded. After all, he hadn't let go of the possibility that she was somehow involved. Could she be bipolar? He hadn't seen any signs of it, but he was no expert. Simply psychopathic or neurotic? Neither of those fit either, but again, he was a detective, not a trained profiler.

"What about Scott? He might be able to corroborate her story."

"Who's Scott?"

"Summer's best friend from college. He and his wife, Lisa, live in Houston. I thought I gave you their names already."

"Hold on." Lank heard the shuffling of paper before Jim came back on the line. "Yeah, you did. I'll give them a call."

"Thanks, Jim. I appreciate the help. And the snake?"

"Nothing so far, but it's a deep well, the black market. It might take some time."

They agreed to talk again the following day before disconnecting the call.

Lank sat in front of Summer's house, watching the dust land on the hood of the car. He was lost in thought when Summer walked outside. She was wearing brown cowboy boots, not the fancy red ones she'd had on the night before. She had on jeans and a mint green t-shirt with an unbuttoned, lightweight denim shirt over it. She wore her lacy cowboy hat above the red braid that trailed down her back. She waved and motioned for him to follow her to the barn.

Lank wore tennis shoes and jeans with a plain black t-shirt. He had a Baltimore Orioles cap on his head, and it occurred to him once again how different he and Summer were and how different their lives were. He followed her into the barn and was surprised to see another horse in the stall next to Black's. Summer led the horse into the open barn. Two saddles were ready nearby, and both horses wore bridles.

"You don't intend for me to ride that thing, do you?" Lank asked, keeping his distance from the tall, suddenly frightening-looking, animal.

"I most certainly do," she said without looking at him. She settled the saddle on the horse's back and began hooking the straps. "I picked him up last night. He belongs to my father." She pursed her lips. "Actually, he used to belong to Johnny. He's old and calm and doesn't get ridden a whole lot anymore. This will be good for both of you." She looked at Lank, her eyes full of meaning, and Lank felt her grief.

"Can't Johnny still ride him? Haven't I seen stories about horses helping people with his type of injuries to heal?"

"Yeah, but Johnny won't even try. He's come a long way, but there are still some things that get to him. He loves Beau, but he hates the idea of all the work that it would take to allow him to ride again. He'd rather be able to stand here, saddle up his horse, and mount him without the aid of people or machines. Doing this," she pointed to the other saddle before picking it up and placing it on Black, "is part of the bonding process. He hates that he can't do it."

Guilt washed over Lank as he thought of Megan's husband and all that he could no longer do. Johnny trusted Lank to help his sister, and Lank was still looking at her as a possible suspect. Jim's call came back to mind as Lank watched Summer talk softly to her horse. Was this woman capable of deceiving them all, of staging this elaborate set up? He found it hard to reconcile that possibility with the woman standing in front of him.

"Ready?" Summer asked, breaking into his thoughts.

"Not really," he said.

"Chicken," she teased. "It's not that hard. Just do what I tell you to."

Lank slowly approached the horse. "I'm not sure this is a good idea," he said. His misgivings were threefold. One, he didn't know anything about horses. Two, he wasn't sure how his back would handle riding a horse. Though the pain was nothing like it had been at one time, certain things still set it off. And three, how easy would it be for Summer to cause him to have an 'accident' on top of the mountain? He sighed. This was an exercise in trust. He needed to suck it up and give it a try.

"Just grab here," she patted the ball at the top of the saddle. "Put your left leg in the stirrup, and hoist yourself up and over. Hopefully I have the stirrups at the right height."

He looked at her for a moment before tentatively grabbing onto the saddle. "I'm not gonna lie. I'm not real thrilled with this."

"You will be. You're supposed to trust me, remember?"

Lank swallowed hard as he looked into her eyes. God, how he wanted to trust her. But how many men trusted Mata Hari, the famed World War II spy? And wasn't it Bonnie who convinced Clyde to become a bank robber? He sighed again and reached for the saddle horn. Heaving himself up on top of the horse, Lank looked down at Summer who was smiling triumphantly.

"Good job," she commended him. He wasn't feeling very accomplished.

The horses maintained a nice, steady pace as they walked up the mountainside. All around him, Lank could see rushing creek beds and snowcapped peaks. Birds called to each other in the trees, and a gentle breeze swirled around him and Summer as they rose in altitude. The air was warm and comfortable, and Lank admitted that he, in no way, missed the heat and humidity of a Baltimore summer. They rode in easy silence, and Lank found himself enjoying the peaceful solitude of the trail.

Every now and then, Summer pointed out some kind of animal, a hawk or coyote, which is much smaller and less intimidating than Lank expected. He learned that the groundhog-like animals that he saw everywhere were called marmots and were relatives of prairie dogs.

At one point, while riding over a creek bed, the horses picked up their pace, crossing over the narrow band of water and back up onto the trail. Lank bounced up and down, his backside throbbing with each hit to the saddle. He thought that some of the pain was probably due to his old injury, but so far, his back was handling it okay. His inner thighs and buttocks muscles were another story.

"If you stand up when he trots, you'll save yourself a lot of bruising," Summer said, demonstrating by standing in the stirrups.

"You could've told me that about thirty minutes ago," Lank said gruffly. He wondered if he would be able to get out of bed in the morning.

They continued for about another half hour until Summer came to a stop in a grove of pine trees.

"Let's stop and take a break for a bit."

Nodding, Lank tried to lift his right leg back over the horse, but his muscles protested and screamed in pain. He

grimaced and made another attempt at lifting his leg.
Summer was already off her horse and untying a bag she
had hooked to Black's saddle. On the third try, Lank was
able to swing his leg over the horse. He was barely able
to keep his balance when his feet hit the ground. His legs
were shaking, and he was sure that all his bones had been
replaced with Jell-O. His back was starting to hurt, too,
and for the first time in years, he wished he was still on
pain killers.

"I've got water and protein bars," Summer said as she
turned around, holding out a bottle of water and a protein
bar for Lank to take.

Afraid to take a step, he leaned forward to reach them,
bracing himself on the horse. Beau, perhaps not taking
kindly to being used as a cane, took a step to the side and
bent over to eat a tall stalk of grass. Lank lost his balance
and grabbed the saddle to steady himself. Summer
laughed.

"Feeling a little unsteady?" She walked over and
handed him the water and snack. Peering at him, her
expression changed. "Seriously, are you okay?"

"Fine," Lank scowled at her as he took the water and
protein bar from her hands. Looking down at the bar, he
felt his stomach asking where the real food was. He
looked for a place to sit and gingerly managed to make
his way to a fallen, rotting tree.

If you only knew how hard that was on my body, he
thought, lowering himself down to sit.

"This is your idea of fun?" he growled as he removed
the cap from the bottle and downed most of the water.

"It is," Summer said, sitting beside him on the log.
"But not just fun. It's relaxing," Lank groaned at her
words. She continued without seeming to notice. "And it
helps me focus and stay calm. It's what gets me through
the day and what has been getting me through this mess.

This and God, of course." She stared off into the mountainous landscape.

Lank followed her gaze and spotted an eagle soaring through the sky. The sun danced off the snow-capped peaks, and the blues and greens of the evergreens dotted the rocky landscape. All around them at eye level, Lank saw wildflowers, several varieties of grass, and a scampering chipmunk or two. He could hear the steady flow of water somewhere nearby.

"I will admit, it's damn pretty out here."

They sat and admired the view while the horses chewed on the grass. After a while, Lank's pain subsided.

"Summer," Lank began, his voice full of gravity. "I've gotten some more information that you should know about."

"That sounds ominous." She turned to look at him.

"It is, I guess." He stuffed the protein bar's wrapper into the empty water bottle and took a deep breath. "Jim, my buddy at the FBI, called me with some news."

Summer watched Lank drive away before walking calmly back to the horses. She put the saddles away and brushed the horses, talking to them in soothing tones. She felt a little shaky when Lank left, but the more she thought about Wyatt, the more her blood boiled. How dare Wyatt say those things about her. They had broken up years ago, yet he was still ruining her life.

She thought about Lank, how he looked at her, how she felt when she was with him. Damn it, what was the matter with her? She knew that she was in no state to be in a relationship. She was better off on her own and had been doing just fine until this stalker mess started. And then Lank came along. He made her insides melt every time he looked at her. She longed to kiss him again, to confide in him, to have a real relationship with him, but she knew that couldn't happen. She would never be able to trust a man again, not after all she had been through.

She stopped brushing Black and blinked. Or was Lank different? Could he see her for her and not try to change or control her? Would he be willing to give up his life back east for her? That was an area where she was not willing to compromise. This mountain was the one place where she could truly be herself. Could he accept that? And what about the fact that he wasn't Catholic? Did he even believe in God? Could she fully trust someone who didn't trust God? Most importantly, could he forgive her for the one thing for which she had never been able to forgive herself? No, she decided. That was too much to ask.

Trying not to let her emotions affect the horses, she finished grooming them and gave them each a handful of carrots before heading to the house. She needed to take her mind off things. She hadn't exercised or prayed yet, and she knew those two things would help her focus.

Just over an hour later, she had completed her Soul Core exercises, taken a long shower, and dressed for dinner with her mom and dad. By the time she and Beau were on the road to her parents' house, she had refocused and knew what she had to do next. She would gain Lank's trust, and she would get through this mess, and someday, she would learn to forgive herself for the past.

CHAPTER NINE

Lank closed his eyes and laid his head back on the inflated pillow as the hot water pulsed from the jets in the enormous spa tub. His body ached in places he didn't know existed. His glutes were on fire, his legs throbbed, and his back hurt like it hadn't hurt in years. He tried to relax, but his conversation with Summer dogged him. He could still see the initial shock on her face and then the way her cheeks slowly turned red. The color flooded her face, and sparks flew from her eyes.

"He said what?" she spat as she stood and began to pace in the little pine grove. With her hands flying in every direction as she went back and forth, she vented, saying every bad thing she could possibly come up with about her ex-boyfriend. At least, bad as far as Summer's vocabulary went. No matter what happened, the woman never cursed. Even when Lank was sure she was about to hurl an F-bomb or expel some other vulgarity, she stopped and changed course. He'd never met anyone, especially in his line of work, who refused to utter a single profane word.

Once Summer seemed to have exhausted her list of inadequacies and personal flaws, she sat back down next to Lank with a huff. Rage poured from her.

"Is that how you really feel about him?" he asked with a laugh.

Summer looked at Lank in confusion. "What's so funny?"

"You are," he said, *reaching over and tugging her braid. "You are the only person I've ever met who can rip a person to shreds without using a single four-lettered word."*

"Well," she sniffed and said matter-of-factly, *"I am a firm believer that one's vocabulary is a clear indication of their intellect. If you can't express yourself without using profanity, then you must have a head full of dirty words and cobwebs but little else."*

Lank laughed even harder. "I'll have to remember that from now on. Though I know an awful lot of highly educated law enforcement personnel who might be able to prove you wrong."

Summer frowned and rolled her eyes. "Anyway, I'm sorry for my outburst. But the things Wyatt said make me absolutely furious."

"I can see that," Lank said.

"Sorry. Now I'm done with my diatribe. I'm upset and having a hard time keeping my cool. I don't know what to do or say anymore," Summer said, *reaching for her necklace. Before Lank knew what was happening, she was sobbing, one tear turning into a steady stream that traced the contours of her face. Unable to resist, Lank held her until she regained control. When she was finished, she pulled away, squared her shoulders and tried to smile. It made Lank's heart melt. She thanked him quietly and stood, going to the horses to prepare them for the ride back to the house.*

Returning to the present, Lank tried to lift his legs out of the bathwater and stretch them as he thought about the conversation that followed. His legs weren't cooperating. He reached beside him and turned up the power on the jets. He closed his eyes and continued to analyze what Summer had told him.

Summer swore that Wyatt was lying about their relationship. And though the woman could lay a mean streak of insults, Lank couldn't see her in the way that Wyatt described. On the other hand, he had seen her as the needy victim, and the events of the afternoon definitely revealed her ability to produce hysterical outbursts, perhaps even a manic episode.

Lank took a deep breath and blew it out. There were two very different sides to Summer Cooper. He just couldn't figure out which one was the real one. He felt like he was trapped in an episode of that old television show that sometimes played on the Gameshow Network, *To Tell the Truth*. He was waiting for the host to come forward and say, "Will the real Summer Cooper please stand up."

"Hey, are you still alive in there?" Megan banged on the door and called to Lank.

"What constitutes alive? Do my legs need to be working? If so, then no, I'm definitely not alive."

"Dinner's almost ready."

"Okay, give me five minutes. No, make that ten. It will take me at least five minutes per leg to get out of this tub.

"Okay, and Abe?"

"Yeah."

"Maybe you and I should go downstairs after dinner and work on Johnny's machines a little. It might help you feel better."

"The last thing I want to do is 'work' on those damned 'machines,'" he growled.

"I know, but I think we should. Please don't argue with me. Remember, I am the professional." Megan said, and he could hear the concern in her voice.

Without answering, he reached over, turned off the jets, and pulled the plug. Moaning in agony, he climbed out of the tub and grabbed the towel from the nearby hook. He thought about his last moments with Summer that afternoon.

After Summer said all she could to try to reassure him, they rode back to her place in silence. Even the beautiful scenery was a blur to Lank as he watched her riding the majestic black horse in front of him. Woman and horse moved as one, Summer's body swaying to an unheard tempo as the horse sauntered at a smooth and steady pace. Lank found himself lulled into a trance-like state, mesmerized by the gentle sway of the horse and rider. When they finally reached the corral in front of the barn, Summer dismounted and went straight to work unbridling her horse. Once Lank was down, she took care of Beau and left the horses to relax while she walked with Lank toward the SUV. Neither said a word until they reached the gate.

"I'm sorry for letting Megan drag you into this," Summer said, unable to meet his eyes. "I'm sorry that your life was put in danger. And I'm sorry that you and I didn't meet under better circumstances." She looked away, and tears once again formed in her eyes.

Lank placed his forefinger on her chin and gingerly turned her face toward his. "So am I," he whispered before bending down to leave a soft whisper of a kiss on her lips. Quickly, before he could do further damage, Lank turned and left Summer standing by the open gate.

He didn't look back as he climbed into the truck and drove away.

Megan looked concerned as Lank walked from the master bedroom to the kitchen table, and she resisted the urge to help him sit down. She knew how stubborn he was. She opened her mouth to say something, but thought better of it and bit her lips together.

"Don't," he warned her, holding up his hand.

"I didn't say a word," Megan said as she turned back to the stove and picked up a tray of fresh, hot corn on the cob.

"It'll feel better tomorrow," Johnny assured him as he set the platter of barbecued chicken down on the table.

"It sure will," Lank assured him. "Because I found Johnny's stash of liquor and picked out a nice bottle of Scotch to help me sleep peacefully tonight. I'm hoping that a few glasses will chase away these aches and pains after I pass out."

Megan looked at her cousin and wondered if he was referring to his body or his heart. She wasn't stupid, and she wasn't blind. She knew that he was wrestling with his feelings for Summer. She wanted to feel guilty about thrusting all this into his life without warning, but she didn't regret it one bit. Ever since she moved to Colorado and started this new life out west, she had longed for a piece of home to join her. No matter how many of her own personal objects she had with her, she missed her family terribly. She knew that her mother would never leave Maryland. She had too many friends and too many memories in their little hometown, not to mention Daddy, who loved his job and would probably work there until the day he died.

It was selfish, and she knew it, but Megan had always secretly hoped that Lank and Summer would meet, take one look into each other's eyes, and know that they were meant for each other. When Summer confided in her about the possibility of a stalker, Megan immediately thought of Lank and wondered if he might be the knight in shining armor who would ride in and save the day.

Well, judging by the pain he was in at the moment, riding in on a white horse was not going to be the way he would save the day, but there was still a chance. Though he hated heights, was obviously not too fond of horses, and didn't trust Summer yet, Megan wasn't giving up hope. She knew that Lank would someday recognize what a great person Summer was. She only hoped that he would figure it out before Summer got hurt. Or before Lank ended up back in the hospital with another broken back.

Lank awoke in the middle of the night with one thought running through his pounding head. Summer.

Trying to lick his dry lips and moisten his cotton-mouth, Lank sat up in the bed. He tried to think clearly through the whiskey-infused haze and the continued throbbing of his legs. Before he could fully wrap his head around the distant melody that had pulled him from his slumber, he heard Johnny yell from downstairs.

"Lank, he's back. Megan said to hurry."

Lank lurched from the bed only to find the need to stop and steady himself. A bass drum sounded in his head, and his legs dragged awkwardly beneath him. It was as if he was back in the hospital living in a drug-induced fog, but he knew that his brain was clouded only by the scotch, the horseback ride, and the dreams about Summer that haunted his sleep.

By the time he and Johnny were on the way to Summer's, Lank was feeling better. The smell of coffee wafting from the house when Megan opened the door further brought Lank into full awareness.

"I figured you might need this," Megan frowned at Lank, shoving the steaming mug into his hand as he entered.

Summer was wearing yoga pants and a long-sleeved John Elway jersey with her hair pulled back in a ponytail. Lank's heart sank as he took in the dark circles under her eyes and the tears on her face. Megan was just the opposite. Lank had seen that look of steely determination in her eyes before. He knew she was angry at the thought of being violated in some way and at what Summer was going through.

"Good boy," Johnny said to Cosmo when the dog ran over to greet him.

"He hasn't stopped looking out the door and growling since he woke us up," Summer told them. "It's really giving me the creeps."

"That's why the lights are still off and the blinds are all closed," Megan said, gesturing toward the floor to ceiling windows.

Summer nodded. "I couldn't stand the thought that he could see me, that he was still out there watching us." She shuddered, and Megan went to her to give her a reassuring hug. It took everything in Lank not to wrap his arms around her as well.

"Are you sure it wasn't an animal that spooked Cosmo?" Johnny asked.

"I'm sure," Summer told him. "He must have stepped into the range of the automatic light by accident and gotten scared when it turned on. By that time, Cosmo had already awakened me with his growling, and I was tip-toing around the house trying to hear whatever alerted him. As soon as the lights came on, I heard someone curse and then the sound of something metal hitting the ground."

"What was it?" Johnny looked toward Megan.

"I didn't hear it. I was still in the bathroom. And we didn't go outside." They turned to Summer.

"I don't know what it was either. I was about to grab my shotgun and go out, but I didn't know who or what I might encounter. I guess I got scared." She blushed and looked away.

"You did the right thing, Summer," Lank assured her. "No need to put yourself or Megan in more danger."

"Let's take a look outside," Johnny said to Lank.

"No offense, Johnny, but I should go alone. There's more of a chance of disturbing the scene if you, I mean, if we both go."

Johnny looked down at the chair. "You're right. You go."

Lank nodded and took a long sip of the hot coffee Megan made him before putting the mug down on the counter and heading outside. Using the heavy-duty flashlight, that he knew from the last middle-of-the-night visit was kept in Summer's hall closet, he carefully looked outside. Summer had pointed toward the driveway when she told them about the noise, and something nudged at Lank from the back of his brain, something he had seen when they arrived but had been in too much of a stupor to process.

Shining the light on the cement walkway leading to the gravel drive, he stopped short before reaching the stones. Lying in the garden, looking as if it had rolled there after being dropped, was a can of spray paint. Careful not to disturb anything, Lank put the flashlight on the ground and shined it on the can of paint while he took a photo with his phone. The can read, *Majic Tractor, Truck & Implement Spray Enamel, John Deere Green,* and Lank took a close-up picture of the label and, after nudging it with his shoe, snapped a shot of the barcode.

A set of headlights turned down the driveway, and Lank picked up the flashlight, shining it on himself and showing his hands so that the officers would see that he was not a threat. When the DOW officer exited the vehicle, Lank recognized him from their last meeting. They must have already been on the mountain because they arrived extraordinarily fast.

"Detective, Lankton," the man said, nodding toward Lank. "What have we got?"

"A can of spray paint," Lank answered, gesturing toward the can on the ground. "When we arrived, I thought I saw something…" Lank's words trailed off as he began walking toward Summer's car. A picture flashed through his head from when he and Johnny pulled up the gravel drive, something that was gnawing at him, and he knew that they overlooked it in the haste to get to Summer. He shined his light on the truck. He and the officers stood silently and looked at the word that was painted on the side of the Ford.

THIEF

After another night with little sleep, Lank watched the sun come up over the San Juan's.

"I thought I might find you out here," Summer said, coming up beside him. Lank tore his eyes from the rapidly changing vista and looked at Summer. Her cheekbones were sunken in, her skin pale, and her hair unkempt in its hastily drawn-back ponytail. She was wrapped in a warm, fuzzy Denver Broncos blanket clutching the ends of the blanket and a cup of coffee in her hands.

"I just can't seem to get enough of it," Lank admitted, turning back to the pink and purple sky. "It's like I never knew what a sunrise was until I came out here."

"They're easy to take for granted when you've lived here your whole life."

"I can't ever imagine taking this for granted," Lank said, shaking his head as he marveled at the orange glow of the horizon.

They stood in silence as the sun ascended from behind the mountains and the pinks, purples, and blues disappeared, giving way to the bright glow of the early morning rays.

"I'm not sure I will ever be able to repay you for all that you've done for me, Lank," Summer said quietly.

Lank noticed that the mug in her hand no longer sent steam into the air as she lifted it to her lips.

"I haven't done much," he told her. "We may be getting closer, but he's still out there, still coming here, still unafraid to target you."

Summer shuddered. "And according to the DOW and the sheriff, he's escalating. He's not waiting in between incidents."

"But he may also have given us a break. That paint had to come from somewhere, and according to the label, it's a specialty paint."

"Yes, but it could have come from anywhere. The local hardware store, the tractor supply store in Gunnison, even online. How can that possibly help?"

"Because it's traceable. Lots all go to the same place. We've got the barcode and can find the lot. Once we do, we know whether it's as simple as getting an address from the online vendor or identifying a photo at the tractor store. And more than that, it confirms that this guy knows about cars, or at least knows something about mechanics and possibly works on cars or other vehicles."

"Are we really getting closer? Can a can of paint really be the break we need?" Summer turned to look at Lank, and his heart melted. She looked forlorn, and he longed to reach out and pull her to him.

"These days, yes," he assured her. "The guy really messed up this time. Even if he wore gloves, we've got him. It might take a little time, but we've got him."

"I hope you're right, Lank. I can't stand to think of him waltzing onto my property any time he pleases, looking through my windows, damaging my things. I just want this to end."

Lank put his hands on her arms. "It will, Summer, I promise." Summer slowly nodded, and their eyes remained locked together.

Lank felt the same urge he had felt the other time he kissed her. He started to bend toward her and then stopped, knowing Johnny and Megan were inside. Clearing his throat, he let her go.

"Johnny's probably ready to head back. I'll be back tonight."

Summer bit her lips and nodded. Lank left her on the deck when he went into the house and mentally cursed himself for not being able to better suppress his growing feelings for her. The sheriff had completely ruled

Summer out as a suspect. Megan swore that Summer never went outside that evening and never spoke to anyone on the phone. Her hands and clothes had no signs of having been near spray paint, and her phone and computer records were clean. Summer had willingly allowed the officers, Lank, and Johnny full access to all her devices.

Lank felt bad for suspecting Summer at all, but even Johnny had come around to understand why Lank had his suspicions. Johnny confessed that, in an effort to clear his sister, he had used his own expertise to search every possible way that Summer might have electronically communicated with anyone. When the sheriff asked for her devices, Megan went back to their house and retrieved all Johnny's research to share with him and with Lank.

The forensics tech the sheriff had called in was gone by the time Lank and Johnny left for home. The can of paint had been taken as evidence, and the barcode, as well as the can itself, were to be investigated by the county crime lab. Pictures had been taken of Summer's truck, Summer and Megan would take it to town later that day to have it cleaned and repainted if necessary.

They had no suspects, but things were beginning to come together. This confirmed their suspicion that the perp knew about mechanics and had a working knowledge of cars or other vehicles. They were in an area where everybody literally knew everyone and everything about everyone; they had the best modern security system money could buy, a top-rated expert in cyber-crimes, and a detective who regularly worked with the FBI. Something was about to give. Lank could feel it.

"Truth time," Megan said, settling onto the couch next to Summer. "Are you okay?"

Summer nodded. "Yeah, I'm okay." She laid her head on the back of the couch. "I just want it to end. I want my life back." She closed her eyes and sighed.

"The same lonely life you had before Lank arrived?"

Looking at Megan out of the corner of one open eye, Summer raised her eyebrow. "What's that supposed to mean?" She closed her eye and let out a long breath, obviously preparing herself for whatever Megan was about to say.

"You know exactly what I mean," Megan poked Summer in the arm. "I know you have feelings for him."

"Megan," Summer groaned. "Now? Really? Can't you just let it go? You've been trying to steer me toward some guy since the day you moved out here. I'm content. Why can't you just let it be?"

"Because nobody wants to live their lives being 'content.' Don't you want to be happy? To be loved and cherished? To have a family?"

"Not everyone gets to have that, Megan." Summer snapped. "Some people aren't meant to find a soul mate. Some of us are better off alone."

Megan stared at her sister-in-law, but Summer refused to open her eyes.

"Summer," Megan said quietly. "Even if you're right, why would you think you're one of them? You're one of the smartest, kindest, most compassionate people I've ever known. Why on earth would you think that you aren't meant for love?"

Summer squeezed her eyes tightly, trying to hold back the rush of warm tears that were ready to burst forth from her eyes. Unable to stop them, Summer took a breath and rubbed away the moisture that escaped.

"You don't understand," Summer said. "I can't be loved."

Megan was stunned into silence. She blinked a few times before taking Summer's hand. "Look at me," she commanded. When Summer refused to turn, Megan tugged firmly at her hand. "Look at me."

When Summer turned toward her, Megan saw the pain in her eyes. "Why would you think that?" Megan asked quietly.

"Because it's true. The only boy who ever really liked me for me was Scott, and he wasn't meant to be mine. And that's okay. I love him, and I love Lisa, and I love them together. This isn't about him. But he understood me and respected me. He didn't try to change me or control me or make me into someone I'm not. He didn't try to hurt me," she added quietly.

Summer closed her eyes, shaking her head as if to make her thoughts go away. Megan wondered what it was that Summer wasn't saying. She was holding back, but Megan knew not to push. She knew that Summer only shared so much, and then she shut down. Why, Megan didn't know, but she had her suspicions, and she knew better than to voice them.

"Summer, Lank won't hurt you."

"I know. It's just that," she sighed. "I don't think I can be with him, Megan, not in that way. I don't think I could ever—"

"Summer, don't. I'm not going to pressure you or ask you why you feel that way, but you're wrong. Whatever you're hiding, whatever has made you think you're not good enough or can't trust someone who loves you, that's not the way it has to be."

"Stop," Summer's voice was shrill. "Just stop. It's not going to happen. Do you understand? I can't be with Lank. I can't be with anyone. Why can't you accept that?"

"Why can't you accept that somebody actually wants to be with you? Somebody might actually want to love you, for you, regardless of anything else."

"And I suppose you think Lank is that someone?"

"I don't know, but neither will you if you don't try."

"And what if it doesn't work out? What if he won't accept me, accept my faults, my past?"

"What past? You've never done anything wrong." Megan had had just about enough of Summer's self-pity. "Maybe it's time for you to grow up and act your age. Stop behaving like a petulant child, throwing a temper tantrum because you want everyone to treat you like a grownup when you're not acting like one. You need to put on your big girl boots and start having some faith. I know how much you talk about trusting in God, saying your daily prayers, going to Church, etcetera. Is that all for show?"

"Of course, not," Summer protested.

"Then prove it," Megan said, pulling the pillow away and forcing Summer to sit up. "'Be not afraid.' How many times did Jesus say that in the Bible?"

"I don't know," Summer said.

"But you do know that He said it more than any other phrase or command. He said to put all your trust in Him, to never lose faith. So why can't you do that?"

Summer swallowed and looked at her sister-in-law. "I don't know," she said quietly. "I just…"

"Don't start searching for excuses because there aren't any. You want to blame all your problems on everyone but yourself. Others want to change you. Others won't respect you. Others say you're too smart or too uppity or too standoffish. I've heard every excuse you've ever come up with. Have you ever thought of looking in the mirror? You're the only one who questions how smart you are. You're the only one who thinks you always must prove that you're making the right decisions, going to the right college, choosing the right career, buying the right land, building the right house. You're the one who insists that you've done something wrong in the past. Stop trying so hard to prove everyone wrong, and start seeing that you've done everything right. Just let things happen. Trust that God has your back."

"I don't know if it's that easy."

"It is," Megan insisted. "I know it is."

If only Summer knew what Megan knew. Megan knew that you only needed faith. Faith in God, in yourself, and in your soulmate. Soon, she would be able to share with everyone just how wonderful life was if you only have faith. For now, Summer would just have to find her own faith and start trusting in God and in herself.

CHAPTER TEN

Johnny was quiet through dinner and went back to his office after discarding his dishes in the sink.

"What's with him?" Lank asked his cousin.

"He's not happy about you staying with Summer tonight," Megan replied as she turned on the water and picked up a saucepan. "How's your back?"

"It's fine, and don't change the subject. I would think that Johnny would want me there. Is it because he feels like he can't help? Because of the chair and all?"

Megan turned and frowned at her cousin. Even with the nap she took that afternoon, she was exhausted. After being up half the night and then going at it with Summer, she didn't want to get into it with Lank, too. Her hormones were going crazy, leaving her tense and cranky.

"Really? You think he's self-conscious about being in a wheelchair? He got past that ages ago, and don't let the chair fool you. If he needed to, he'd crawl on his hands to help his sister. No, you idiot, it's because of the kiss and because of the way you look at his sister." She shook her head and turned back to the pan she was scrubbing. Were they both blind or just fools?

"The kiss? I thought we were past that." Lank closed the dishwasher and leaned back against the counter.

"He would be past it if he wasn't reminded of it every time you look at Summer."

"What's that supposed to mean?" Lank crossed his arms and furrowed his brow.

"Oh, come on," Megan said as she deposited the pan in the drying rack. She dried her hands with a dish towel that she tossed on the counter and placed her hands on her hips. "You've got feelings for her. Anybody can see it."

Lank opened his mouth to protest but thought better of it. Megan knew him too well. If he protested, she'd see right through him. If he admitted it, she'd start conniving to get them together, and neither of them needed that right now. Finally, he shook his head, pushed himself away from the counter, and headed toward the loft to pack a bag for the night. At the bottom of the steps, he paused and turned back to Megan who remained poised with her hands on her hips and her head cocked to the side.

"Fine, I'm attracted to her. I already admitted that to you, but I'm not going to take advantage of Summer or her situation. Summer's your sister-in-law. That practically makes us related. On top of that, I've spent the last several days sizing her up as a possible psychopath, or a mentally ill person at least. She'd never want anything to do with me."

As he walked up the stairs, Megan, in a low commanding voice, said, "Watch yourself, Lank. Summer needs you more than you think, and you're in deeper than you're willing to admit. Someone's going to end up hurt, and it better not be Summer. She's gone through enough already."

❦

It's one big game of musical cars, Lank thought, as he parked the Jeep in the driveway. Summer had rented it while her truck was being painted but had left it at Megan's for Lank to drive to the house. Megan needed her rental for work, and Johnny didn't want to be left without his SUV. It was becoming a hassle to not have a vehicle, and Lank needed to think about getting one of his own.

He knocked on the front door, but Summer didn't answer. Still not sure of his place, he didn't want to walk in the door uninvited, so he walked around the house toward the back deck and looked through the kitchen window. Summer was doing push-ups on a mat on the floor. In front of her, the television was on, and a woman on the screen was pushing herself up from a mat as well. The woman changed to a standing position, raising her arms, and stretching to the sky. In one fluid, graceful motion, Summer moved with her, her gaze to the ceiling, arms outstretched, her mouth moving as if she was speaking.

Lank noticed her toned body beneath the spandex workout shorts and athletic tank top. Her red hair was pulled back, and she was the definition of poetry in motion as she smoothly changed position. She and the woman on the screen bent forward, their hands grasping their elbows, arms slowly swaying back and forth as they gently turned their bent bodies from side to side. Summer's eyes were closed, and she appeared as if she was in a trance; but, as if she felt his presence, her eyes opened, and their gazes locked. With a sudden jolt of panic, Summer sprang completely to her feet and screamed. It only took a moment for her to recognize

Lank, and she took a deep breath as she walked to the back door and unlocked it.

Lank moved from the kitchen window and met Summer at the back door, feeling embarrassed at being caught watching her.

"Hey, Summer. Sorry to scare you."

She grabbed a small towel and wiped her face. "Do you always stare at women through their kitchen windows while they're working out?"

"I don't usually make it a habit." He looked toward the TV, confused by what he was hearing. Music played softly in the background as the woman on the screen softly said familiar words. He thought it was a prayer that he'd heard before but not one with which he was personally acquainted.

"Is she praying?" he asked

Summer turned toward the TV.

"Yeah, the Rosary. It's called Soul Core. It helps keep me grounded."

Lank nodded and watched the woman move into a submissive position, knees bent, body folded over them on the mat, head down, and arms outstretched with the palms up. She continued to pray.

"I've never heard of praying while doing yoga. At least, not like that. I thought yoga was for meditation or something."

"First of all, this is more like Pilates than yoga." Summer picked up the remote control and turned down the volume on the video. "Second, I'm pretty sure you can pray anywhere, anytime. I think it's a major issue in our world today. Most people have forgotten how, or weren't taught, that everything should be done as a form of prayer." She reached for a glass of water on the table and took a drink before rolling her head from side to side and stretching her arms.

Lank wasn't sure how to respond to her words about prayer. He was pretty sure that he was taught at some point, how to pray, but it wasn't something he was sure he could do anymore. Making everything he did a form of prayer was a completely foreign concept that he didn't know where to begin contemplating.

"Sorry, to interrupt," he said, feeling uncomfortable with his thoughts – those about prayer as well as those about Summer in her spandex. "Maybe I should wait in the truck."

"Don't be silly," Summer said. "I can finish my prayers later. I was almost at the end, so I'm feeling pretty limber and at ease."

Lank winced and looked away. He was positive that prayer and exercising women did not go together. He swallowed and tried to maintain his senses as Summer bent in front of the TV and stopped the streaming video that played through a laptop connected to the television.

"If you don't mind, I'm going to go upstairs and do some cooling stretches before taking a shower."

Lank nodded but was unable to speak as he watched her go up the stairs. She moved like a mythical creature, toned and muscular, with grace and beauty. It was obvious that she had no idea the effect she had on him. He was sure she had no idea that she had that effect on all men. He knew because he had seen it in their eyes and on their faces the few times they had been together in public.

She was beautiful yet modest, confident yet humble, and an enigma to Lank. She kept her feelings to herself, rarely talked about her own life or her past without being prodded into it, and could shift her mood in the blink of an eye. When she wasn't scared to death, she exuded self-confidence and assurance, but she never wanted to be the center of attention. On the contrary, she lived behind a well-guarded barricade that few people could penetrate. And every minute that he was with her, Lank felt himself falling even harder for the woman he believed to be hidden inside the wall she had built around herself. Maybe Megan was right and he was in over his head. The question was, what was he supposed to do about it?

Restless, Lank paced the floor of Summer's living room while she tried to concentrate on reading her book. Every now and then, she could feel him nonchalantly glance at her, but neither said a word. Finally, Summer put down the book and stretched.

"How 'bout a beer?" she asked.

"I'd love one," Lank answered and headed to the adjoining kitchen without waiting for Summer to get up.

She watched him reach into the fridge, grab two beers, and twist off the caps. He took a long, healthy drink before heading back to the living room area and handing her the other bottle.

"What's got you so worked up?" she asked. "My bet is he won't come back tonight. Last night was too close a call."

After taking another swig, Lank looked at her and nodded. "Yeah, I think you're right."

"Are you bored? We can turn on the TV."

"Nah," he said as he settled into the recliner across from her. "I'll probably head to bed soon."

"You won't sleep. Not until you get whatever is bothering you off your chest. I'm a trained expert at reading people and counseling them, remember? Want to talk about it?"

Lank stared at Summer for a minute before taking another drink of his beer.

"Nothing to talk about," Lank said curtly.

"Suit yourself," Summer said and returned her gaze to her book, pretending to read but unable to concentrate.

They sat in silence for a few minutes before Lank spoke again. "Mind if I get another?"

"Be my guest, but if you down the next one as quickly as you downed that one, you won't need to worry about not sleeping. You'll pass out before you make it to the bed." She watched him walk to the kitchen and retrieve another beer.

"After two beers? I don't think so," he said as he twisted off the cap and took another, this time smaller, drink.

"So, what's up? Is it me?"

The bottle stopped halfway to his mouth, and Lank looked at her with eyes the color of the January sky, blue with clouds of grey; smoky eyes, her mother would say.

"What do you mean? Is it you?"

"I mean, are you still thinking that I might be doing all of this for attention or that I'm crazy? Do you still not trust me?" she asked quietly. Pulling her outstretched legs in toward her body, she curled up in the corner of the couch.

"As far as I'm concerned, Summer, you're off the hook." He walked back across the room and sat on the edge of the recliner, holding her gaze steady. "You understand, don't you, that I had to look at every angle, every possibility. The first rule to solving a crime is ruling out those closest to it."

"I get it, and I truly thought we were past that. But something is bothering you. If not me, then what?"

She mechanically took a sip of her beer and watched him as he watched her. The clouds in his eyes were certainly present tonight. They looked more grey than blue at the moment, and he needed a shave. They stared at each other the way a mountain lion and a mule deer would have stared at each other; and though she felt her body heat rising, Summer shivered, feeling even more like *his* prey than that of the stalker.

"I, um, I think I'll head to bed," Summer said though she made no attempt to stand. She suddenly felt exposed even in her t-shirt and jeans.

"I think that's a good idea," Lank said, taking another sip, and Summer watched his Adam's apple as he swallowed. Her heart began to beat faster, and she felt the need to retreat to the safety of her bedroom. Without looking back, Summer stood and fled up the stairs, away from everything that the look in Lank's eyes implied. When she locked the door behind her, she wasn't sure if she was locking him out or locking herself in.

Breakfast was a solitary affair the following morning. Lank scrambled himself a couple eggs and toasted two pieces of bread. He ate in silence and wondered if he would see Summer at all before he headed back to Megan's. The vibration of his watch alerted him to a text, and he reached across the table for his phone to read his update from Jim.

Barcode old. Lot was from a few years ago, but it was shipped to the Ace Hardware in Montrose. Hope that helps.

By the way, Scott and Lisa vouched for Summer. They say Wyatt is a narcissistic jerk and potentially dangerous. I'm keeping him in

my sights. And no news on the snake. Still looking, but I think it's a
dead end and waste of time.

Grateful that Jim was going to continue following up
on Wyatt and the snake, Lank called the county sheriff's
department to relay the news about the paint. Their
experts had turned up the same information and were
pulling registration records for all John Deere tractors,
combines, and other vehicles sold in the area that might
use that color paint. Now they were getting somewhere.

Certain that Summer must have heard him talking on
the phone, Lank glanced up at the closed bedroom door
in the loft. The second door was open, as it had been all
night. Unable to bring himself to sleep in the room next
to hers, Lank laid down on the couch to sleep. Or tried to.
After just small snatches of sleep here and there
throughout the night, he dragged himself from the couch
just as the sun was cresting over the mountains. Having
no desire to enjoy the view, he rolled toward the back of
the couch and put a pillow over his head until his stomach
began to rumble.

Lank made himself eggs and toast and ate in silence,
looking over his notes. When he finished eating, he
downed four Ibuprofen for his still aching back, he
washed his plate and mug and put on his shoes. He gave
the loft one last glance before walking out of the house.
Waiting for Johnny to pick him up, he looked at
Summer's rented Jeep in the driveway where Summer's
truck belonged. He could still picture the word scrawled
across the side of the Jeep. While he was glad that the
accusation was being stripped away, he wished he knew
the meaning. How was Summer a thief? It was just one
more piece to the damned puzzle in which none of the
pieces fit.

Summer stayed in bed until she heard Johnny's SUV head down the driveway. She felt guilty for hiding in her room, but she couldn't bear to face Lank. She knew he wanted more than she could give. Even if she was willing to give a relationship a try, she didn't know if she could be the person he would want her to be, if she could do the things he'd expect from her. And even if she could, would Lank ever be able to look at her with love and trust instead of lust and suspicion? Would she be able to do the same? Was Megan right? Was it time to just trust God and see where things might lead?

"I sure do prefer this way off the mountain more than the other one," Lank said as he watched the flat ranchlands roll by, their gradual descent almost unnoticeable. Megan had left for work, and Johnny and Lank, with permission from both the Montrose and Gunnison County Sheriffs, were headed to Montrose to visit the businesses that may have used the tractor spray paint. Then they were also heading to the airport so that Lank could get a rental vehicle of his own. He had decided the evening before that he needed to bite the bullet and get a car.

"Not a fan of the switchbacks, huh?" Johnny asked.

"Not at all. I much prefer the smooth, steady descent where I don't have to see the world drop away right outside the car door."

Johnny laughed. "I guess it can be somewhat disconcerting for someone who didn't grow up out here. I don't even notice it, to tell the truth."

"Yeah, well you're lucky." Lank replied as he watched some men and boys repairing a fence as a group of cows stood nearby, feeding on sage and sparse patches of grass. He wondered, again, about the Ute Indians who lived on the land.

The ride was quiet, both men lost in thought. Every now and then, one of them would bring up the incidents, and they would try to piece them together. They were close, and they could feel it. If they could just figure out where the paint came from, they could narrow down the body shops and repair businesses and start looking at suspects.

The Ace Hardware was bustling with shoppers when Lank and Johnny went through the store to the administrative offices in the back. While Lank had no authority as a law enforcement officer here, the county police force was small, and they welcomed any help he could give them. They had arranged for him to meet with the manager of the store, and he was grateful to have the chance to follow up the one and only solid lead they had.

"No, sir," the elderly man told them, shaking his head. "Those cans don't sit on the shelves too long around here. Somebody always has some piece of equipment in need of repair and painting."

"So, there's no way that a can of paint from this 2015 lot would have been recently sold," Lank clarified.

"That's right. They would have been gone by the end of the summer. October at the latest."

The old man pulled a handkerchief from his pocket and wiped his brow.

"Is there a way to trace this barcode?" Lank asked.

The man thought for a moment. "Not that I know of. We ain't got no fancy computer programs that track purchases or anything like that. Just discount cards. I wouldn't use one of them things myself." He looked around, leaned toward Lank, and lowered his voice. "My wife read an article that said that every time a person uses one of them grocery store cards, the store makes a list somewhere of everything she buys. Then they sell it to the government so that the Feds can see what every person buys. That's how they supposedly track terrorists, but I think it's just one of the ways they keep track of what we're all doin' and buyin'. We ain't got no secrets from the Feds. It's like that book by Orson Welles."

Lank and Johnny exchanged confused looks before the reference made sense to Lank.

"I think you mean, George Orwell," he offered.

The old man wiped his brow again and looked up at the ceiling, presumably giving that a thought. "Nope, I'm pretty sure it was Orson Welles."

Lank and Johnny smiled to each other. "Okay, well, thank you, sir," Lank said, reaching his hand out to shake the man's hand. "We appreciate your help. Oh, one more question," Lank said before leaving. "Can you tell me if anyone bought any cans of that brand and color recently?"

"Just about every day," the man said with a smile. "Like I said, somebody always needs to repair or paint something."

"Thank you, again, Mr. Brice."

"More than happy to help, boys. Let me know if you need anything else."

"Not likely," Johnny muttered under his breath.

"That was a grand waste of time," Johnny said when they exited the building.

"Maybe not," Lank said. "Mr. Brice said it definitely would have been sold back in 2015. How many places around here work on farm equipment that would have been open back then? We're assuming this guy walked in and bought the can and took it home, but what if he works for a place that uses the paint. He could easily lift an old can without anyone noticing."

A quick search on Lank's phone produced six businesses. Of the six, one dealt only with tires and did no vehicle repairs. Three sold only orange Kubotas, red Masseys, and/or blue New Hollands. Only two places sold and repaired John Deere products.

"This one's the closest to where we are now," Lank said, pointing to a name on the screen.

"Then let's see what we can find out from the local John Deere retailer," Johnny said as he put the SUV into drive.

Fifteen minutes later, they were seated with the owner of the sizable lot featuring at least a dozen each of tractors, riding lawn mowers, combines, and other massive farm equipment.

"Most of my people have been here for at least that long, but I'd bet the store that none of them is the one you want."

"Why is that?" Lank asked. "You don't even know what they may or may not have done."

The middle-aged man shrugged. "I know my employees. They're all hard-working family men, fathers, wives, mothers, or good kids trying to make an honest dollar."

"I'm sure they are," Lank told him, "but you see, somebody took a can of paint, the kind meant to paint a John Deere tractor or mower or other product, and they used the paint as part of an on-going effort to terrorize a single, young woman. And that can of paint has been traced to the Ace right here in Montrose. The same Ace where you probably buy the paint you use in that parts and repair building right next door."

"Then I can assure you, Mr. Lankton, that it didn't come from my place of business. I haven't bought a single can of paint from that Ace since it opened. All of the paint we use here is bought in bulk from the manufacturer."

"We hit one damned dead end after another," Lank said before stabbing his steak with his fork and stuffing it into his mouth.

"Maybe the sheriff is having better luck," Megan offered.

"Maybe," Lank conceded. "I don't see how it could be any worse."

"What did your boss say?" Megan asked, referring to a call Lank had received earlier in the day.

"He wants to know when I'll be back." Lank didn't make eye contact with Megan. He could feel her gaze on him as he chewed his well-done sirloin. Although it was McCain who convinced Lank to go to Colorado in the first place, he wasn't very happy that things were taking so long to wrap up. He'd already assigned the recent case he had for Lank to another detective, but there was bound to be another one soon. Lank knew that the longer he stayed to help Summer, the less likely it would be that he'd have a job waiting for him when he returned to Maryland.

"What did you tell him?" Megan pressed.

Lank shrugged and shoveled a large chunk of a baked potato into his mouth. After he swallowed, he looked at Megan.

"I told him that things weren't going as well as I'd hoped and that I might need some extended leave time." That hadn't gone over well. Lank could still hear the background noise of the station as McCain let the silence say what his words did not. After what felt like an extraordinarily uncomfortable eternity, McCain cleared his throat, and simply said, "I see." Lank could see, too. His boss's patience had come to an end.

"Did he say okay?" Megan broke into his thoughts.

Lank looked up and blinked. "Huh?"

"Your boss, did he say it was okay if you took extended leave."

"He didn't say it wasn't okay," Lank hedged, taking a long drink of iced tea. What he had said was that Lank had until the end of the week to decide on which side of the country he preferred solving crimes. "Is there more tea in the fridge?" he asked, standing up from the table. He went to the refrigerator and bent down to look for the tea pitcher.

"So, what time are you going to Summer's?" Megan asked, changing the subject.

Lank hit his head on the freezer as he pulled the tea off the top shelf in the fridge. "Ouch," he yelped, rubbing his head with his left hand and kicking the door shut with his foot.

"You okay?" Megan turned to see what was going on.

"Yeah, fine. What did you ask me?"

"What time are you going to Summer's tonight?"

"Oh, yeah." He refilled his tea and thought about Summer. He would rather Megan stay at her sister-in-law's, but in a surprise move, Johnny put his foot down and said that his wife needed to be safely home with him, and his sister needed to be guarded by the police. Since

Lank was the policeman they'd brought out to do the job, he agreed.

"Summer's having dinner with her parents. She said she'd call when she was on the way home. She's meeting me there."

"I'm glad Johnny took you to get your own vehicle this afternoon. The car situation was already complicated." Megan said as Lank sat back down. "The insurance company called today. My truck is totaled, as suspected. They're going to process a check so I can buy a new one, but who knows how long that's going to take."

"Yeah, I'm glad to have my own set of wheels. I just hope I don't have to rent it for too long."

"As soon as we get to the bottom of all this, you can take back the truck and head home to your job and your own life." Megan said, as if it was that simple. "If that's what you want." She glanced at Lank, but he didn't take the bait.

Lank needed to solve the case of Summer's mysterious stalker and figure out exactly what he was going to do with his job and his life. Because he knew one thing for sure. Summer *was* a thief. In the midst of everything that was going on, and despite his distrust and misgivings, she had somehow managed to steal his heart.

CHAPTER ELEVEN

Lank gripped the wheel and rode the brakes as he made the hairpin turn on the switchback. He cursed under his breath and hoped that he wouldn't lose traction on the gravel road.

"Damned mountains. Why does Megan have to live at the top of one?" he asked out loud. "She couldn't have chosen a nice little house in the valley on level ground?"

His white knuckles tensed as he eased the truck down toward the county highway. Once he was down, he took a deep breath and willed his heart to slow its rhythm. At least his back wasn't hurting him this morning. So, he had that going for him even if his heart was about to give out.

He drove another half hour until he hit Route 50. He still marveled at the fact that this was the same Route 50 that ran just twenty miles from his home in Lakespring. He didn't believe Megan at first, but sure enough, she showed him, using Google Maps, that Route 50 did indeed run from Ocean City, Maryland, to Sacramento, California, cutting right through Gunnison County, and along the beautiful Blue Mesa Reservoir where they turned to head up the mountain to Megan's cabin. Megan told him that it gave her a bit of comfort that she was still connected to home via this highway, and that if she ever felt the need, she could drive straight from here to home. Of course, Route 50 in Maryland was a 55 to 65 mile per hour, three and four lane highway, while Route 50 in Colorado was little more than a dual lane country road connecting one mountain pass to another. Lank thought about all the other differences between here and home as he drove. The one that kept coming back over and over was Summer. She was here, and there was nobody like her back in Maryland, as far as Lank was concerned.

There was only one body shop in Lake City, the same one where Summer's car was being repainted. Megan, Johnny, and Monica were all taking turns staying with Summer when Lank was away, now that she didn't have a car. Lank stopped at the body shop and asked for the manager. Thomas Hiller introduced himself as manager and owner, having taken over the business from his father. He was the same age as Lank and had gone to school with Johnny. Lank had no need to fill him in on the case or beat around the facts. There were few secrets in Lake City.

"How's Summer holding up?" Tommy asked.

"As good as can be expected," Lank told him, though Lank honestly had no idea. He beat Summer to her house the night before, let himself in with the key, and prepared himself to apologize, once again, for his impulsiveness. Instead, Summer arrived about ten minutes later, thanked him for coming, and hurried upstairs to bed. That morning was the same as the morning before. Lank got up early, ate alone, and left before Summer was out of bed.

"I hear Mr. Cooper is trying to get her to move back home. Sounds like a good idea if you ask me."

"Yeah, he wasn't too happy about her trying to keep it all from him."

"She should've known better than to try. Word travels fast in a small town."

"Yes, it does," Lank agreed. Though they may seem worlds apart in many ways, Lakespring and Lake City were both small towns, and Lank knew all too well how quickly word could get around, especially when someone didn't want it to.

Lank asked Tommy a few questions, expecting another dead end. He was pleasantly surprised, though, when he asked about the spray paint.

"Yeah, we buy that brand from Walmart now and then. I don't do a lot of farm equipment in here, mostly cars and trucks and four-wheelers, that kind of stuff. Every once in a while, I get a riding mower or something that calls for special paint. It makes more sense to buy it from Walmart than to order it from my regular suppliers."

"Would you still have a record of a purchase from 2015?" Lank asked hopefully.

"Yeah, I should. I just have to pull it up."

Lank followed Tommy to a room behind the counter, expecting to find a row of filing cabinets amid the grease and grime of the auto-body shop. Instead, he walked into a nicely furnished office equipped with a computer setup that even Johnny would have admired. Tommy tapped the mouse, and the three monitors on the desk lit up. After a few clicks, Tommy's printer started spitting out paper.

"I'm printing a copy of the purchase receipt as well as the invoice for the repair done."

Lank took the papers and saw that a full description of the work done, and the cans of spray paint used, were on the invoice, right down to the barcode number. It was a perfect match to the one in the picture on Lank's phone. His heart skipped a beat at the find.

"Does that help at all?" Tommy asked.

"Does it ever," Lank responded. "Any chance you still have these cans here?"

"Maybe," Tommy told him. "Hold on." With a few more clicks, Tommy nodded his head. "Looks like we have one can left. We only bought three, and like I said, we don't use a whole lot of it."

"Would you mind checking to see if the can is still on the shelf?"

"No problem," Tommy said. "We're pretty good at keeping track of our inventory, so it should be there. Let's take a look."

Lank and Tommy went to the repair shop where a radio played country music, and a pair of legs stuck out from under a jacked-up Toyota 4Runner. Tommy perused the shelves from one side to another and then backed up and began again. He reached up and turned down Randy Travis.

"Hey, Al," he called.

The legs propelled out from under the 4Runner to reveal an older man, wearing the same overall jumpsuit as Tommy and covered in grease. "Yeah?" the man answered.

"You use any John Deere paint lately?"

"Nope. Why?"

"There's a can missing. Did you clean out the old cans?"

"Not me, sorry."

"Okay, thanks," Tommy said, an odd expression on his face. Lank's heart began to race.

"That's strange. We don't usually misplace stuff around here."

Lank looked around the shop, with its tools scattered across the workbench and the floor with grease splashed on every surface, and that dry, Rocky Mountain dirt that seemed to be everywhere, dusting the floor and everything in between. Despite the appearance of the shop, Lank believed Tommy. This was a man who knew how to run a business, and Lank instinctively knew that he was much more organized than appearances would suggest.

"Is it just the two of you that work here?" Lank asked, his hope beginning to rise.

"Well, kinda," Tommy said, scratching his head.

Lank's heart sank. "Kinda?"

"It's just the two of us who are employed here, but we've got a partnership with the local high school and with Western University in Gunnison. The local kids use the shop for school projects and can work here on the weekends for credit. The school provides their supplies, and they're stored in a separate part of the shop."

"I'm going to need the name of every person who has worked here for the past six months. No, wait, can you tell me when the last time was you used that paint?"

"Yeah," Tommy said, furrowing his brow in question.

"Great. I need a list of every person who has worked in this place since that can was last seen."

Lank stood at the back door and watched the lightning. The mountains were invisible, shrouded in black from the ground to the heavens. Each bolt of lightning illuminated the sky with an iridescent glow that gave clear understanding of the term, electric blue.

"This is spectacular," Lank said.

"It is pretty incredible," Summer agreed. It was the first time they had seen each other in forty-eight hours, and Lank couldn't help but see the irony of them being together during a lightning storm. Every time he thought about her lately, he felt like he'd been hit by a bolt out of the blue.

Another strike hit a distant mountain with offshoots of light emanating from the bolt like the long, spindly branches of a tall, pine tree.

"The lightning is seriously intense," Lank said, feeling like a kid mesmerized by his first storm.

"And dangerous. One strike to a dry, dead tree can start a fire that would spread for miles and lay waste to everything in its path."

Lank marveled once again with his new appreciation for nature. "I guess that's something I've never given a thought to. Forest fires are pretty non-existent on the east coast."

"And pretty common out here. We had one about seven or eight years ago that spread all the way up to the base of the San Juan's. You could see the haze and smell the smoke even with the doors and windows closed."

Lank was speechless. He'd never seen such a beautiful storm, and it was hard to reconcile that with the destruction that he knew a forest fire could create. He turned to Summer.

"Why do you stay up here? So far from civilization? With bears and mountain lions and lightning that could burn down your house? Why, with everything you've gone through over the past couple months, do you stay in this house, on this mountain, alone?"

Summer looked at Lank and then turned back to the light show. She fiddled with the cross dangling below her throat as she watched the light flash across the sky. When she finally spoke, her voice was low, and her gaze was fixed on the black horizon with its intermittent blue light.

"Once, when I was younger, my parents took us to Disney World. It was a dream come true for me. Even Johnny, who acted like it was a stupid trip for his baby sister, had the time of his life. We went to all the parks, rode all the rides, watched the shows, and had our pictures taken with every Disney character imaginable."

Lank watched her as she spoke. Her red hair hung loose around her shoulders, and the occasional flash of light made her eyes even greener than usual. She was the most beautiful sight he had seen since he'd arrived in Colorado. He watched her lips curve into a smile as she remembered her family trip.

"One night, we went to see Fantasmic, the light and water show. Have you seen it?" She turned and looked at Lank who shook his head, too awestruck by her to speak.

"It was this amazing show of lights and lasers and water spouts. But as I watched it, all I could think about was that it was made up. It was a technological wonder of grand proportions, but it was a show." She turned back to Mother Nature's show outside the window. "This," she said as she gestured to the sky, "this is the real deal. This is a light show of epic proportions that Walt Disney could only dream of portraying with his fancy lights and music."

Summer turned to Lank and smiled. "I wake up every morning with a heavenly masterpiece painted across the sky outside my window. I drive to work amid the majesty of the most beautiful mountains in the world. I see God's version of a magical light show every time we have a storm. If I'm lucky, Black and I can spot a bobcat or a mother bear and cubs up on one of our rides. I walked through Cinderella's castle, rode the Matterhorn, watched Fantasmic, and met creatures of all kinds in their costumes and wigs, but I never once saw anything that compares to what I have on top of this mountain."

Without thinking, Lank reached up and tucked the stray lock of hair behind her ear. He felt Summer catch her breath at his touch. His hand lingered near her face before he gently touched her cheek and let his finger trail down her face.

"I've never seen anything as beautiful as what's standing in front of me at this moment," Lank said quietly as he lightly caressed her cheek with the back of his fingers.

"Lank, I," Summer began to speak, but Lank put his finger on her lips.

"Shh," he whispered. "You don't have to say anything. I think you know how I feel, but I don't think you know how you feel. Not yet." He felt her shiver and saw the relief in her eyes. It was all he could do not to take her into his arms.

"As far as I'm concerned, I'm here on business. God help me, I might not sleep a wink waiting for you to decide what you want, but once you can see clearly and choose me for who I am and not what I can do to save you; once you're no longer the damsel in distress but the strong woman I believe you to be, then I'll be here."

Lank leaned down and placed a soft, gentle kiss on her lips before backing away and heading upstairs to the room next door to hers. He had made up his mind, right or wrong. Summer was the only woman who had ever made him feel this way – focused yet confused, secure yet unsteady, manly yet like a child in need. He was too far gone to turn back now.

Summer's heart raced, and her body tingled with as much electricity as was in the lightning over the San Juan's. She closed her eyes and swallowed. As much as she wanted to deny it, she felt it, too. All her life, she had heard about this feeling. Scott hadn't done this to her. Wyatt hadn't come close. After all the making out and close encounters she'd had, nothing left her wanting more like Lank's touch, his kisses, the way he looked at her. It almost made her forget....

Suddenly very thirsty, Summer went to the kitchen to get a glass of water. Her hand shook as she brought the glass to her lips.

Darn you, Lank. I had no idea you would be more frightening than a stalker.

Like the previous two mornings, when Summer woke the next day, Lank was already gone. She showered, dressed, and ate before heading to the barn. She needed time to think. It still gave her the creeps each time she entered the barn. Her gaze immediately went to the stall where she had seen the snake slither into his hiding place. Every morning, she expected to see it there again, to hear its deadly hiss and haunting rattle.

She talked to Black as she saddled him up and walked him to the far side of the corral. For so long, Black was the only male she wanted in her life. After being manipulated by Wyatt and attacked by Jeremy, she had sworn off all men. She bought her own piece of property and worked with an architect to design the perfect house with the best view on the mountain. She was able to support herself and liked what she did. But she was lonely, and lately, she was beginning to wonder if she'd been wrong. About a lot of things.

As she rode off into the trees, Summer tried to calm her own fears and doubts. Could she do this? Could she let herself trust a man? Enough to tell him about her past? And then, would he forgive her for what she had done?

CHAPTER TWELVE

Lank stood by the fence and watched as Black and his rider sauntered out of the trees, down the path, toward the paddock. He unhitched the gate and walked out to meet Summer as she dismounted. Cosmo followed at his heels.

"You look like you've had a good day," Summer said with a smile. "Hello, baby," she said to Cosmo, bending down to scratch under his chin.

"I could say the same about you," Lank said, resisting the urge to take her in his arms. A small part of him hoped that his admission the previous night would allow Summer to open up to him. The rest of him was still trying to decide if her opening up would be a good thing with promise for the future or a bad thing, causing upheaval and chaos in his quiet, solitary life. "I hope you don't mind that I let Cosmo out."

"No, I appreciate it. Thanks. And it was a good day," she said as she turned back to Black and stripped him of his riding gear. "I went for a ride this morning, then did some laundry, worked on some paperwork for school, did a little spring cleaning, and still had time for another ride. I needed the fresh air after cleaning all afternoon. And some time to think," she added.

"Think about what?" Lank asked, avoiding looking at her.

"Things," she replied nonchalantly as she carried the saddle into the barn. Lank waited, rubbing Black's neck, more comfortable with the animal than he had been when he'd arrived, until Summer returned a few minutes later with a bucket of soapy water and two brushes. She threw one to Lank.

"If you're going to stay, make yourself useful."

For a few minutes, they bathed Black in silence. Lank hoped she would say more about the "things" she referred to, but after a while, it was obvious that she wasn't going to elaborate. He experienced a small feeling of relief. Until the situation was resolved, he couldn't let his desire for her cloud his judgment any more than it already was.

"So, I didn't tell you about the break I caught yesterday."

"Another one? Really?" Summer stopped brushing Black and looked expectantly at Lank.

He told her about his visit to the auto body shop in Lake City and the phone call he received from Tommy this morning.

"Tommy Hiller," Summer smiled. "That boy always was smart. The most organized person I've ever known. And computer skills like you wouldn't believe. A lot of people around here think he's wasting his time and talents working on cars, but I get it." Lank stopped working and watched Summer over the horse's back. She smiled as she spoke about Tommy, but her gaze never left Black. She lathered and brushed him with great care and attention.

"There are two kinds of smart people in this world. The kind who spend their entire lives working hard to make money or gain power because that's what they're expected to do with their brains. And the kind who use their intelligence and talents to do what makes them happy. I think the latter ones are the smartest ones."

"You're part of that group." It wasn't a question. Lank sensed her meaning and knew that, though she spoke in general terms and in reference to Tommy, she was really speaking about herself.

"Yeah, I think I am. I know I could have started my own business like Johnny, or moved to Manhattan and taken over Wall Street, or done any one of a hundred other things I was expected to do, but I didn't want any of that."

Without thinking, Lank walked around to the other side of the horse and stood beside Summer. He placed his hand on hers to stop her from tending to Black.

"And what is it that you want, Summer?" he asked quietly.

Slowly turning to face him, she gazed into his eyes for a moment before licking her lips and biting her bottom lip.

"I," she started. "I want what I have. To help kids figure out who they are and what they want in life. To live here, on this mountain, with Black. To spend my days and nights however I wish without having to answer to anyone."

"Is that really what you want?" he asked, taking a step closer.

"I, I think so. That's always been my plan," she said with uncertainty.

They stood so closely that they were almost touching, so close that Lank could practically feel her body against him, her heart pounding next to his. Their eyes were locked on each other's, Lank's Orioles cap brushing Summer's cowgirl hat. Then Lank abruptly took a step back.

"Good plan," Lank said, adjusting the cap on his head. "Until you get lonely." He looked into her eyes again. "And I bet there are times when this mountain can get awfully lonely."

"Well, it's a good thing Megan and Johnny are nearby." Summer turned quickly and went to the side of the barn to retrieve the hose. "Good boy," she said to Black as she rinsed him. The horse snorted and pawed at the ground but allowed Summer to hose him off until he'd had enough and shook, starting with his mane and shaking all the way down to his tail, sending droplets of water raining down on Lank and Summer. Summer squealed and laughed before turning the hose on Lank.

"Your turn," she yelled.

"Whoa, what the—" Lank darted away from the stream of water and chased after Summer. She didn't get far before he grabbed her from behind, sending the water up into the air, creating a fountain above them. Cosmo ran around them, barking and trying to join in the fun but retreating to a safe distance each time the water rained down on him. Laughing, Summer held firm to the hose, but Lank was able to wrestle it away from her. The hose fell to the ground, and Lank spun Summer around to face him. He held her tightly against his chest, his cap falling to the dirt behind him. She breathed heavily in his arms, but her body stiffened and her eyes pleaded with him to let her go.

"You're playing with fire," he told Summer through clenched teeth and a steely gaze. She gasped but held her wide eyes steady. He cursed as he turned her loose. "I'm going to change. Meet me inside, and I'll fill you in on Tommy."

❧

Lank turned, bent down to grab his hat, and walked briskly to his rental truck where he grabbed his bag from the front seat. He headed into the house and slammed the door behind him.

Summer shivered, despite the warmth of the sun, and ran her hands up and down the denim sleeves that covered her arms. She turned to look at Black, who had thrown himself into the dirt and was scratching his back on the rough ground, undoing all the work that she and Lank had done to bathe him.

"Really?" she said to the horse. "You couldn't at least wait until I was inside?" She shook her head and glanced back at the house.

Summer was confident, by the time she returned from her ride, that she would be able to resist Lank and deny her feelings for him. But each time she was with him, resisting him moved farther and farther from her mind.

If only the events of the past couple months had never taken place, then everything would be as it was. Summer would be content to live alone on the mountain for the rest of her life, without a man to complicate her life, without feeling the guilt over what she had allowed to happen with Jeremy.

But now, nobody would allow her to live alone or take care of herself, and the longer Lank was around, the less she wanted to. His words replayed in her head as she closed the gate and walked to the house.

I bet there are times when this mountain can get awfully lonely.

Summer scanned the list of names that Lank placed on the table before her. There were twelve high school students and five college students who had done work at the auto body shop in the past year. It was a small list, which was both good and bad. Small meant that Summer could probably identify everyone on it; however, it could be too small a list to include all potential suspects. But Lank figured they only needed one—one name, one suspect. If he was right, then they didn't need to look any further than the names that were right there in front of them.

"They're all local kids for the most part."

"For the most part?"

"Some of them are from Gunnison County. Lake City is much too small to field a football team on its own. About a year ago, some of the parents worked with our school and some of the ones in nearby Gunnison County to establish a team. Kids who live just over the county line, like this one, Luke, are allowed to go to school in Lake City and be starting players on the team. Having the garage nearby lets them still obtain a trade license even though we have the shop facilities on campus like some of the bigger schools."

"So, these are kids with athletic promise?" Lank asked.

Summer frowned. "I'm not sure I'd say that. I think Luke might. The others just want to play, and they have that opportunity here whereas they might not in a larger school." She leaned over Lank's shoulder to get another look at the list.

"These are all just kids," Summer said with a sigh. "None of these can possibly be the person."

"Wasn't Jeremy a kid?"

Summer turned pale. "Well, yes, but,"

"No buts. Sometimes kids have issues. They act out. It happens."

"But to try to kill you and Megan? Why…" Summer stopped. There had been plenty of kids in the news in the past twenty years who had killed people, who had stalked, raped, shot, and more.

Lank, who had been leaning down to look at the paper over her shoulder, pulled out the chair next to her and sat down.

"Summer, you need to look at these kids, not as students, but as potential suspects. Does anyone on this list stand out to you as someone who might not like you, might hold a grudge against you, might see you as taking something that belonged to them?"

"What do you mean?"

"I don't know, anything. Whoever is doing this thinks you're a thief. Why?"

"I don't have any idea," she said, shaking her head. "I've never taken anything from anyone. Not ever."

"Okay, a jealous girlfriend, perhaps. A couple of these names are girls."

Summer looked at the list again and shook her head. "These are good kids. All of them. It can't be any of them. It just doesn't make sense."

"Well, whether it makes sense to you or not, I'll be talking to every kid on this list, and his or her parents, teachers, and anyone else who might be able to shed some light on this. It's one of these people. I know it is. I can feel it in my gut."

Summer shook her head again and pushed the paper away.

"It's not possible," she said. "It's just not possible."

"Think about it," Lank urged.

"Okay. Let me go back out to get Black settled for the night. I'll be able to focus more after that."

"All done out there?" Lank asked as Summer walked into the house.

"Yep, Black has eaten, taken care of business, and is in the barn for the night."

"I guess you can't get pizza delivered up here, huh?"

Summer laughed. "Not unless you want it stone cold by the time it gets here. I guess there are one or two disadvantages to living up here, but I'll take the view over those few things any time."

Lank watched her take her hair down and shake it loose over her shoulders. She reached into the freezer and took out a frozen pepperoni pizza. After unwrapping it and putting it on a pan, she turned on the oven.

"So, tell me another advantage, besides the view." Lank stood and took a beer from the fridge. He held up another in an offering to Summer, but she shook her head and took a glass from the cabinet. She filled it with water and downed the entire glass before answering.

"It's peaceful. Well, most of the time. Recent events notwithstanding."

Lank acknowledged the reference with a roll of his eyes.

"I have access to the BLM without having to load Black into a trailer and drive up there."

"Okay, that's one."

"That's two," Summer corrected.

"I'm not sure about the peaceful one yet," he replied as he straddled a kitchen chair, sitting backwards to face her.

"Okay, I love my neighbors." She leaned back against the counter and crossed her ankles.

"The human ones or the animal ones?"

She smiled. "Both."

"Fair enough, what else?"

Summer thought about it for a minute as she placed the pizza into the heated oven. "I'm independent up here, nobody to answer to but myself, enough distance between lots to have privacy, plenty of room to move around, quiet Saturday mornings, majestic sunrises, magnificent lightshows on stormy nights, cool breezes during the day, and good, cold nights for sleeping all year long. I can sing at the top of my lungs, shout at the TV during a Broncos game, or walk around in my birthday suit if I want. Which I don't," she hastily added as Lank raised his brow. "But I could. I'm free to be and do whatever I want up here."

"But couldn't you be and do whatever you want down there?" He motioned in the direction of the highway.

"It's not the same," Summer answered. "Up here, I can just, be. I'm not Ms. Cooper, or Steve and Monica's daughter, or the smart girl who threw away her future to be a teacher. I'm just a girl with a horse and a world that's wide open for possibilities."

Lank thought about his life in Lakespring. He could relate.

"You know, it seems like every time I turn around back home, I run into someone who asks about the accident. I appreciate that they care, but it was ten years ago. It's not something I want to talk about to everyone I meet."

Summer moved across the room and leaned on the back of the loveseat near Lank's chair.

"Care to talk about it now?"

Lank stood and walked to the French doors that led to the deck. After a few minutes, he turned back to Summer and motioned to the couch. They both sat down.

"I was sixteen, the fall of my junior year, and I had everything in the world going for me. I was already being looked at by some pretty big colleges, Notre Dame, Oklahoma State, A&M." He smiled at Summer, wondering what would have happened if they had met in college. "I was going to have my pick of any D1 school in the country. I was sitting at the top of the world until Friday, October twelfth, 2007.

"I was a cornerback, a tough spot to be in for a high school kid, and an especially tough one for me. I was tall, lean, and fast. I spent my entire life as a running back. Then, my first year of high school, Coach O'Neil says, 'hey, Lankton, you're playing corner this season.' My first thought was, 'holy cow, I made the team.' I was a freshman and had no real hopes of being picked." He looked at Summer to be sure that she was still following him. She motioned for him to continue. "My second thought was, 'did he just say corner?' Mind if I get a glass of water?"

"Go ahead," Summer said. He felt her eyes on him as he stood, crossed the room, and got a drink. Once he was back on the couch, she shifted so that she was looking directly at him.

"So, anyway, I'm kind of bummed that first season, even though I'm on Varsity, because I'm a corner, not a big deal position in the eyes of a high school kid. Not a guts and glory position, so to speak. But I give it my all, and lo and behold, I'm good. Coach O'Neil was a genius. Most cornerbacks aren't noticed until college, and some not even until they're in the NFL, but he knew what he was doing, and I was the lucky SOB who got noticed."

The memories came flooding back. The recruiters, the news interviews, the folks cheering for him when he ran onto the field.

"By sophomore year, I'm reveling in my own glory, too much I suppose. I was cocky, not a nice guy, not the kind of person you would have liked, more like the kind of person who would have spent a lot of time in your office getting warnings about slipping grades."

"And did you spend a lot of time getting warnings about your grades?" Summer asked with a smile.

"Yeah, for a while, until Coach calls me into his office one day, early junior year, and tells me that I'm off the team."

"What?"

"Yeah, that was my reaction, too. I got really upset, started yelling, even thought about throwing something at him, and then it hit me. I didn't know who I was anymore. I didn't have any friends because I was too good for my old friends, and a lot of kids were jealous of me. I went through girls like Grant went through Richmond. They were nothing but jewelry, something to wear on my arm and show while I used them for my own pleasure. Megan hated me."

"I doubt that," Summer said soothingly.

"You know Megan better than that. She was furious with me. I'd hurt a couple of her friends, and I was acting like I was better than everyone. She was embarrassed to be my cousin.

"When it sunk in that Coach was sending me a message, I just sat down and started crying. This big, tough, star cornerback with his whole life ahead of him, was sitting in his coach's office crying his eyes out. Coach and I had a long talk after that. I saw the error of my ways and promised to do better. He was counting on me, and so was my mom." Lank looked at Summer and frowned. "My dad died of cancer the year before. I needed to make it to the big league so that I could take care of my mom, and failing algebra wasn't going to get me there.

"Anyway, I got myself straightened out just in time for the biggest game of the year. We're facing our rival, and both teams were aiming for states that year. They had this receiver who was the fastest kid in the state. He could run over you so fast, you'd still be looking forward while he's catching the ball behind you." Summer smiled, and Lank continued.

"So, I'm covering this kid, and we're racing down field when I look back, and I see the ball coming straight toward me. As I said, I grew up playing receiver. I knew what a catchable ball looked like, and I knew it was mine. I caught the ball and started running up the field like a rocket. I can still see it all, like I was watching a movie. The yard lines were flying by—30, 40, 50, 40, 30. I was almost to the twenty-yard line when I felt the most tremendous pain I'd ever felt in my life. It was like someone lit a fire to my upper back. I hit the ground hard and literally saw stars as two guys fell on top of me, pinning me to the ground. After all the other guys were up and walking away, I was still on the ground, still stunned, but feeling nothing in my back. I mean nothing. It was surreal."

Lank leaned his head back and closed his eyes, reliving the night for the thousandth time. He looked up and shook his head.

"Do you know how many cornerbacks sustain major injuries?"

Summer shook her head, and tears glistened in her eyes.

"Less than one percent, .06% to be exact. And most of those injuries are broken fingers, fractured hands, sometimes a broken wrist. But a broken back? It's almost unheard of. But there I was, being carried off on a stretcher. Megan and my mom met us at the back of the ambulance. Megan was hysterical, but mom, she was the picture of calm. She just kept telling me that everything was going to be all right, that God had a plan for me. Hell if I know what it is, but she still says that."

"She sounds like a great woman," Summer said.

"Yeah," he smiled. "She's a strong woman, too. And despite her hysteria, so was Megan. She was there for me every day for almost two years. I spent months in the hospital and then my whole senior year in rehab. Megan brought me my work every day and helped me get through my studies. She pushed me to keep trying on the days when physical therapy was too painful to bear. Sometimes, I hated her. Other times, she was the best friend I had. She and Coach O'Neil. He never gave up on me either. It was because of the two of them that I was able to walk across the stage to accept my diploma."

"And your mom's faith," Summer added.

"I guess so," Lank frowned. "I never really thought about faith having anything to do with it, hers or anyone else's."

"Faith has everything to do with it," Summer said. "Sometimes, it's all we've got."

The oven timer sounded, and Summer went to take out take the pizza. She laid it on the top of the stove and rummaged through a drawer for the pizza cutter.

"When have you had to rely on faith?" Lank found himself genuinely interested.

Summer shrugged as she cut the slices. "All the time. If I have a student who I'm just not getting through to, I say a prayer to St. Thomas Aquinas."

Lank raised his brow as Summer prepared their plates and put them on the table, refilled her glass, and took a seat. Lank sat beside her and nodded his head as she said the blessing.

"So, who is this Thomas person?" he asked before taking his first bite. He sucked in air to cool his tongue and regretted being in such a hurry to eat.

"St. Thomas Aquinas, patron saint of students. When Johnny was in Iraq, I prayed to St. Michael the Archangel, patron saint of those in battle. And when he was hurt, I prayed to St. Gemma, patron of back injuries."

"How the hell, sorry, how the heck do you know all that?"

"I look it up." She shrugged and took a bite of her pizza after blowing on it. Lank watched her lips with interest. "Whenever I have a special intention, I look to see who the best saint is to pray to."

"I never got all that stuff about praying to saints. It doesn't make sense to me."

"Why not?"

"Why not just pray to God?"

"I do, but I believe that having a few people in Heaven put in a good word for me can't hurt."

"I guess so. I'm not real familiar with all that churchy stuff."

Summer laughed, "Well maybe that's your problem, Lank. Maybe you're looking for help and guidance in all the wrong places." Lank had no answer for that, and they fell into a companionable silence for the rest of the meal."

"I need a shower," Summer said once she had finished eating. "Would you mind cleaning up?"

"Not at all," he answered honestly.

"Thanks, Lank."

Lank watched her go and thought about their conversation. Summer didn't judge him, lecture him, or pity him. She listened, even cried a little, but didn't interrupt or tell him he was a jerk like Megan often told him back when he was too full of himself to think straight. And then there was the saint stuff. Though it still seemed somewhat strange to him, he could see her point. There was a lot more to Summer than he gave her credit for. She was more than a hot body with fiery hair and a fiery temper. She was highly intelligent, adventurous, an individualist, brave, compassionate, and passionate about her work and her students. Despite all of that, she was humble and unassuming. And she had just pulled off a major crime right in front of his face. She managed to steal another piece of his heart.

CHAPTER THIRTEEN

After Summer showered, she and Lank played a game of Scrabble, in which Summer killed him, and that led to an early evening with both of them going to their rooms. Summer said she was going to read, and Lank went to bed with Summer's words on his mind. Lank managed to sleep through the night in the guest room without pain. It was a deep sleep without dreams, and without any stalker incidents pulling them from slumber before dawn, but Summer's words slipped in and out of his consciousness.

Maybe you're looking for help and guidance in all the wrong places.

What did that mean? Was she referring to the case or to his personal life? By morning, it was still a mystery to him, but he had work to do that day and not a lot of time to ponder the philosophical quandaries of his life.

With the aid of the Montrose and Gunnison County Sheriffs' offices and the Hinsdale County Sheriff in Lake City, Lank managed to set up interviews with five of the boys on the list. He would use Sheriff McCoy's office in town to meet with each boy and their parents and have official police status. With police forces made up of so few personnel, the sheriffs were happy for Lank to take the lead in Summer's case and were giving him as much leeway as they could. As he drove to Lake City, Lank thought about life on the mountain and how it compared to life back home.

For the first time in his life, he questioned his position with the Baltimore Police Department. He was tired of working drug busts and prostitution and human trafficking. When he was offered a position as a city police detective, he kissed his little job in Lakespring goodbye and whistled on his way to work the first morning he reported in Charm City. But after a while, he started wondering if he was doing any good. For every criminal he put away, three more cropped up.

Out here, police dealt with some of the same types of crime, but the crime rate was much lower, the types of crime more easily handled, and the criminals less violent. Not to mention the views and the fresh air. Lank could spend every day of his life waking up to the sunrise over those mountains. He'd always wanted to learn to fly fish, and he might even try his hand at hunting. That is, if he actually lived out here. Right now, it was all just a comparison scenario he was running in his head.

Until he thought of Summer. The idea of her leaving Colorado to live anywhere else in the world was not just laughable; it was downright offensive. And the more he was around her the less he thought he could live without her. Lank was just beginning to think about what it would be like to wake up every day next to the most beautiful redhead he'd ever seen, when he spied the "Welcome to Lake City" sign.

Pulling into the sheriff's station, Lank put Summer out of his mind. At least the Summer who was lying in bed next to him. He had to focus on Summer the victim. He had a feeling that things were about to get real hot real fast.

ৡ

"Your first interview is here, Mr. Lankton," Maybelle said, poking her head into the sheriff's office.

"It's just Lank, ma'am," he told the secretary, or office manager, or whatever she was to the sheriff.

"Yes, sir, Mr. Lankton," the grandmotherly woman nodded as she held the door open for the first young man and his parents.

Parker Novey was a good-looking kid. He had a big smile and an even bigger personality. He introduced himself and his parents, clearly taking control of the situation. Was that the sign of a very mature young man or a controlling sociopath?

A local college student at Mesa State in Montrose, Lank wondered why Parker was wasting his time taking a class on auto body repair.

"I thought it would be interesting," Parker told him. "And you never know when that kind of skill might come in handy."

Lank questioned the kid about whether he knew Ms. Cooper, his whereabouts on the dates in question, and if he'd ever been in trouble before. The kid was squeaky clean. Lank asked if he had seen anyone else in the shop using the green paint, but Parker said he had not. The first interrogation had been a waste of time. Lank thanked Parker and his parents for coming in and told him he might be in touch with some follow-up questions.

The next two kids were clean as well. One was hoping to open his own shop someday, and the other was just looking for an easy A. Both knew Summer and seemed to like her. They acted concerned that she might be in danger and said they'd let their parents and teachers know if they thought of anything or heard anyone talking about her.

Strike two and strike three. Luckily, Lank had two more times at bat that day, and Maybelle was able to schedule more interviews for the following day. He had time to grab food between interviews and strolled over to the local café. When he walked through the door, all eyes turned toward him. Telling himself that he was imagining it, Lank sat on a stool at the counter and perused the menu.

"Hello, there, sugar, what can I get for you?"

A waitress in a pink uniform stood behind the counter and took a pencil from behind her ear. Lank smiled and thought of a character from a show he once saw on TV Land. She was a sassy waitress with bright orange hair and a Southern accent. She had some kind of signature saying that he couldn't quite remember.

"Could I get a buffalo burger, please, well done, and a side of French fries?"

"Sugar, I'll get you whatever your little ol' heart desires." She winked at him and turned to go before turning back. "How 'bout a drink to go with that?"

"Sure, a Coke, please."

"You got it, sugar."

Lank played with his phone and tried to ignore the stares and whispers around him. In less than ten minutes, his food was placed in front of him.

"Can I get you anything else?" the waitress asked, placing a bottle each of ketchup and mustard beside his plate.

"No, thank you, Ma'am. I'm all set."

"You're welcome, sugar. We want to keep you well fed so that you can go back to work taking care of little ol' Summer."

"Excuse me?" Lank said as he held a French fry up to his mouth.

"Sugar, you don't think a guy as good-lookin' as you can walk in here wearing that badge on your hip and talkin' with that East Coast accent and not have everyone knowin' who you are, now do ya?"

"I guess I hadn't thought of it that way, Ma'am," Lank said after swallowing the fry. Apparently, he was correct that everyone was talking about him. The whole town must have known who he was and why he was there.

"We don't normally take too kindly to some city slicker coming in here, poking his nose in our business, but any friend of Johnny and Summer is a friend of ours, especially one who looks like you." She winked at him before walking away, and Lank almost choked on his soda.

When he was done eating, Lank left a nice tip for the waitress, who he learned was named Sally, and headed back to the sheriff's office. Luke Froelich and his parents were waiting for him and chatting with Maybelle when he walked in. Luke was a sizeable kid with well-toned muscles and access to tractors on his family's ranch; and he knew how to handle a gun.

He introduced himself and apologized for keeping them waiting.

"No, it's fine, son, we're early," Luke's father said. Luke looked sullen and angry as they followed Lank into the office. "Can you say hello to the detective, Luke."

"Hey," Luke said without making eye contact.

"Manners, boy," his father said. "Luke here is angry that he's missing football practice."

"Football, huh? What position?" Lank asked, hoping to get the kid to open up and start talking.

"Corner," the kid said. "But I'm aiming to be a running back."

"Really?" Lank said. "Why's that?"

"Corner's for sissies. That's where the little guys play. Ain't no scholarships for corners."

"Hmmm," Lank nodded. "I guess things have changed. When I played corner, I had coaches from A&M to Florida State and everywhere in between trying to court me."

Luke gave Lank a sideways glance. "You messin' with me? You didn't play no corner position."

"The hell I didn't. Excuse me, Ma'am," he apologized to Luke's mother. "I was the best cornerback in the whole US between 2005 and 2007."

Luke sized up Lank and pursed his lips. "You 'Long-legs Lank'?"

Lank laughed. "Wow, that's a name I haven't heard in a long time."

"But you're walkin'. I thought you got your back crushed. I've seen the films."

"I did. It took a long time to get back on my feet, but here I am. And I sure wish I hadn't taken my days as a corner for granted."

After a little more football talk, and a few pointers offered by Lank, they moved on to more serious matters.

"Yeah, I know Miss Cooper. Me and her had a meeting in the spring about my grades. I told her I'd work harder, and I did. Got all Bs on my last report card."

"Have you ever had a problem with Ms. Cooper? Been angry with her?"

"Nah, she's cool. It's Mrs. Jefferson I got a problem with. She's the meanest teacher in the school."

"Luke, I don't think you should talk that way about your teacher," his mother interjected.

"Sorry, ma." Luke's cheeks reddened, and Lank thought the kid might be embarrassed at being scolded in front of him now that they had established a rapport.

"Do you like to hunt, Luke? Ever hunt on the BLM up near Blue Mesa?"

Luke's eyes widened. "I love to hunt, but not up there. We've got plenty of mule deer on our land."

"What about cars? Other than working in the body shop, do you know much about cars?"

"Sure, I do," Luke said. "I've been tinkering with cars since I was tall enough to look under a hood."

"What about brakes? Ever fix someone's brakes?"

"I, uh, I replaced my mom's brakes for her last month." Luke shifted in his seat, and his face turned red. Lank noticed perspiration on his forehead.

"Did something happen to Miss Cooper's car?" Luke asked, not looking Lank in the eye.

"As a matter of fact, it did, Luke. Have you heard anything about it? Care to let me in on anything?"

Luke's parents exchanged looks.

"Should I call an attorney?" his father asked. "It seems like this questioning is getting a little out of hand. We thought this would be a general inquiry into the trouble his teacher has been having. Is there something we should know?"

Lank looked at Luke, sizing him up. He sat back and folded his hands in front of him. "Luke, you heard your dad. Is there something we should know?"

"No, sir," the boy said quietly. "I don't know anything."

Lank waited for a moment, letting the tension build in the room.

"One last question, Luke," Lank said, clasping his hands on the table in front of him and moving his head closer to the boy's. "Have you ever heard of anyone buying animals illegally online? Or somehow catching and relocating snakes? Specifically, rattlesnakes?"

Luke squirmed, and his face reddened. "No, sir," he answered without looking at Lank.

"You sure about that, Luke?"

"Yes, sir, I'm sure," the boy said nervously as he licked his lips.

"You look a little nervous, Luke."

"Snakes," he said uneasily. "I hate 'em. Never go near 'em."

"Well, then, I guess we're done here," he said as he continued to look at the teen. Glancing at Mr. and Mrs. Froelich, he nodded. "I'm done for now, but I may need to question him again."

Luke's father rose from his seat. "In the meantime," he said to Lank. "I think I'll call my wife's brother. He's an attorney in Gunnison."

"You might want to do that," Lank said. He made several notes on his legal pad before he heard Maybelle greeting the next family.

Samuel Groves was the last kid to meet with Lank that afternoon. Like the others, he was a normal, American high school student. He liked cars and enjoyed his class time at the shop. He didn't participate in any extracurricular activities because he worked at the ice cream parlor in town, a tourist favorite among the row of shops on the main street. On the surface, he seemed clean and too busy to spend his nights prowling around Summer's house. But he had a car, a fair amount of knowledge about mechanics, and a rather loose curfew, so his name stayed on the list.

❧

"He's definitely not your guy," Summer said as she set six places for dinner on the table on the back deck.

"I agree that he would not be the obvious choice, but I can't rule him out due to logistics." Lank turned the steaks as he recapped his day.

"Sam's a good kid. He works hard in school and out. Now Luke, there's a kid who's been in all kinds of trouble. He'd be at the top of most people's list." She set a basket of bread on the table and went back inside for a tray of condiments. Lank raised his voice so she could hear him.

"But not your list, right?"

"Nope, I'm afraid not," she agreed, pushing the door open with her hip. Lank turned to face her.

"None of these kids would be on your list, would they?"

Summer bit her lips and sighed. "I hate to say it, but no, none of them would be on my list. I can't imagine any of these kids being that angry or jealous or anything else to make them do the things this guy has done. How do we even know it's a kid? Why not a grown man?"

Lank shook his head. "I don't know, gut? I just have this feeling that we're heading in the right direction. It just feels right."

"Hello, anybody home?" a now familiar voice called out from the front door.

"Later, okay?" Lank said.

Summer nodded and turned to go inside. "Out here, Mom."

"Oh, good. I'd hoped you were using the deck furniture your dad and I gave you. It's such a nice night. Hello, Lank." Summer's mother walked onto the deck and flashed the same brilliant smile as Summer's. They had similar builds, both were of average height and slim, but Monica had Johnny's dark hair.

"Hello, Monica. Where's Steve?"

"He's coming. He baked one of his special recipe cakes for dessert and is bringing it in. Ever since he retired, I can't seem to get him out of the kitchen."

"Better him than me," Johnny said, wheeling himself onto the deck. "Give me a grill and a roasting fork any day, but don't make me bake a cake."

"Don't worry," Megan assured him as she walked out carrying two bottles of wine. "I'll never forget the time you attempted to bake a pie."

"Hey, you were the one who wanted a homemade pie for your birthday."

"But you didn't have to make it yourself. You ruined me for cherry pie for the rest of my life."

Lank smiled as he watched Megan, Summer, Johnny, and their parents interact. He missed this. His father had been gone for more than twelve years, and, like Lank, his father was an only child. His mother had one sister, Megan's mother, and they were extremely close. He wondered what it would have been like to have a brother or sister. Megan was as close as he got, and that wasn't the same.

"Whatcha thinkin'?" Megan asked quietly.

"I miss Mom, believe it or not. And Dad. Times like this do that. Looking back, we didn't do things like this enough."

"You're right, we didn't. But it's not too late. Maybe someday we'll have our own families to do this with." Megan looked at Lank with a twinkle in her eye, and he wondered what it was that she wasn't saying.

"Megan, is there—"

"Not now, Lank." She winked and walked away, caressing Johnny's arm as she passed his chair. Lank saw the look they gave each other and wondered if it was possible....

The meal looked and smelled delicious. Once everyone was seated and the blessing said, conversation ensued, and Lank enjoyed it all very much. His mother would love Summer and Johnny's parents, and he enjoyed seeing how well Megan fit in with the family. He even felt like a member of the family himself.

"A toast," Johnny said once there was a break in the conversation. It was then that Lank noticed that Megan lifted a glass of water while the rest held up wine. "To my beautiful wife and baby."

For a moment, the only sound was the beating of the wings of the hummingbirds as they came and went from the feeder like traffic at a busy intersection. Then it seemed as if everyone began talking at once congratulating them and asking questions.

"Baby!" Monica exclaimed.

"How did that happen?" Summer asked, then blushed when Monica giggled and Johnny looked incredulous.

"How do you think it happened?" Johnny said to his sister.

"I don't mean that," Summer gushed, and Lank smiled as her cheeks tinted to a bright red. "I mean—"

"He knows what you mean," Megan said. "We weren't sure it would happen. There are, issues, so to speak, but the doctor said it was possible, and he was right."

"How far along are you?" Monica asked.

"About six weeks," Megan said. "I was pretty positive last week, but the doctor just confirmed it today. We were going to wait another month to tell everyone, but we just couldn't keep it from you all."

"Does Aunt Dot know?" Lank asked.

"Mom was the first person I told," Megan assured him. "I'm sure your mother was the next one to know."

"And to think that she kept it a secret when I talked to her on the drive back today." Lank was surprised that his mother hadn't mentioned it. She was probably as excited as his aunt was.

"Well, this sure is good news," Steve said. "And we could use some of that these days."

"We sure could," Monica agreed. "To the marvels of modern medicine," she said as she raised her glass.

"Actually, it was really just good, old-fashioned biology, Mom," Johnny corrected.

"We don't need to know the details, Johnny," Summer said, rolling her eyes as she clinked her glass to his.

Lank felt privileged to share in this moment. Summer caught his gaze and smiled, her eyes twinkling and her cheeks turning rosy. Was it the news, the wine, or his hand reaching under the table to squeeze her thigh that caused it? The intimate moment lasted but a second before Lank and Summer were pulled back into the conversation, and he withdrew his hand; but a knowing look from Megan told him that she was on to him, and her words echoed in his mind that perhaps this might be their families someday.

The joyful meal stretched into the evening. Megan brought candles to the table and lit them and then served dessert and coffee. Conversation flowed as easily as the dinner wine, and Lank thought, perhaps, he could get used to nights such as this.

"I heard Sherriff McCoy is retiring," Monica said over her coffee cup. "Has he mentioned anything to you, Lank?"

"Not much," Lank responded after swallowing a bite of Steve's homemade carrot cake. "He's done some interviews. There's a young woman fresh from college, who grew up in Denver, that he thinks might be a good fit. But he doesn't know if she would take the job."

"Has he asked you?" Monica asked nonchalantly, peeking over at Lank.

"Mom," Summer said, sounding shocked and embarrassed. "That's a personal question, and Lank has a job back in Maryland. Why would you even ask that?"

Monica shrugged. "He might decide that he likes things out here." Monica looked pointedly at Summer, cocking her head to one side.

Lank watched the exchange. Summer blushed and looked away.

"No, Ma'am," he answered Monica. "Like Summer said, I have a job back home. And, to be honest, the sheriff has his hopes set on this young woman. He seems to see something in her that he thinks is just right for Lake City."

Talk turned to whether or not a young woman in her early twenties, who grew up in the big city, would be able to find happiness in a small town like Lake City. The conversation faded into the background as Lank ate and quietly watched Summer. He had no desire to be the sheriff of a small town, that was for sure, but he could certainly think of one thing that might make him want to stay in Colorado.

Later that evening, after all was quiet, Summer put her book in her lap and turned to Lank who sat at the opposite side of the couch watching a baseball game on TV. She was growing more comfortable with his presence but still kept her distance from him. She didn't want to send mixed signals when she wasn't sure how much she had to give in a possible relationship.

"Exciting news, huh?" she asked him.

"What?" he asked. "You mean about Johnny and Megan?" She nodded, and he smiled. "Yeah, that was quite a surprise, but a good one. Megan always wanted a house full of kids. She never wanted the lonely childhood that the two of us had."

"But you had each other, right? You were always close from what I understand."

"We were, but it wasn't the same, I guess. I never really thought much about it until lately. Watching you and Johnny together has opened my eyes to what I was missing."

"Do you want kids, Lank? Someday, I mean?"

"Sure, when the time is right. With the right person." He swallowed and turned back to the game.

"Of course," she said quietly. "I guess you're still looking for the right one," she said, not looking at him.

"I guess so," was all he said, but she felt him looking at her.

"I'm sure you'll find her someday," She said, trying to sound casual.

She turned toward him and found Lank looking at her. Butterflies filled her stomach, and heat rose from below her waist as she felt herself blush from the intensity of his stare.

"Maybe I already have." His response was barely above a whisper.

Neither moved, but Summer could feel the current in the room pulling them toward each other. She swallowed and noticed his eyes follow her tongue as it darted out to moisten her lips. Her breath quickened, and the flesh on her skin began to crawl.

Tearing her gaze from his, she closed her book and stood up from the couch.

"I think I'll head upstairs. Can I get you anything?" she asked as she turned to leave the room.

Though she never heard him move, she felt Lank suddenly standing behind her. She froze and closed her eyes, feeling the heat from his body just inches from hers. She inhaled and took in his scent, musk mixed with beer and a dose of desire. Slowly and gently, he placed his hands on her arms. Summer was torn between the urge to run and the desire to fall back against him. Doing neither, she stood still, breathing deeply, her eyes still closed. Both longing and fear coursed through her.

"You know that I want you," he said, his voice low and husky. "I've made it clear how I feel about you."

Heat flooded her as goosebumps continued to crawl the length of her body. When she didn't answer, he bent down and slowly nudged her braid out of the way with his chin before tenderly kissing the back of her neck. She held her breath as he trailed the kisses along the collar of her t-shirt and began to turn her toward him.

Once they were facing each other, Summer looked up into his eyes and let out a small gasp before Lank pulled her to him and pressed his mouth against hers. Without thinking, Summer's arms moved to his neck, and she was pulling him in tighter as his tongue parted her lips. His arms moved over her back until they came to a stop at the base of her shirt. As soon as she felt his warm palms graze her bare skin, Summer's eyes flew open. She put her hands on his chest and gently pushed him away.

Summer saw the confusion in his eyes when she stepped back. "I'm sorry," she whispered. "I didn't mean to…. I can't do this, Lank."

Summer's Squall

She left Lank standing by the couch as she fled up the stairs to her bedroom. She closed and locked the door, then turned and pressed her back against the hard wood. Closing her eyes, she breathed deeply several times until she could feel herself regaining control. She heard his words in her mind, *I've made it clear how I feel about you.* But the truth was, he hadn't. He'd made it clear that he was attracted to her and that he would join her in bed any time she gave the signal. What he hadn't made clear was whether the feeling in his groin matched the one in his heart. She shook her head and told herself that it didn't matter. No matter what his feelings were, she couldn't, wouldn't, return them.

Hours later, Summer stared at the ceiling. The clock by her bed read 3:38AM. Sleep was not coming easily tonight with Lank in the next room. At moments like this, she wanted him to go back to Baltimore so she could have her house back, and life could continue as normal, according to her plan to live happily without a man. He frightened her more than the stalker, more than Jeremy. His touch did something to her, made her want what she thought she would never want again. Maybe, just maybe…

Summer blinked. It had been a very long time since she had thought about those kinds of things. Once she moved back home and built her house on the mountain, she began to plan her life without a man in it. Now, here she was, thinking about what her life could be like if she met the right man. She just had to decide if Lank was that man. Did she trust him? More importantly, did she trust God?

But there was so much that Lank didn't know about her. As much as she wanted to open up to him, as good as his touch felt, she couldn't be with him. As soon as she felt his hands on her skin, she was taken back to another time and place. A time she never wanted to revisit again. With anyone.

She sighed and closed her eyes. *Please, God, give me strength and wisdom to know how to handle this,* she began to pray. Then she thought for a minute about what Megan had said a couple days before and changed course. *God, lead me down the right path. I'm willing to try to give my worries and fears over to you. It's all in your hands now.*

CHAPTER FOURTEEN

Lank got up and left the house early on Saturday morning. He had another full day of interviews with young men and their families, and he wasn't ready to face Summer. He had overstepped. Again. She just did something to him that he couldn't deny and put him in a place beyond his control. When he was with her, all he wanted to do was touch her, kiss her, hold her in his arms, and make love to her. He knew she felt the same. He could see it, heck he could feel it, every time she looked at him. Why the hell was she holding back?

He took a deep breath as he unlocked the door to the sheriff's office. Maybelle was off on Saturdays, so he had the office to himself until the first kid arrived. He was determined to not think about Summer. He had work to do, and thinking of her only clouded his judgment. Of course, it was going to be hard not to think about her when he knew that one of these kids he would be questioning was likely out to hurt her. Once he figured out which was the right one, it would take everything in him not to throttle the kid.

Trying to put Summer, and the way she felt in his arms, out of his mind, Lank put on a pot of coffee in the well-worn coffee maker sitting atop a gray metal file cabinet in the cramped reception area of the Sheriff's office. He went over his notes from the day before and prepared himself for the day ahead. Shortly before ten, the door opened, and a fearful looking young man walked in, followed by his parents. Lank stood and introduced himself and started another long day of trying to find Summer's stalker.

The day dragged on, and Lank found it hard to keep his eyes open and his mind clear by the time the last family left at 3:30 in the afternoon. The teenage girl, who just closed the door behind her, was the least likely of the suspects, and Lank was glad when the questioning was over. He rubbed his eyes and tried to decide whether he would eat alone or accept Megan's invitation to join her, Johnny, and Summer for dinner after Mass.

When the church bells rang at 3:50, Lank locked the office and found himself walking in the direction of the little white church on top of the hill on the back side of town. He stopped when he reached the doorway and hesitated. It had been many years since he'd joined his mother in church, and his understanding was that a Catholic Mass was a far cry from the non-denominational services he was used to.

"Welcome to St. Rose of Lima. Will you be joining us?" a friendly voice said from behind him. Turning around, Lank realized that he was blocking the way for the priest.

"I'm sorry, Reverend. I guess I was just asking myself the same question."

"It's Father Glenn," the young man replied with an outstretched hand. "Our door is always open, at least on Saturdays at four," he said with a smile.

"Thank you, Father. Maybe I'll just sit in the back and observe, if that's okay."

"The Lord is just happy that you're here," the priest said joyfully, and Lank wondered how a man, close to his own age, could find that much joy in what he regarded as a lonely profession.

Lank nodded and let the priest go past before entering the tiny church and finding an empty seat in the back pew. He looked around and wondered what all the statues and paintings were meant to symbolize. It was all unfamiliar to him, and he found himself not only intrigued but comforted by the songs, prayers, and readings.

When it was time for the faithful to go to the altar for Communion, Lank moved out of the way to allow others in the pew to go past him. He wasn't sure what he was supposed to do, but he didn't feel right going up with the others. As he stood in the back, his height put him head and shoulders above most of the congregation, and he saw Summer as she approached the altar, bowed her head, and accepted the bread. She ate it and made the sign of the cross before turning to go back to her seat. As she turned, it was as if something propelled her to look his way, and her eyes locked on his. He saw her catch her breath and stop short in the aisle. When the man behind her bumped into her, she blushed and hastily moved to her seat next to Megan. Lank continued to stare at the back of her head for the rest of communion and the final blessing, but she never turned around, and Lank wondered what she thought of his being there.

"Are you ready?" Megan asked when, after Mass, Summer remained standing in the pew.

Her thoughts interrupted, Summer turned toward Megan with a quizzical look.

"Are you ready to go?" Megan prodded.

"Um, sure," Summer said even though her feet seemed reluctant to move.

"Are you okay?" Johnny asked from the end of the pew where the seat had been shortened to allow for a wheelchair.

"Did you see him?" Summer asked, looking toward the back of the church.

"See who?" Megan asked, looking around anxiously. "Did you see someone suspicious?"

Megan stood on her tiptoes and stretched to look over the last few people making their way down the aisle.

"Never mind," Summer said. "Maybe I imagined it." She wasn't sure why she didn't tell Megan that she had seen Lank, and she felt that she had just sinned by omission while standing inside the church. Maybe she had imagined him. Maybe it had been a sign from God, a vision of some sort. She shook her head, feeling as if she truly was going insane.

When the three walked outside, Summer spotted Lank, leaning back against Johnny's SUV, his legs outstretched and crossed at the ankles. No, it wasn't a vision. She was certain he'd been in the back of the church.

"Well, look who's here." Megan said.

"What are you up to?" Johnny asked as they made their way over to where Lank was waiting for them.

"Just thought I'd see if that invitation for dinner is still open."

Summer eyed Lank and waited for him to say more, but he avoided her gaze.

"It's always open," Megan said. "Why didn't you come in and join us?" she asked, motioning to the church. Summer looked at Lank, curious as to what his answer would be, but he just shrugged.

"Maybe someday."

An awkward silence fell over the group as Summer and Lank looked at each other. Megan glanced from one to the other and clicked her tongue.

"Okay, then, are you ready for dinner?" Megan asked.

"Sure, lead the way," Lank said, pulling himself away from the vehicle.

"Where's your truck?" Megan asked.

"Back at the sheriff's office. I walked up here."

"Then get in the back, and we'll go together." She told him.

Once they were all in the truck, Johnny and Megan in the front, and Summer and Lank in the back, Summer made a point of sitting as close to the door as possible. She avoided looking at Lank but could feel him staring at her as they drove the short distance to the barbecue place in the middle of town. She wasn't sure why he was keeping his presence at Mass a secret, but she would follow his lead. She was beginning to realize that she would follow him anywhere.

Over dinner, Lank told the others about his interviews. Skye Yidi was a hard-working, honor student who worked in the shop because her father wanted her to know how to take care of a car. She wasn't crazy about it at first, but she grew to really like Tommy and Al and enjoyed her afternoons at the shop. She liked and admired Summer, and Lank could see the genuine concern written on her face for her teacher.

Mongwau Begay, who goes by Monty, was an interesting kid, at least that's how Lank described him to the group.

"Have you ever worked with him?" He asked Summer.

She shook her head. "No. Most of the kids on the reservation are schooled there. He's one of the exceptions. He keeps to himself, plays football, and gets decent grades. I've often gotten the impression that he doesn't want to be there. I believe his parents sent him to school because he's very smart, and they think that an education would be good for him and for their people. Signing up to play football allows him to attend school in Lake City even though he's out of the district. That gives him an advantage over going to the bigger school in Gunnison."

"Yeah, he seems like a smart kid, quiet, well-mannered, and small for a football player. He maintains the cars and trucks for 'his people,' as his father put it. The father's an interesting guy, too. Nibaw is his name, and I got the impression that he speaks for his tribe on many issues. And for his son. Monty looked at his father before answering any questions, and it was obvious that they had rehearsed all his answers. Nibaw must tow a hard line."

"Yeah," Johnny agreed. "He's strict from what I can tell. And a smart one. He's known for giving it to the government. He keeps a keen eye on the people driving in and out of the subdivision and makes sure that everyone stays on their own side of the fence, literally and figuratively. Their family is one of the few Ute families who live on that property all year and take care of their own crops and livestock. Most of the Utes live in Tocowa, where the Ute Headquarters is, and work as migrant laborers. Nibaw's family has lived in these parts, though, for hundreds of years, if not longer."

"Huh." Lank took all that in and wondered what kind of place they lived in and how well they fared. It surprised him that, with a high level of intellect and an eye for political matters, they would continue to live on the reservations and not assimilate into the many aspects of modern culture. Of course, he surmised that blood is thicker than water and that their background and upbringing meant a lot to them.

Their dinner arrived, and all was quiet for a few minutes as the hungry foursome began eating their steaks and burgers.

"So, what about the two others you interviewed today?" Summer asked, wiping her mouth with a napkin before taking a swig of her beer.

"Not much to tell. Neither kid seemed to be a likely suspect." Lank shrugged and downed his beer before motioning the waitress for another.

"So, we're still at an impasse?" Megan asked.

"Maybe, maybe not," Lank told her. "I still think we're heading in the right direction. Three of the kids know a fair amount about cars and mechanics, so I'm considering them suspects. Plus, I've got three more kids to talk to on Monday. We'll see where that leads."

Lank could tell by the look on her face that Summer disagreed with him about his suspects, but she didn't argue. Perhaps she was beginning to realize that not all the teenage boys in Lake City were cut from the same cloth as Johnny.

The mood was somber for the rest of the meal. After they ate, Lank and Summer followed Johnny and Megan out to Johnny's SUV.

"Do you want a ride to your truck?" Megan asked.

"No, it's too nice a night not to walk. Thanks for the offer."

"No problem. Summer?"

Summer looked at Lank. He shrugged and answered for her. "Makes more sense for her to go with me. We're both going to the same place."

Over the past week, Lank had moved what few number of belongings he had with him to Summer's. He had no need to go back to Megan's to get anything, and Summer had no reason not to ride with him, unless she was trying to avoid him, which was entirely possible.

"He's right," Summer agreed. "It makes more sense for me to ride with him."

Lank detected some reluctance in her response, but she hugged Megan and Johnny goodbye before walking with him to his truck.

Neither Lank nor Summer spoke for the first fifteen minutes of the ride home, but curiosity prompted Summer to asked, "So, how'd you like church?"

Lank shrugged and watched the road ahead. "It was fine, I guess. I didn't really understand everything that was going on, but I liked the music and the prayers and all."

"Father Glenn is really awesome. It's been a long time since we've had a young priest, and he brings a whole new dimension to the Mass and a welcome breath of fresh air to the parish."

"His sermon was a little long, but it was good."

Summer laughed. "Yeah, he likes to take his time getting to his point, but you should have been here for the last priest. He gave homilies that were about theological matters hardly anyone understood. Father Glenn's homilies are relatable stories about God's presence in our everyday lives."

"I'll admit that he gives you a lot to think about," Lank said, still staring at the road. They sat silently for a few minutes before Summer ventured to ask what was apparently gnawing at her mind.

"Why didn't you want Megan to know you were there?"

"At church?" Lank asked after a moment.

"Yes. You acted like you hadn't been there."

"I don't know," he admitted. "I guess I don't really know where I am with all that stuff, and I want some time to think about it without having Megan pressure me." He glanced at Summer. "She's like that you know."

A genuine laugh rolled off her tongue. "Don't I know it," Summer said, and Lank smiled as her laughter filled his senses. Without thinking, he reached over and took her hand. When Summer tried to pull away, Lank squeezed tighter.

"Relax," he told her. "Just let it be for once. It's the only time I can touch you without you running away."

Even in the darkness, he felt she was blushing, and though he knew it was probably his imagination, he thought he could feel her pulse quicken as her hand relaxed in his.

Summer found it hard to stay calm. Her heart raced, and her throat went dry as currents of electricity ran up and down her body. She tried to ignore the sensations and dispel her thoughts, but the truth was, she liked the way her hand felt in Lank's. She liked the strength that he exuded as he gently squeezed her hand. She liked the pulses that his touch sent through her. She liked his touch. Darn it, she liked him. More than liked him.

Closing her eyes, Summer leaned back on the headrest and closed her eyes. She felt safe with Lank. And she felt loved. While he hadn't said the words, in her heart, she knew. He was falling for her, and she found herself tumbling right behind him.

CHAPTER FIFTEEN

"Something has changed," Dr. Zamora said when Summer took a seat on the couch in her office.

"What do you mean?" Summer asked.

"You look different," the doctor said, eyeing her client. "You look, I don't know, a little more relaxed than you were last week."

Summer took a deep breath and let it out. "Maybe I am," she conceded. "At least, as far as this crazy situation goes. I mean, it looks like Lank has some solid leads. He left the house early this morning to interview some potential suspects."

Dr. Zamora raised a dark eyebrow sharply. "He left *your* house early this morning?" Summer blushed, and Dr. Zamora continued before Summer could clarify her statement. "You're sleeping with the man who is trying to find your stalker?"

Summer sucked in a deep breath and nearly choked on the air. "No! I am most definitely not sleeping with him."

"Last week," the doctor checked her notes, "you said you had feelings for him."

"No," Summer corrected. "I said, I might be attracted to him. I also said that I was not going to pursue anything." She set her jaw and looked at her therapist.

Putting down her notepad, Dr. Zamora looked at Summer.

"Summer, we've talked about this. It's okay for you to open yourself to the possibility of a relationship. In fact, you should be open to it. It's not healthy for you to decide, at this age, that you're going to spend your life alone. You are letting Jeremy run your life from the grave."

"I am not," Summer said indignantly. "I am taking charge of my own life."

The doctor shook her head. "No, Summer, you are giving the reins to the man, boy really, who hurt you the most."

Tears sprang to Summer's eyes. "Dr. Zamora, I've told you. I don't see the point in being in a relationship. I can't stand to be touched by any man. The very thought of it makes me want to curl up and disappear. How can I even entertain the thought of…" her words trailed off, and she looked away.

"Do you feel that way when Lank touches you?" the doctor asked gently.

"I used to," Summer said quietly. "But lately, I don't know. I can't stop thinking about that kiss." She gave the doctor a weak smile.

"A kiss that you admitted to me you enjoyed."

Summer's cheeks burned. "Yes, for a moment, and then the memories came back, and I…."

"You fled," the doctor finished the sentence. "And since then? You said he left this morning. Did he stay the night?"

"Yes, in the guest room. He and Johnny thought it would be best." Summer bit her lips.

"And how does that make you feel?"

"At first, I felt angry, betrayed even, like my family doesn't think I can take care of myself. But now, I kind of like having him around. We have some really good conversations, and it's actually nice to have someone to come home to. Not that I'm making this into something it isn't. I know that he will go back to Maryland soon, and I'll be on my own again; and that's okay." Summer wasn't sure her heart agreed with her words, and she stared at the artwork on the office wall as she thought about what life would be like once Lank was gone.

"You'd like him to stay," Dr. Zamora stated after a moment of silence.

"I think," Summer hesitated. "I think I would," she sighed. "But how do I get past everything that happened with Jeremy?"

"One step at a time," Dr. Zamora told her.

Lank finished his interviews on Monday morning and spent the afternoon going over everything with Sheriff McCoy and Deputy Santoyo from the Gunnison County Sheriff's Department. They talked about the possibility of any of the kids being capable of hurting Summer, ran through possible motives, and began checking alibis.

"Only three of the kids have questionable alibis," Lank told Summer when they sat down for dinner that evening. "Samuel Groves, one of the kids with mechanical know-how, seems to be a decent kid; but he can't account for his whereabouts on any of the nights in question. He says he spends a lot of time just driving around, thinking about his direction in life. Doesn't seem to add up to me."

"That's because you don't know Sam," Summer said, placing a large bowl containing a mass of something unrecognizable, that resembled yellow noodles, covered with a light marinara sauce. She took a seat across from Lank.

"What the heck is that stuff?"

"Spaghetti," she answered. "Try it. It's good."

"It sure doesn't look like any spaghetti I've ever seen before."

Summer sighed. "It's healthy spaghetti. Just try it." She scooped a large helping onto his plate and offered him a gadget with a crank on it. He took the gadget and eyed it suspiciously.

"What's this for?"

Rolling her eyes, Summer sighed again. "It's parmesan cheese. Don't you ever eat anything besides pizza and burgers?"

Lank began cranking the cheese onto the food on his plate. "Yeah, I eat a lot of different foods. They just never looked like this."

Summer smiled and waited for her turn with the cheese. After spreading the white shreds on her own food, she watched Lank, a knife in one hand and a fork in the other, try to figure out how to tackle his meal.

"Oh, for goodness sake," she said as she picked up her fork and demonstrated. "You eat it like you would regular spaghetti." She twirled the noodle-like food onto her fork and took a bite.

Looking skeptical, Lank followed her directions. His eyes widened as the taste of the dish filled his mouth.

"Mmmm." He nodded his head as he chewed. Once he swallowed, he gave Summer a look that showed he was impressed. "This isn't half bad."

"Not half bad?" Summer retorted.

"Okay, better than half bad."

"Really?" she asked with annoyance.

"It's good," he smiled. "Really good."

"That's better," Summer said though there was still a hint of exasperation to her tone.

"Seriously, what is it?" he asked as he heaved another forkful in his mouth.

"Spaghetti squash," she answered, taking a sip of wine.

Lank's fork stopped in mid-air. "Squash?" he repeated. "You made me eat squash?"

"What?" Summer said. "You have a problem with squash?" She stared at Lank over her glass.

"Yeah, I have a problem with squash. It's gross."

"You just said it was really good." Summer pursed her lips and eyed him, daring him to change his assessment.

Lank looked down at his plate. After several seconds, he shrugged. "Yeah, I guess it is," he said before taking another large bite.

"So," Lank said after a few minutes of silence, during which they both enjoyed their meal. "Back to Sam. Why do you think he's a no-go as a suspect?"

Summer wiped her mouth with her napkin and took a long drink of wine. Licking her lips, she set her glass back on the table.

"He's a hard worker, never in trouble, and aiming to get out of Hinsdale County and on to bigger and better things. There's no reason for him to go after me. He'd have nothing to gain from it."

Lank nodded and guzzled a large swig of beer. "Not satisfying, but I'll let it go. For now. So, then, Luke Froelich. He knows a lot about cars. How does he look to you?"

"Sullen, angry, always has a chip on his shoulder and an attitude, like he has something to prove to everyone."

"He acted nervous when I asked about the snake, like he knew something."

"The snake?" Summer said, her brow raised in question. "Why would you ask about that? I thought that was a random coincidence."

"It might be," he said, "but I haven't ruled out a connection."

"Why haven't you mentioned this before?"

"Because it's just a hunch, nothing more. But I got the impression that Luke knows something about it. Any history between the two of you?" Lank asked, leaning back in his chair and stretching his legs. He raised his hands and entwined his fingers behind his head.

"Not really," she said as she shifted nervously in her seat.

Lank noticed the way Summer turned to avoid his outstretched legs.

"Putting the snake aside, he's everything I said, but still a good kid. A few months ago, I noticed his grades were precariously low in several classes and called him in for a meeting. We had a long talk about his future and how he would never be on any college's radar if he didn't get his grades up." She looked pointedly at Lank. "I'm sure everyone who knows him thinks it's a waste of time to talk to him about college, but he's a bright kid. He has a lot of potential if he'd only learn to harness it. Football helps, but it's not going to be enough. He needs to straighten up and get himself together. If he does, he could really make something of his life."

"You really care about these kids." Lank sat up and put his arms on the table, pushing his empty plate out of the way and folding his hands in front of him. He leaned forward and looked hard at Summer. "This is more than a job to you. You would fight heaven and earth for these kids, most of whom probably don't even give a damn about themselves."

Summer blinked and slowly nodded. "Someone has to care. Some of these kids come from great homes with families who really care about them. Others have nobody in their corner." She looked determinedly at Lank. "Did you ever see the movie, *The Outsiders*?"

Lank nodded. "Yeah, what about it?"

"In some ways, the people around here are still living in 1965. When these kids read the book in school, so many of them identify with it, not only because it's a classic tale of teen angst, but because Tulsa, Oklahoma in 1965 and Lake City in 2017 aren't all that much different. It's a small town in the middle of nowhere. Kids can find a way to go to college and make something of themselves, or they stay here and work as cattle hands or rodeo cowboys or mechanics. Don't get me wrong." She shook her head and started gathering the dishes on the table. "There's nothing wrong with any of those jobs, but there are only so many to go around. There are some really smart kids here who deserve to get a taste of life outside of Hinsdale County, whether it's by going to college or by joining the military. Either way, it's my job to get them there."

Lank admired the way she cared for her students and the passion she displayed when she spoke about them. And he saw something that he hadn't really seen before as she talked.

"Johnny was one of them," he said. "He was a local kid just trying to get out of Hinsdale County. You had a ticket out with that brain of yours, but you decided you wanted to stay. Johnny, on the other hand, despite all his talk about the two of you never wanting to leave, he thought the Army was his way out."

Summer looked away, and Lank noticed a faraway look in her eye as she reached for her cross. After a minute, she turned back toward Lank, a small, sad smile on her lips. She nodded.

"Johnny is smart, too, don't think for a second he isn't."

"I know. I've seen his set-up and watched him work."

Nodding again, Summer continued quietly. "He just wasn't book smart. He was good with his hands and could work circles around anyone with a computer. He just didn't enjoy school. Like a lot of the boys I see, including Luke. Johnny wanted to be career military. It wasn't about war or fighting or anything like that. He wanted to find a way to learn everything he could without having to go to college. He would never have been a Steve Jobs or Mark Zuckerberg, who went to college and dropped out only to become billionaires. He didn't want that. He was more than content with serving his country, working his way up through the ranks while he learned a skill and saw the world."

When she blinked, a tear that had been threatening to fall, squeezed out from under her lid and slid over her cheekbone, leaving a shiny trail down her beautiful face to her chin. Her hands trembled as she reached for his knife and laid it on top of the collection of dirty plates and utensils in front of her.

"When he ended up in Iraq, we all feared the worst might happen, and it almost did." She looked at Lank and tried to smile. "I guess we got lucky, if you could call it that. At least he came home."

"And he's married, and happy, and soon to be a dad," Lank reminded her. Summer nodded and wiped the wetness from her cheek.

"Anyway," she said, standing and picking up the dishes. "That's why I work so hard to help these kids. They all have a dream, even if they don't know what it is yet. I saw mine come true. Johnny is seeing his come true, though it's different from how he pictured it. They all need to know that it's possible, no matter what life throws your way."

Lank stood and followed Summer to the sink. Coming up behind her, he waited for her to put down the plates and then took her shoulders in his hands, turning her to face him.

Looking deeply into her eyes, he spoke quietly, "Have all your dreams *really* come true, Summer? Is this what you want? To live here, alone, forever? You talk about these kids needing someone to be there for them and help them find where they belong. What about you?" He ran his hands down her arms until he moved them to her waist. Pulling her so close that scarcely a whisper of air was between them, he leaned down toward her. "Don't you want someone to be there for you? Don't you want what Johnny and Megan have? What they're going to have?"

He felt her intake of breath and saw her eyes moisten before she closed them. It was barely audible when she breathed the words, but he heard them.

"I do."

Without wasting another second, Lank pressed his lips against her, and like the first time, she responded. First with her mouth, as it opened just slightly, to welcome him. Then with her hands as they found their way around his neck. Then with her body as she pressed herself against him. Lank gently pushed her against the kitchen sink, and she ran her fingers through the short hair at the base of his neck. He moved his hands up to her neck and entangled them in her hair. When he shifted his body so that she felt his need, she inhaled sharply.

Forcing himself to stop and pull back, Lank looked at Summer. Her lips were red and swollen, her eyes wide, her cheeks flushed. He could see her quickened breath as her breasts heaved up and down beneath her shirt, and he wasn't sure if her quick breathing was caused by desire or fear.

"Tell me you don't want this, Summer, and I'll stop. Once and for all. I'll never touch you again. I'll finish helping you and then go home, and you'll never have to see or hear from me again." He watched her eyes as she processed his words. "But just say the word, and I will be your someone. I will be the one you come home to. The one who listens to your dreams and tries every day to make them come true. I will be the one who takes care of you every day. *I will be your someone*. It's your call."

Though his mind and body were both urging him to sweep her into his arms, carry her up the stairs, and show her exactly how much he cared, he was afraid to rush her. He didn't understand why it was taking her so long to admit what he already knew was true – that she was falling for him as fast and hard as he was for her – but he knew that she needed to come to the realization on her own. As much as it killed him to not take her back into his arms and begin where they left off, he took a deep breath, released her, and walked back to the table to get the rest of the things that needed to be put away.

As he stood at the table gathering the cheese, wine glass, and empty beer bottle, he could feel her stare. Just as he turned around, though, she turned back to the sink and began reaching for the plates. He watched her hands shake as she rinsed them in the sink and began to wash them. He knew she wasn't going to give him an answer tonight, but he smiled anyway. Her words might not say what he wanted to hear, but her body, her lips, and her eyes spoke loud and clear.

Summer quickly washed the dishes and laid them in the rack. Without speaking, Lank picked up a dish towel and dried the dishes, putting them neatly away as he finished. Summer tidied the kitchen and then turned to Lank.

"Thank you." She managed to say. Taking a deep breath, she continued. "For helping me. Not many people would risk losing their job, and fly across the country, to help someone they've never met. I appreciate it."

He stood looking at her, no doubt waiting for her to say more. And she wanted to. Part of her wanted to tell him that she was just fine, alone on the mountain, and that he should put any thoughts of changing her mind to rest. She wanted to smile with confidence and show him just how good she was at taking care of herself.

But the other part of her wanted to grab him and pull him back to her and take up right where they had left off. She wanted to accept his offer and let him take care of her for the rest of her life. She wanted him to be her *someone*. She needed him to help her feel whole. She thought about her admission earlier that morning. She *did* want him to stay. But every time he touched her, she responded and then recoiled with the memory of that fateful day. How could she ever get past it? That thing that she kept hidden from everyone except Dr. Zamora. How could she allow herself to enjoy what should come so naturally but didn't?

The indecision that put her mind and heart at battle was ripping her in two. With the exceptions of Johnny and Scott, every male she ever knew treated her like there was something wrong with her. They didn't know how to deal with her intellect or her looks (though she'd never admit it, she wasn't blind to what she saw in the mirror). Not until Wyatt, did she think she'd met someone who was her equal in intelligence and humble ambition. But it was all a show. There was nothing humble about him, and the cold manipulation that he wielded was deadlier than any physical weapon.

Then there was Jeremy. He was nothing more than a troubled kid, and he almost destroyed her. Nobody knew what she went through after the attack. All the hours she spent seeing Dr. Zamora all the way up in Crested Butte where nobody would recognize her. Nobody else knew that the story she told was a lie. The custodian hadn't shown up that day until it was too late. He found her on the floor of her office, just gaining consciousness and bleeding after the brutal rape. She begged him to take her to the hospital but not to say a word to anyone at the school. Sometimes she wondered if his early retirement at the end of that year was due to guilt because he hadn't stopped Jeremy and because he had helped her cover up what happened. She refused to identify her attacker at the hospital, refused to even confirm what all the professionals knew had taken place. And she couldn't bring herself to tell Jeremy's parents what he had actually done. It was a lie she had sworn to herself she would take to her grave. A lie that she knew she couldn't keep from the man she loved. Which meant that love was out of the question.

"Summer?" Lank repeated. "Are you okay?"

She blinked, and the memories of that horrible day, and of his father's accusations at the funeral, faded from view. Lank was looking at her with concern mingled with fear. She hadn't even noticed until that second that his hands had a death grip on her arms; but her heart was racing, and she felt the urge to flee, so somewhere in her mind, she must have registered his touch.

"Where were you?" he asked, his voice full of emotion.

"I," she faltered. "It's been a long few weeks. I think it's all just catching up with me."

"I shouldn't have pushed you," Lank said quickly. "About the kids, about Johnny, about…" He let his words trail off into the evening air.

"No, it's okay," she assured him. She wiggled her arms, and he let her go. "Would you mind if I went for a ride? It won't be dark for a couple more hours, and I need," she looked away.

"To be alone," he completed her sentence.

When she looked back and nodded, he saw that she was holding back tears.

"I'm sorry," she whispered before running toward the door.

She grabbed her jean jacket from the hook by the front door, pushed through the screen and jammed her feet into her boots and her hat on her head. Without looking back, she raced to the barn. As the tears flowed down her cheeks, she frantically readied Black for an evening ride. Unlatching the gate at the back of the paddock, she heaved herself up onto her most trusted confidant and kicked him into a gallop as she felt Lank's eyes watching her from the front porch of the house.

It wasn't until after Summer was long gone that Lank realized they had only discussed two of the three likely suspects. Monty Begay was still on the list. His father provided his alibi for every night in question, which bothered Lank. It was too tidy, and too abnormal for a teenage boy. Was he really at home with his father every night? It didn't sit right with Lank, especially knowing that he knew a lot about cars and was the reservation's resident mechanic.

Lank's watch vibrated, and he reached into his back pocket for his phone to read the message from Jim.

No luck on the online snake purchase. Sorry.

"Damn," Lank said out loud. "Another dead end."

Feeling restless as well as frustrated, Lank walked onto the back deck. The evening air had grown chilly, and Lank watched as dark clouds gathered in the distance. How long would Summer be gone? He swallowed as he watched lightning strike far into the distance. He knew that, while the storm seemed miles away, distance perception was nebulous in the mountains, and storms tended to move quickly as they crossed from one peak to the next.

As he stood and watched, the landscape shifted and changed as an ominous black shroud was pulled across the mountains toward him by unseen hands. A shiver ran down Lank's back as the wind picked up around him, and he was reminded of their conversation a few weeks back about the squalls that sometimes blew across the Rockies. Johnny said they could be deadly if someone was caught in one on top of the mountain.

A long streak of lightning ripped through the clouds on the next peak over, and Lank's heart began to pound. How long had she been gone? One hour? Two? He looked at his watch. He wasn't sure what time she had left. Certainly, she was watching the skies. It was nearly dark. Check that. With the clouds rolling in faster than he could think, it was already dark.

Suddenly, Cosmo, who had been by his side, turned and sprinted across the deck, heading to where the deck wrapped around the side of the house. Following quickly on his heels, Lank ran around the house to the front porch. With the wind whipping through her red hair, Summer fought to get the gate closed at the back of the paddock. She hastily led Black to the barn as Cosmo paced back and forth along the fence.

Lank breathed a sigh of relief at the sight. He found himself saying a silent prayer that she was safe and waited for her to emerge from the barn. After a few minutes, Summer ran across the paddock as the rain began to fall. She unlatched the gate, and followed Cosmo onto the porch. Just as her feet hit the wooden planks, the sky burst open, and torrents of rain poured down all around the cabin. A loud crack of thunder accompanied the zig-zag bolt that reached from the heavens to the earth.

Already soaked from the short run from the barn to the house, Summer ran her fingers through her wet hair and smiled at Lank.

"Made it just in time," she said.

Lank's jaw hardened, and his teeth clenched.

"Just in time?" he repeated. "Just in time?" His voice rose. "Do you know how worried I've been? Do you know how long you've been gone? I've been watching the sky and trying to figure out how to find you if you didn't make it back 'just in time.' What if you'd gotten lost in the dark? What if you had fallen? What if lightning had caused a tree to fall on you? What then?"

Summer's eyes widened, and she looked at Lank like he had lost his mind.

"Lank, I ride every day, often in the evening as well. You've never had a problem with it before. What is wrong with you? You know that I know my way back and that I'd be okay. Give me some credit." She walked around Lank and held onto the bench as she worked her foot out of her boot.

Lank stood watching her, seething, annoyed that she didn't see what he had been going through. All that time, not knowing if she was okay, not knowing what she was thinking or feeling, not being able to comfort her while she cried. And then, seeing the storm approaching and knowing that she was still out there, had almost driven him mad. Once she had both boots off, she stood and looked at him as if for the first time.

"Hey, you're really upset. What's wrong? Did something happen?"

He didn't know whether to yell, punch something, or grab and kiss her again. Willing himself to calm down, he did to her just what she had done to him. He walked away. Pushing past her, he swung open the front door and stormed into the house as nature unleashed its fury on the mountain.

CHAPTER SIXTEEN

"I still don't see what the big deal was," Summer told Megan over lunch the following day.

Lank was gone when she awoke that morning, and Summer was both upset and angry about the way the night had ended. She thought about it while on her morning ride and even prayed about it while doing her Soul Core workout.

"Lank obviously thought it was a big deal," Megan told her sister-in-law.

"I told him that I was going for a ride. I needed time to cool off and to think. He knows that riding calms me down and helps me gain perspective." Summer shook her head and took a drink of water.

"What aren't you telling me?" Megan asked.

The glass stopped halfway between Summer's mouth and the counter where they were seated. She swallowed the cool liquid and sat the glass down, a pink blush creeping into her cheeks. She pursed her lips and looked away.

"Oh, my gosh. It happened again, didn't it? You kissed." Megan sat back against the hard rim of the barstool and shook her head. "Or was it more than a kiss?" she asked, her eyes narrowing as she looked at Summer.

"No," Summer sighed. "It was just a kiss. Well, it was more than *just* a kiss." She shook her head and blushed even more. "It was, I don't know, an extremely *intense* kiss." She grabbed her glass, stood, and crossed to the glass door that looked out onto the deck.

Following her, Megan continued to press for information. "What does that mean?"

Summer gathered her thoughts and shrugged. "I don't know what it means," she said as she turned back to Megan. "It means that Lank has deep feelings for me, I guess."

"You guess? Did he say anything, or did he just grab you and lay on an 'intense' kiss?"

"We were talking, and it got pretty, uh, heavy, I guess you could say. He brings that out in me. Without thinking, I end up telling him things that I wouldn't dream of telling other people. He just has this way." She closed her eyes and shook her head. Turning back toward the glass door, she stared at the peaks in the distance but didn't really see them. "Anyway, we were talking, and then the next thing I knew, we were by the sink, and we were kissing, and it felt so good."

Megan waited for Summer to continue.

After a moment, Summer whispered, "I didn't want him to stop." She closed her eyes again and dropped her chin to her chest. "I know it's wrong, but I couldn't help it." Turning toward Megan, she tried to smile.

"I was feeling so vulnerable, and it felt so right. I know I shouldn't have responded, but...."

"Summer, there's nothing wrong with giving in to your feelings. I told you that you need to trust him, trust your feelings, and trust God. He won't lead you astray."

"Lank or God?" Summer asked.

Megan pursed her lips in thought. "Both," she affirmed. "They're both in your corner. It's okay to follow your feelings as long as they're true, and you're not leading him on."

"That's just it," Summer said, her heart aching as she remembered the kiss and how much she wanted to stop and keep going at the same time. "I was leading him on."

"How so?" Megan pressed. "Do you have feelings for him?"

Summer licked her lips and walked back to the counter. She put down her glass and gripped the edge of the counter. She looked down, and, staring at the bits of salad left on her plate, she shook her head. "I don't know." When she looked back at Megan, it was all she could do to hold in the tears. "No, I do know. I do have feelings for him. I'm falling hard and can't stop myself, but I can't go there, Megan, I just can't."

"Why not?" Megan said, grasping Summer's arm and looking at her with confusion and concern.

"Because, I can't. Don't you see?" Summer pulled her arm away from Megan, picked up both plates, and went to the sink. Without thinking, she turned on the water to wash them but put them down in the basin instead. She turned back to Megan while the water ran behind her. "Lank has a life back in Maryland. Mine is out here. Once this is over, he will go home, and that will be it for us. There's no sense starting something." She hoped that she sounded convincing.

"But it doesn't have to be like that, Summer. Lank could stay here."

"And resent me for the rest of his life? Why would I want that?"

Megan shook her head and furrowed her brow. "Do you think that I resent Johnny? Don't you think I'm happy? What makes you think Lank couldn't be happy out here?"

Summer thought about it. "He hates heights," she said with conviction. "He could never live on top of a mountain."

"Well he's been doing a fine job of it for the past couple weeks," Megan countered.

"And he has a job back home that he really likes. Law enforcement around here is pretty dull compared to what he deals with back there." Summer was growing in confidence as she tried to convince Megan, and herself, that she was right. "And his mom is back there. He would feel terribly guilty if he abandoned her."

"Aunt Sue would feel even more guilty if she thought that he left the woman he loves because of her."

Megan's words caused Summer to freeze. They repeated themselves in her mind, drowning out the sound of the running water. Megan reached behind her and turned off the faucet.

"He hasn't told you, has he?"

Summer swallowed but didn't give in. "Told me what?" she asked quietly.

"That he loves you," Megan gently answered. "Because he does. I know Lank better than anyone in the world, and he does love you."

"No," Summer protested. "He might think he does, but he doesn't. He's projecting. He's trying to save me, and it gives him the notion that he's my savior. It's not really love."

"You keep telling yourself that if you want, but it's not going to change anything."

Megan began to walk away, pausing to grab her purse off the back of the couch. Before rounding the corner toward the door, she stopped and looked at Summer. "But if you do keep telling yourself that he's not really in love with you and that you can't love him back, you're going to regret it."

Summer heard the front door close and Megan's SUV start up. With her heart pounding in her chest, she closed her eyes and fought to hold back the tears. Once again, Lank had made her cry. Or was she the one who was causing all the pain?

The view from the Froelich ranch was almost as good as that from Summer's cabin. Nestled between BLM lands, like those near Summer and Megan's homes, the ranch had more crops than Lank thought possible in the Rockies. Lank recognized corn and wheat in the fields, as well as tomatoes and even grapevines in the well-tended garden near the house. The house was just inside the Gunnison County line but only about ten miles from Lake City.

Lank and Deputy Santoyo shook hands with Dan and thanked him and his wife, Debbie, for cooperating.

"This is Debbie's brother, Gene," Dan said, introducing Luke's attorney.

"I trust that everything is in order with the warrant?" he asked.

"You can take a look for yourself, sir." Santoyo answered. "It's all routine."

The attorney looked over the document and handed it back to the officer.

"It looks good," he confirmed.

"We'll do anything to clear Luke," Dan said. "He may have his issues, but he's a good kid. He just needs to find his way."

"You don't need to talk to them," Dan's brother-in-law advised. "Just let them do their job."

"We've all been there at one time or another," Lank said to Dan without acknowledging the attorney.

"Thank you," Dan said as he led the men into the house.

The search of the house turned up nothing. Dan was a hard-working, God-fearing man who seemed to want only what was best for his family. He walked with Lank through his farm fields as a tech crew scoured the rest of the property. Dan worked as an agronomist, which Lank learned was a scientist who works to find ways to increase soil productivity and improve the seed and nutritional value of crops. He had worked hard to pay for his education and knew the value of a dollar. He and Debbie tried to instill that knowledge in their own children, Luke and two older sisters. So far, they seemed to be successful. Though Luke was a work in progress, his sisters were both stellar students, one studying law, and the other heading to medical school in the fall.

"Hold on," Lank said, stopping Dan's story about his daughter's decision to go to med school. He turned his arm and read the text on his watch. He reached for his phone and read the text again, confirming the message. "I'm sorry, Dan, I hate to tell you this, but they may have found something."

When they reached the barn, two techs were standing with Santoyo, who held a large evidence bag.

"Take a look," he said to Lank.

Peeking into the bag, Lank shrugged and looked back at Santoyo. "What is it?"

"A snake tube," one of the techs answered. "Used for catching poisonous snakes."

"We'll need to take this with us," Santoyo told Dan.

Dan started to say something, but his brother-in-law laid a hand on his arm. "It's best not to say anything," Gene advised.

Lank feared that Luke's father might suffer a heart attack on the spot. The anguish in his eyes told Lank that the man was shocked and shaken.

"We'll be in touch," Lank said gently. It was the first time he'd ever felt sorry at the possibility of having to arrest someone.

Climbing back into the rental truck, Lank couldn't let go of the look on Dan's face. The search warrant allowed them to look through the house and barn and all of Luke's possessions. Dan and Debbie had offered them the run of their home, even when the attorney advised them to stick to the scope of the warrant. But Dan and Debbie felt they had nothing to hide and were certain that their son hadn't either. Deputy Santoyo had Luke's laptop in his possession and was taking it to the crime lab for further inspection.

Lank couldn't stop thinking about the things Summer had said the night before – that Luke wasn't any different than Johnny was at that age, a good kid with a bad attitude just trying to find his way off the mountain. This changed everything. Still waters run deep, as the saying went, and Lank had no idea what kind of kid Luke really was underneath it all.

Though they had almost enough evidence to get an arrest warrant for Luke, they still needed motive, and Luke didn't seem to have one. Thirty minutes later, Lank followed Deputy Santoyo as he pulled up in front of the Groves' home. Lank and Santoyo agreed to stick to their plans to search the homes of Sam Groves and Monty Begay, just in case. At this point, they still couldn't rule out a conspiracy. Everything was still on the table.

Sam Groves lived in the town of Lake City, in a house much different than Luke's. It was small and old, and Lank detected a hint of embarrassment when Peggy Groves answered the door. She'd been working double shifts at the steakhouse that week, she explained, and hadn't had time to clean. Dishes littered the kitchen, the trash overflowed in the can by the back door, and laundry was piled high in the hall bathroom that also contained a washer and dryer.

"It's not a problem, Ma'am," Lank said with a smile. "Mind if we take a look at Sam's room?"

"Well," Peggy hesitated. "He's still sleeping. He doesn't have to be at work for another hour or so."

"We have a warrant, Mrs. Groves," the imposing-looking Deputy Santoyo was kind but firm.

Sam's mother swallowed as she looked over the piece of paper he presented to her.

"Let me wake him up first," she said as she nervously bit her bottom lip. Lank and the deputy looked at each other, conveying a silent message.

"Ma'am, we'll do that," Santoyo said. "Just point out the room."

Hesitating for just a moment, the worried mother raised a shaking finger to point to the door on the left in the small hallway. "It's that one," she said with a tremor in her voice.

Lank nodded to Santoyo, and the deputy knocked loudly on the door before calling out. "Sam, Deputy Santoyo and Detective Lankton here. We'd like to search your room."

Without more than thirty seconds passing, the door flew open, and the disheveled, wide-eyed teen stood in the doorway looking at them. He held his hands in front of his boxer shorts. His hair stood on end.

"I'm sorry, sir," he said. "Can I get dressed first? Please?" he added. He looked nervous, but there was no pretense of guilt, just a bit of confusion.

"We won't be long, Sam," Lank told him. "Do you have a pair of shorts or something close by you can grab?"

"Yes, sir," he answered and bent to the floor to retrieve a discarded pair of sweatpants. With a red face, he pulled them on as the two men looked past him into the room. As he moved from the doorway to the hall, he looked back and asked, "Am I in trouble? I told you everything I know and answered all your questions."

Santoyo didn't respond as he took the boy's inexpensive laptop and put it into an evidence bag.

"We hope not, Sam," Lank said. "We're just doing our jobs."

Sam nodded and looked at his mother. He swallowed and said, "I have to go the bathroom. Is that okay?"

"Sure, go ahead," Lank answered as he looked around for evidence that Sam might be the one stalking Summer.

Twenty minutes later, Lank and Santoyo stood outside the house by the police car.

"Not a thing here," Lank said, shaking his head.

"We'll see what the tech team finds on his computer. Want to grab something to eat before we head to Monty's?"

At that moment, Lank's stomach began to growl, and he realized how long it had been since he'd eaten. The piece of toast and banana he grabbed for breakfast hardly constituted a meal. He was surprised at how filling the spaghetti squash had been the night before, but now, he was famished.

They headed to the same diner where Lank had met Sally, and she smiled and waved as the men entered.

"Any luck finding the perp who's after Summer?" she asked as she placed a hot cup of coffee in front of each man.

Lank smiled and winked at Santoyo. "Not yet, Sally. Anything to report?"

Her eyes twinkled as she leaned closer. "Well, word around town is that you've been asking a lot of questions to the kids who work for Tommy Hiller. Some folks think that Luke Froelich is a strong suspect. I hear you even went to his ranch this morning."

Lank looked at Santoyo with surprise. Word traveled even faster here than it did in Lakespring. How was that possible?

"Luke is sweet on Skye Yidi. You questioned her, too. Anyway, her ma works at the grocery store, and she told Alma, who works next door. I expect the whole town knows by now. And I wouldn't be surprised if it was him. That kid's got major issues, if you know what I mean." She looked around to see that nobody had heard her.

"I'm not sure I do," Lank said. "What kind of issues?"

"Well, Skye's not allowed to date him because he was caught drinking with a bunch of boys under the footbridge crossing Henson Creek near the ball diamond." She looked at Santoyo. "The police weren't involved. The parents took care of punishing the kids. They weren't hurting anybody after all." She looked back at Lank. "Anyway, he's known for being a little wild and bucking authority. I've heard he was called into Summer's office more than once this year. I bet he's none too happy to have been called on the carpet."

"Hey Sally, you workin' or visitin' today?"

"I'll be right there, Joe," she called to the man behind the lunch counter. "I've got to get back to work. Anything else I can get you fine gentlemen?" she asked loudly, casting a look at Joe.

They ordered and sipped their coffee before Lank spoke.

"What do you think? Any bearing?"

"What? That?" Santoyo asked, jerking his head toward Sally.

"Yeah. You think we've got the right kid after all?"

"Could be. Town like this? People tend to know each other pretty well."

"I was thinking the same thing," Lank said, sitting back against the booth and taking a long swallow of his coffee.

❧

Lank was surprised to see how close Monty's home was to Summer's. Though not in the same subdivision, it was on the lands that he and Johnny crossed on their way to Montrose. Lank wondered if any of the kids he saw that day were Monty's brothers or sisters.

The house they pulled up in front of was not much more than a shack with several additions. Rooms had been added on here and there, letting Lank see what people meant when they referred to cookie-cutter houses. It was an odd-shaped building with crooked windows, but there were gardens all around it with flowers of every color just starting to bloom. Curtains blew in the open windows, and Lank could smell something good cooking inside. When they knocked, Monty's father, Nibaw Begay, opened the door. He didn't say anything. He merely stood in the doorway with a disapproving frown on his face and his arms crossed over his chest.

"We have a search warrant to look for evidence of stalking," Santoyo said after introducing himself.

"Your warrants have no jurisdiction here," Nibaw told him.

"sir, I can get a federal warrant, if you insist, but we can clear things up much faster if you'd just cooperate." Santoyo said. He had told Lank that the warrant might be a problem. On the reservation, only tribal and federal laws applied.

"My son has done nothing wrong." Nibaw shifted his gaze toward Lank and set his chin firmly in a scowl.

"Then there should be no reason why we can't search his room," Santoyo reasoned.

"He shares his room with his grandfather. It would be a violation of my father's rights."

"We're not interested in your father's things, Mr. Begay. We only need to check to see if Monty has anything that might tie him to Summer Cooper."

Lank saw the man's resolve slip just a bit before his steely gaze returned. "Only if I am there. You cannot enter alone."

Knowing they had no other choice unless they wanted to go through the hassle of getting a federal warrant, Santoyo agreed.

The room Monty shared with his grandfather was small but well-kept. The bedding reminded Lank of the blanket his mom brought back from Tijuana. It was thick and warm with bright, geometric patterns. The drawers of the dresser and small desk were neat and organized. The desk, judging by the collection of schoolbooks, supplies, and small laptop, belonged to Monty.

"We'll need to take his laptop," Santoyo said. Unlike the others, he didn't put it into an evidence bag. Instead, he looked at Nibaw for permission to open it.

"You can look, but only if you tell me what you are looking for."

"I'm not sure I'll know what I'm looking for unless I see it."

Nibaw thought for a moment. "Okay, you may look. But here. You will not take it."

Santoyo sighed but nodded. He opened the laptop and was greeted by the password request. He looked to Nibaw for help. Nibaw pushed his way between Santoyo and the desk and typed in the password.

"I require that there be no secrets in this house," he said as he backed away, and the desktop lit up.

"Good rule," Santoyo said as he began clicking through the folders and Internet cache. After several minutes, he stopped. "It's been wiped clean," he said to Lank.

"How recently?"

"It's set to delete the cache every night. Interesting, don't you think?"

"Why?" Nibaw asked. "Many people clean their computers regularly."

"Not kids. Unless they have something they don't want you to see."

"It means nothing. You have searched enough." He stood by the door, and his message was clear.

As the men walked back through the house, Lank was struck by a picture that hung in the living room. It was of a coming storm on top of a mountain, and, for some reason, it struck a nerve. It was very old and in black and white, but there was something about it that was disarming. He stopped and gazed at the photo.

"It is from my ancestor's mountain," Nibaw said with unmistakable pain and resentment in his voice. "It was taken many years ago by my great-grandfather, before there were any houses built on these mountains but long after the government took the land. He had always hoped that the land would be given back to our people."

"It's remarkable," Lank said.

For the first time, Nibaw let his guard down. "It is," he agreed. "The Thunderbird was very angry on that night. Why? We do not know, but the lightning in the photo shows his fierceness. And the light shows the trees almost bent in two. It was a bad squall, to be sure."

Lank wasn't sure what he meant by all the talk of the Thunderbird, but he knew that Nibaw was right about the storm. He had seen firsthand how fierce the lightning was on the mountain, and it had to have been quite a massive wind to bend the trees that far. The squall was exactly the way Johnny had described it, and Lank hoped he would never be on the top of a mountain in a storm like that.

That night, Lank ate dinner at Megan and Johnny's for the first time since he had moved his things to Summer's house. Summer had left Lank a note that she was having dinner with her parents. He wondered if her mother had extended the invitation to him, as it seemed likely that she would have; but if she had, Summer had obviously declined for him. It was just as well. He and Summer hadn't seen each other since the night before, and he still harbored a grudge for her lack of understanding. Yes, he was angry, and yes, something had happened. He had become acutely aware that if anything ever happened to her, he wasn't sure he could go on living.

"So, how are things at Summer's?" Megan asked casually. Too casually. Lank locked eyes with his cousin, trying to sum up how much she knew. *Yep*, he surmised, *she knows everything*.

Johnny's brow shot up. "Something I should know?" He was obviously as in tune with Megan's mood as Lank was.

Shrugging, Lank reached for the garlic bread. "Everything's good. Is this your mom's lasagna recipe?"

Megan gave her cousin a look that said, *don't even try to get out of this one*.

"Yes, it's mom's recipe. What's going on between you and Summer?" No more beating around the bush.

"What do you mean, 'between you and Summer'? I thought we established that there was nothing between you and Summer." Johnny's jaw hardened as he scowled at Lank.

"There is nothing going on between me and Summer." He glared at Megan. "Trust me, nothing."

Johnny sat back and looked back and forth from his wife to her cousin. When nothing else was said, he shook his head. "Dammit, Lank, what the hell is going on? Don't think that I don't know when Megan has something on her mind. You promised me that there would be no more kissing."

"Actually, Johnny, I never made that promise," Lank said, wiping his mouth with his napkin.

"Don't be smug with me. What's the story with you and my sister?"

"Okay, if you must know," Megan said. "Lank and Summer had another fight."

"How do you know? You weren't there," Lank said. "You have no idea what happened. And there was no fight."

"Summer said you got angry because she went for a ride and cut it too close to the storm by the time she got back. She said you weren't willing to hear her out and stormed upstairs for the rest of the night. Pardon the pun."

"Oh, really, is that what Summer said? Well, did she tell you that when she went out on the ride, she was upset and starting to cry, and I was worried about her?"

"Oh, great, this just keeps getting better and better," Johnny said.

"We were talking about the kids I've been questioning. It got personal." Lank put up his hands to stop Johnny from speaking. "Personal as far as Summer talking about the kids and how much she wants to help them find their place in the world."

"Why would that make her upset and go off crying?" Johnny asked.

Not wanting to tell the whole story, the kiss notwithstanding, Lank shrugged. "Something about the conversation got to her. I don't know what it was. One minute she was fine." *Lank vividly remembered just how fine she was, and how fine she felt in his arms.* "The next, she's staring off into space, starts crying, and runs out. Honestly, I have no idea what happened."

Megan furrowed her brow. "Hmmm, she didn't mention that part. What do you think it was?"

"Hell if I know," Lank said. "I can't figure that woman out. Every time we seem to be making progress and getting along, having a good time, she suddenly turns on me or bursts into tears. I have no idea what's going on in her head."

"Maybe it isn't what's going on in her head that's the problem," Megan offered. "Maybe it's what's going on in her heart."

The room was silent as they all thought about what Megan said. Johnny didn't look pleased, but Lank felt a small tug at his own heart. Perhaps Summer was just trying to figure out how she felt about him. The question was, why did it make her so sad?

"So, you're thinking that this Luke kid may be the one?" Johnny asked later as the three of them sat on the back deck, enjoying the night air and the occasional call of a great-horned owl.

"It sure looks that way," Lank said. "He's been in trouble more than once, normal stuff, drinking, mouthing off, you know. He knows his way around a car, and he definitely has a chip on his shoulder. But the snake tube was the real clincher. I really thought we were barking up the wrong tree, relying on circumstantial evidence at best, until we found that."

"And is it enough?" Megan asked. "What's the phrase you cops are always looking for? Motive and Opportunity?"

Lank nodded. "He definitely had the opportunity. His alibis are pretty shaky. It's the motive that we can't quite figure out. As far as I can see, he has no reason to go after Summer. And why spray paint 'thief' on her truck? It makes no sense. We just have to see what shows up on his laptop."

"Yeah, that's what has me puzzled. Why would he do all this?" Johnny asked. "I mean, I wasn't that different from him at that age, but I never stalked anyone. Summer called him on the carpet, but he seemed to shape up. What's the point?"

"None that I can see," Lank agreed. "I really don't have any idea why he, or anyone, would go after Summer like this."

They sat in silence, staring at the multitude of stars in the clear sky.

"You sure can see a lot more of the sky out here than you can in Baltimore, or even in Lakespring, can't you?"

"You sure can," Megan agreed with her cousin. "Kind of makes you want to stick around, doesn't it?"

Though it was dark, Lank knew exactly which look Megan was giving him. The view from the back deck was almost enough reason to make him want to stay. But the view that sat across from him at dinner the night before was the only reason he needed.

CHAPTER SEVENTEEN

"I'm sorry, Lank, I really am, but my hands are tied," McCain said through the phone.

"I get it. No worries," Lank said, closing his eyes and rubbing his forehead. He was sitting at the kitchen table, his phone pressed to his ear, with the morning light pouring in through the glass doors and windows.

"When I encouraged you to go, I didn't think it would be for this long."

"Neither did I." Lank sighed and looked up.

Summer stood at the bottom of the steps, and the sight of her caused him to miss the rest of McCain's comments. "Thanks for everything. I'll let you know what happens," Lank said, oblivious to anything but Summer.

She stood, with her red hair braided down her back, wearing tight jeans and a shimmery white top that showed off her tanned skin and made her green eyes sparkle.

"You don't look dressed to ride this morning," Lank said, putting his phone down on the table and trying like mad to control his breathing and the beating of his heart.

"I'm going into work this morning. But speaking of looks, you look like you just lost your best friend," she answered.

"Just my job," Lank said, shaking his head.

"Oh, Lank." She walked toward him and sat in the chair next to him. Reaching out to take his hands in hers, she breathed deeply and slowly blinked her eyes. "I feel terrible. I'm so, so sorry."

Lank looked down at the small hands that held his in a tight grasp. They weren't the hands of a model. They were rough, with short, well-manicured nails with no polish, and were covered with freckles. And they were beautiful. Sometimes at night, he watched her smooth them with lotion and wondered what it would feel like for her hands to be on his body.

Pulling himself out of his thoughts, Lank looked up into her mesmerizing, tree-frog green eyes.

"It's okay," he said, his voice hoarse and choked with emotion. "It was worth it." And he meant it. No matter what happened to him or his career, no matter what may or may not happen between them, it was worth getting to know her and spending time with her, worth helping her to get her life back, with or without him.

Summer let go of one hand and slowly raised her fingers to his face. Lank's gaze never left hers as she lightly caressed his jawbone. She seemed unsure of herself, but she didn't pull back even as Lank leaned closer to her. Unlike the other times, Lank moved slowly, gently reaching his hand behind her head and pulling her toward him. He saw her eyes close as their faces neared. When their lips met, it was soft and gentle. She stopped caressing his face and slowly let her fingers trail to the back of his neck. They continued to hold each other's hand as their lips slowly and carefully explored each other. After a few minutes, they both pulled back, gazing into each other's eyes.

"It took me a long time to decide to do that, Abe Lankton," Summer whispered. The sound of his name on her lips caused his groin to tighten.

"It sure did," he agreed. "It's all I think about doing these days."

Summer blushed, but she didn't pull away. "I'm not sure I can do this," she admitted.

"Then, why are we? What changed?" Lank asked.

"I'm not sure," she admitted. "Maybe the fact that you're willing to give up everything to help me."

"I don't want to be your hero, Summer. I'm not Superman. I won't just walk away after this thing ends. That's not me."

Summer licked her lips. "I'm beginning to realize that." She gave him a shy but heart-melting smile. "But the truth is, I'm not sure I'm what you're looking for. I'm not ready for what you want, Abe, physically, I mean. I'm not like that."

"Neither am I," he assured her, liking the way she was calling him by his name rather than his moniker. "I can wait it out. I want all of you, Summer, not just a show of gratitude or a night of passion." Though he was happy to take either if she offered it. "I want the whole nine yards, a home, a future, a family. I never knew I wanted all that, but I do. With you."

"Then I need you to promise me that we'll take it really slow. There are things," she looked away, inhaled, and turned back. "I need us to take it slow."

Lank nodded. His hand caressed her neck as he took in the fear in her eyes, the almost imperceptible twitch in her cheek, and the way she raked her bottom lip through her teeth. Letting go of her hand, he traced her bottom lip with his finger and wondered what it was that she was afraid of.

"I'll wait for you for as long as it takes," he said quietly before pulling her back in for another tender kiss.

The drive to Lake City seemed to take longer than usual. Several things were eating at Lank, and he was feeling at a loss as to what to do about any of them.

He wondered about Summer and what she was holding back. What in her past had her so afraid and skittish when it came to being with him? She wasn't afraid of commitment. She'd had long-term relationships, but none since returning to Colorado. While that had not seemed important before, Lank now wondered if there was a reason. But as much as he wanted to get to the bottom of it, he had too many other things on his mind.

He had lost the best job he ever had or ever thought he would have. He liked McCain and admired him, and it pained Lank to think that he'd probably lost the man's respect.

He was anxious to meet with Santoyo and the tech team to hear what they discovered on the laptops. He hoped it would lead them to some answers.

He worried that Luke seemed the most unlikely of suspects, but the evidence was stacking against him, and Lank found no reason not to believe what he'd seen with his own eyes.

And somewhere, in the back of his mind, was the thing that bothered Lank the most, a nagging of sorts, something he was missing. Was it something about the case, or about Summer in general? What was it? A clue? A warning? As much as he tried to focus, nothing was coming to him.

When Lank finally pulled up in front of the small sheriff's station, he couldn't shake the feeling that he had really screwed up, and that things were about to go terribly wrong.

He checked his phone for messages, but he had none. He wasn't sure why he was checking. Summer rarely texted him, and Megan was working. Johnny had a client that was keeping him busy, and he was about to meet with everyone else on the case. Still, that nagging feeling wouldn't go away.

"It's about time," Santoyo said when Lank walked in. Excitement gripped him as he looked at the expectant faces.

A young woman with a blonde ponytail sat at the table with Santoyo, McCoy, and Officer Harris, the computer tech.

"Lank, this is Jordan Kyle," McCoy said. "She's going to be taking over for me at the end of the summer, and I thought it might be good for her to sit in on our meeting."

Reaching to shake her hand, Lank nodded. "Nice to meet you, and congratulations."

"Thanks," she said. Jordan was awfully young, and Lank wondered what McCoy saw in her that gave him the confidence to give her the approval needed to take over for him. But it wasn't any of his business, and Santoyo looked ready to burst.

"Before we begin, I have something to tell you," Lank said. "I've been fired. My boss called me this morning to let me know that they've given my caseload to someone else. When I told him I didn't know how much longer I'd be gone, he said they couldn't wait on me. So, I no longer have any credibility as a police officer." Lank looked away and waited for the response from Santoyo.

After a pause, McCoy spoke. "Well, I'm in no position to be making any permanent hiring decisions with Jordan taking over soon, but I think we could use a temporary deputy to help with this case." He looked at Jordan for affirmation.

"Agreed," she said. "From what I've heard, you've done so much of the legwork already, it makes sense for you to continue."

"And you're definitely going to want to hang in there for this," Santoyo said.

"Really? You found something?" Lank said, taking his seat at the table and then feeling like he was too excited to sit still. "And thanks," he said to both sheriffs, not sure who had more authority at the moment.

"We found something," Santoyo said. Lank's heart jumped.

"What is it?" Lank ran his hand over his hair and realized he badly needed a haircut. He looked around at the faces of Santoyo, McCoy, Harris, and Jordan Kyle.

"Take a look at the search that Luke did a few weeks ago," Harris said, pushing the laptop toward Lank.

Lank's eyes widened. "How to tamper with brakes? Tamper, not fix. He told us that he replaced his mother's brakes last month, but that's not what this is."

"Yep. Keep reading," Santoyo coaxed.

Lank read the report and blinked. One of the sites actually gave specific instructions as to how to tamper with the brakes so that they would work just fine for a time and then completely stop working.

"You've got to be kidding me," Lank said, shaking his head.

"Yeah, it tells exactly how to make it happen, which hoses to cut, and how to time it."

Lank sat back and shook his head. Had he really been that blind? Did he let the fact that Luke played corner and came from a good family influence his feelings about the kid? How could he have done that? The kid had actually done a search on 'how to tamper with brakes.' Lank was in shock.

"I'm ready to get an arrest warrant," Santoyo stood and looked at Lank. "We've got rather damning pieces of evidence that speak for themselves. I think it's time to wrap this up. Care to join me?"

"What about motive?" Lank asked. "We still don't have one. The kid is troubled, but he has no priors, and he's never made so much as a joke about wanting to hurt Summer."

"Hopefully we can find that out once we have him in custody." Santoyo said. "I highly doubt his work at the body shop has him enabling brakes to give out at the precise moment needed to kill somebody. And, by the look on his father's face, that tube wasn't a standard tool on their farm."

Lank had to agree. They had more than enough to arrest the kid. He had searched for information on how to kill someone through brake failure. He knew about cars. He worked at the shop from where the can of spray paint was stolen. His alibis for all the times in question were shaky, at best. And he had the means to capture and release the rattler. All doubts aside, the kid was as good as sentenced.

"You ready?" Santoyo asked, breaking into Lank's thoughts.

"Yeah, I guess so. What do the rest of you think?" Lank looked at the faces of the other law enforcement officers in the room.

"It seems pretty cut and dry to me," McCoy said, shaking his head. "Was there anything found in any of the other searches?"

Santoyo shook his head. "Nothing. We ran searches on all the computers except Begay's, and I checked that one. Groves was clean. This is it."

"It can't hurt to bring him in," Jordan offered. "I agree with Santoyo. Motive or not, he looks guilty. Bringing him in might cause him to crack and tell us why he did the things he did."

"Then, let's do this," Lank conceded but still found himself bothered by the thought that he was missing something important.

Hours later, Lank arrived at Summer's cabin feeling both exhausted and relieved. The drive to the Froelich family ranch seemed to take even longer than the drive to Lake City earlier that morning. Lank was restless and unable to focus. Something didn't feel right to him. He guessed it had to do with the case coming to an end and him not knowing what that meant for him. His future looked hazy. He had nowhere to go, no job, and no guarantee that Summer would get over whatever was holding her back from being with him. She had let him kiss her and said she was willing to try, but what if she changed her mind once the case was closed?

"What's eating you?" Santoyo had asked. "I thought you'd be overjoyed."

"I wish I knew. I can't shake this feeling that we've missed something." Lank looked out the window and cracked his knuckles, something that, until the last few days, he hadn't done in years.

"Whatever it is, it will come out. Once we tell him what we found, he'll come clean."

"Yeah, you're right," Lank said.

But he hadn't. Luke maintained his innocence even as the cuffs were being put on him. The kid's parents were distraught, and nothing felt right about the arrest. When Lank walked into Summer's cabin, he didn't feel any better.

"Is it really over?" Summer asked anxiously. She had a glass of wine in her hand, and while she had a smile on her face, the slight crease in her brow let Lank know she was cautiously optimistic.

"Yep, it's over," he said.

Summer held the glass still and studied Lank. "Then why do you look so unsure?"

Lank went to the refrigerator and took out a beer. Twisting off the cap, he shook his head.

"I don't know," he admitted. "When we pulled up in the police SUV, Debbie Froelich opened the door and immediately burst into tears. She cried the whole time we were reading Luke his rights, and by the time Dan walked in, Luke was crying, too, and begging his mother to stop. He kept telling her over and over that it was a mistake; that he would never do the things we said. The last thing he said before we closed the truck door was, 'I love you, Ma. I'm sorry.'"

"Then he did do it. Why else would he be sorry?" Summer asked hopefully.

Lank exhaled and shrugged. "I have no idea, but it didn't seem like that kind of apology. It was killing him to see his mother in pain." Lank looked at Summer and shook his head. "I know what he was going through. I'll never forget the look on my mother's face when the doctor told her my father was dead or when they carried me off the field that night. Twice, I watched my mother as she realized that the world, as she knew it, was gone, and her life would never be the same. I've seen that same look of grief, of disbelief." He took a seat on one of the barstools, and his shoulders slumped in defeat. "Damn, I hate this part of the job."

Lank felt helpless and weary and wanted more than anything to finish his beer and collapse into bed, pull the covers over his head, and pretend he was asleep, like he did when he was a child. He propped his elbow on the counter, dropped his head into his hand, and closed his eyes. Then he felt the soft, warm, comforting embrace that soothed him like a hot bath.

With her arms wrapped around him, Summer rested her forehead against Lank's head and murmured soft, consoling words against his skin, much like he'd seen her do with her horse.

"It's all right, Abe, I'm here if you need more. I'm not going anywhere."

Lank opened his eyes and shifted his head slightly to face her. With their foreheads touching, and their eyes so close he could see the tiny gold flecks amid the bright green of her irises, Lank whispered, "Do you mean that?"

As she nodded, he felt her hair brushing against his neck. "I do," she whispered back.

The sweet, tender kiss they shared was all Lank needed to console him. Job or no job; case closed or not; no matter what else happened, he was home.

Megan stopped by a short time later. Lank and Summer had fallen into the comfortable ritual of making dinner together and were waiting for their grilled chicken to be ready to eat.

"So, that's it? It's over?" Megan asked as she came up behind Lank as he grilled chicken on the back deck.

"We hope so," Lank told his cousin. "By now, Luke is probably awaiting arraignment. I can't imagine what it's doing to his parents." He cut into a chicken thigh to check it, and flipped it over for a few more minutes.

"You don't sound too happy. I thought you'd be thrilled to have this all over."

"I am," Lank smiled. "In fact, we're celebrating. Have a glass of wine, oh, never mind."

Megan grinned. "Thanks, but no thanks." She took a seat in a nearby chair. "So, tell me what you're really thinking."

"I don't know," Lank said. He absent-mindedly turned the chicken over again. "It just doesn't feel right."

"Yeah, I got that impression last night. You really don't think it was Luke, do you?"

Lank looked up over the grill and stared at the mountains. "I don't know, Meg. I just don't know."

"Well, you did your job, which is all you could do. Everyone else seems to think it's him. For now, let's assume they're right and that this is all over. Even if it's not him, whoever did it will think he's off the hook. Maybe he'll give up."

"Is that really how you want it to end, Meg?" Lank turned and looked at her. "Would you really want an innocent sixteen-year-old kid to take the fall for someone else?"

Megan bit her lip. "Well, no, of course not." She looked uncertain. "But he doesn't look all that innocent, does he?"

Lank shook his head. "No, he doesn't. I don't even know why I'm doubting what's right in front of me. We'll just have to see what happens with the judge and whether it goes to trial, and then hope that the truth comes out, whatever it might be."

"And then what?" Megan asked. "Will you head home and go back to being a Baltimore City detective?"

Lank shook his head without speaking and went back to staring at the mountains. After a moment, he turned off the grill and moved the chicken to a plate.

"I'm not sure," he told her as he took the plate to the table and set it down. He turned toward the house. "I guess Summer didn't tell you."

"Tell me what?" Megan asked, standing and walking over to Lank.

"I got canned," Lank said matter-of-factly.

"Canned? You mean they fired you?" Megan's eyes were wide with disbelief.

"Yeah, and I can't blame them. McCain warned me a couple weeks ago that he was on the hot seat for letting me come out here. I had cases getting cold, and he had people to answer to." He shrugged. "It is what it is."

"Lank, I'm so sorry. This is all my fault."

Lank turned toward his cousin and smiled. "Don't worry about it, Megan. It's all going to work out."

"How?" Just as she asked, Summer walked onto the deck with a large bowl of salad in one hand and a plate of baked potatoes in the other. Megan looked from Summer to Lank and back again. Lank saw the look of understanding as she smiled and nodded. "I'm guessing you two worked out your *differences*?"

"You could say that," Summer said. "At least, we're working on it."

"Does that mean you're staying out here?" Megan asked Lank, and he saw the hope in her eyes.

"I'm not sure what it means just yet. I've got a temporary job with the Lake City Police so that I can stay on the case. After that..." he cast a look at Summer.

"After that, I'd like him to stay out here," Summer said. She smiled at Lank. "That is, if he wants to."

Megan nearly knocked Lank over when she lunged at him to give him a hug.

"I knew it," she said. "I'm so happy for you."

"Let go, I can't breathe," Lank teased as he gently pushed her away. "Slow down. We're just taking this one day at a time."

"That works for me," Megan said. She beamed as she told them that she had to get home. "Johnny has dinner ready, I'm sure, and you two don't want your meal getting cold."

Lank laughed as he watched her leave. "That girl is way too excited."

Summer went to Lank and wrapped her arms around him. "I think your cousin is very happy," she said, looking up at Lank.

"She is," he said as he leaned down and kissed her. "Are you?"

Summer bit her lips and took a deep breath. "I am," she said. "I'm still not sure about this, but I'm happy, and that's a start."

"That's good enough for me," Lank said, leaning down for another kiss.

CHAPTER EIGHTEEN

"He's out on bail," Santoyo told Lank.

"I figured," Lank said, holding the phone against his shoulder as he made himself a cup of coffee.

"How's Summer?"

"Relieved. She's at the school today. She was tired of working at home and said she needed to go to her office for a few hours. She'll be back around lunch time."

"Mind if I ask you something personal?"

"You can ask," Lank said as he sipped the steaming hot Colombian blend.

"You and Summer. Is there something there? I know it's none of my business. I'm just asking because, well, hell, because I'm curious."

Lank laughed out loud. "I tell you what, Santoyo, if and when there's something to tell about Summer and myself, you'll be among the first to know."

"Fair enough." He paused, and Lank could hear Dierks Bentley, in the background, singing about being drunk on a plane. "By the way, Lank, we're always looking for good men like yourself. That is, if you ever decide there's something out here that's worth saying goodbye to the drugs, gangs, and turmoil back in the big city. I'm happy to put in a good word for you with the sheriff."

"Good to know," Lank said. "I'll keep that in mind."

When they disconnected, Lank called his mom to give her an update. She wasn't thrilled about his job, but perceptive as always, she did what mothers do best.

"Is there anything you'd like to tell me?" she asked. "Any reason at all as to why your voice changes just a bit whenever you talk about Johnny's sister?"

Lank shook his head. "Despite Megan's claims to know everything there is to know about me, nobody knows me like you do, Ma."

He could hear the smile in her voice when she spoke. "What's she like, Abe? Not all the basics that you've already told me. What's she like inside?"

Lank pushed open the screen door and went onto the deck, which had become his favorite place to do just about anything.

"Well, Ma, to tell the truth, I'm still figuring that out myself." He smiled as he watched two hummingbirds fighting their way to the feeder. "She's a lot like you. She's feisty and set in her ways, but she has a heart of gold that she guards fiercely but opens to those she feels need and deserve it the most. She's painfully shy and insecure but can hold a room's attention when she talks about something she's passionate about. She cares deeply about the kids she works with and her family, and she'd fight a mountain lion to protect any of them. She's got a short temper but doesn't hold a grudge. And she's probably the most beautiful woman I've ever laid eyes on."

There was silence on the other end, and Lank thought he'd lost the connection until he heard his mother sniffle.

"Ma, are you okay?"

"I'm fine, Abe," she said through tears. "It's just that I now know how your Aunt Dot felt when Megan told her she was moving to Colorado. I'm so happy for you, but I'm also sad. I wish you were coming back to Lakespring, but I know that you've finally found your way home."

Funny, Lank thought, that's just the way he feels every time Summer walks into the room.

It was almost two o'clock by the time Summer's freshly-painted truck rolled into the drive. Bypassing the house, Summer drove straight to the paddock gate, jumped out of the truck, unlatched the gate, and drove the truck and trailer into the barnyard. Until that point, Lank hadn't noticed that the trailer wasn't parked by the barn. His stomach dropped as he realized what that meant.

The barn smelled like fresh hay when Lank walked up beside Summer, who was soothing the big brown horse with her soft, gentle tones.

"That's a good boy, Beau, good boy. You're a good traveler."

"So, Beau's back," Lank said as he tentatively reached to rub the animal's nose.

"Yeah, I told mom and dad that I wanted to keep him here for a while." Summer continued to coo to the horse without looking at Lank.

"I guess that means you want someone to ride him."

"That was the plan," she said as she finally looked his way. She flashed him a smile that was part 'I'm glad to see you' and part 'Please, say yes.'

Letting out a long sigh, Lank closed his eyes and shook his head before looking back up at her. His heart leapt, and he knew that he would always wage an inner battle when it came to telling Summer no.

"I guess I can give it another try."

Summer threw her arms around Lank and hugged him fiercely. "Thank you. But you look like you're going to be sick. The first time around wasn't that bad, was it?"

"You have no idea," he said to her as he resigned himself to the fact that he'd better learn to like horses or learn to tell her no. He wasn't sure which would be harder.

By the time they reached the pine grove, where they had stopped the time before, Lank was feeling pretty good. His legs were sore, but his back felt okay. He had remembered to lift himself from the saddle when Beau trotted, and it made a big difference. He also found himself loosening up and enjoying the ride more this time than he had the last. He didn't know if it was because he knew what to expect as far as the riding went, or if it was because he now trusted Summer on a level that he hadn't before.

Managing to climb down on his own without feeling like he was going to collapse, Lank felt better than good. As soon as the horses were settled, he went to Summer and took her in his arms.

"We've come a long way since our first ride, haven't we?" he asked.

Smiling, she pulled him toward her and kissed him. While the fire and passion were still there each time they kissed, the urgency was not. Instead, their kisses held more now—trust, honesty, tenderness, and a promise of things to come. There was an easiness there that hadn't been there before. They had moved past sexual desire to a deeper, longer-lasting sense of contentment. While Lank now recognized that feeling of being in love, he stopped just short of saying it out loud. He wasn't sure if either of them was ready to hear the words.

When she pulled back, Summer continued smiling at Lank. Taking his hand, she began to lead him away from the grove.

"I want to show you something," she said, and he willingly let her lead him.

They passed through the trees toward the sound of rushing water that Lank remembered hearing the last time they were there. As they followed a path toward sunlight, the sound of the water intensified. Stepping into a small clearing, Lank came face to face with a rock wall that loomed about thirty feet above them to the top of the mountain. Gushing down from the peak was a waterfall. It was a far cry from the falls of Niagara, but it was fresh and clear and absolutely beautiful.

"This is one of my favorite spots in the world," Summer told him as they stood in front of the fall, holding hands. "Sometimes I ride up here just to think. It's as if the water cleans my soul and clears my mind. I always leave feeling fresh and renewed."

"I can see how that could happen," Lank said, and he wondered what else he would learn about this beautiful, remarkable woman. "Thank you for sharing it with me."

Summer turned and looked at Lank. "Someday, I'd like us to come back here. When I'm ready. I'd like us to…" she blushed and looked away.

Lank took her chin in between his fingers and tilted her face back toward his.

"Don't ever feel embarrassed when you talk to me. You can tell me anything, especially what you're feeling, what your hopes and dreams are, and what you're thinking about me, about us." He wondered if he was ready, if she was ready. He felt that the time was right. "Summer, I love you."

He felt her tense, her hand tightened her grip, and he watched her swallow. A small, slow smile tentatively made its way onto her lips.

"I love you, too, Abe. I wanted to fight it. I wanted to prove that I could survive on my own without you or any man. I had this insane plan to live up here forever, like some crazy mountain lady, making my own way in the world. I knew as soon as you walked into my life that was never going to happen. As much as I tried to convince myself otherwise, something in me knew I could never live without you."

As the sound of the water filled the air around them, love filled their hearts. And despite the ache in his legs and height of the mountain, Lank had never felt so strong, secure, and loved in his life.

After another long kiss and tight embrace, they watched the water cascade down the sheer rock face. Then they turned and walked, hand-in-hand, back to the horses.

On Saturday night, after Mass, everyone gathered at the home of Johnny and Summer's parents. Monica and Steve still lived in the same house, in Lake City, where Johnny and Summer had grown up. Not much seemed to have changed over the past several years since the kids moved out. Their bedrooms were still very much the same as they must have been when they lived at home. Though most of their personal belongings were gone, and a treadmill had been added to one room and a sewing machine and table to the other, both still reflected the tastes of the teens who once occupied them. Johnny's old room was painted green and brown and reminded Lank of

Army camouflage. Summer's was turquoise and lavender, and Lank could picture her sitting at the little desk in front of the window, doing her homework while the moon hung low over the mountain.

As he walked through the family room, Lank stopped to look at every family photo. There were studio portraits of the four of them mixed in with photos of Johnny on a motor bike and in his Army uniform. Summer sat on top of Black, holding a blue ribbon, in one photo, and stood in front of the little white church, wearing a white dress and veil in another. Other family pictures dotted the wall-length bookshelves, and Johnny guessed they were Summer's grandparents and other extended relatives.

"Seeing anything interesting?" she asked, coming up behind him and wrapping her arms around his waist.

"What's this from?" Lank pointed to the photo of Summer in the white dress and veil.

"My First Communion," she said.

"What's that?"

"It's when a child, or it could be an adult who is new to the Church," she added. "Anyway, it's when he or she receives the communion host for the first time."

"Why were you dressed like a bride?"

"I wasn't dressed like a bride. I was dressed like a little girl receiving her First Communion."

Lank examined the photo. "Looks like a bridal veil and wedding dress to me."

Summer shook her head. "When we're baptized, we wear white to symbolize purity and new life in Christ. First Communion allows us to continue that same journey in the Church. The white is to remind us that we are children of God, promised to Him in baptism."

"Interesting," Lank said, nodding. "You were a cute kid," he commented, enjoying the feel of her body against his.

"Is there a backhanded compliment in there somewhere?"

Lank turned around in her arms so that they were facing each other. "You were a cute kid," he repeated, "but you're a stunning, sexy adult."

"Shh," she suppressed a giggle as she squirmed out of his embrace. "My parents are nearby."

Lank laughed, but then he turned serious, frowning as he looked at Summer. "Don't they know? About us, I mean?"

"Of course, they do. I mean, they know there's more to our relationship than the victim and the cop. Mom has been watching *Days of Our Lives* her entire life. This kind of thing happens all the time on that show. She wasn't the least bit surprised." Summer shrugged, a devilish grin on her face, and Lank laughed again.

"Well, then, I guess she knows everything."

Taking his hand, Summer began to lead Lank away.

"Hold on," he said, tugging at her hand. "I've been thinking," he said hesitantly. "I'd like to learn more." He gestured toward the photo. "About that stuff, I mean, First Communion and saints and that prayer you say when you exercise."

Summer laughed, "You mean the Rosary."

"Yeah, that," Lank said. "I'd like to learn more about your beliefs and your Church."

"The best person for you to talk to is my mom. She's been teaching catechism classes for years and leads a Bible study. But if you're not comfortable talking to my mother, you could see Father Glenn. He's very approachable."

Lank thought about the young priest they had just heard at Mass before heading to the house for dinner. Lank enjoyed his sermons, or whatever they were called.

He'd have to think about contacting Father now that the stalker had been caught.

"I may do that," he told Summer with a smile and felt his heart beat a little faster when she beamed at him.

"I'd like that," she said, squeezing his hand.

Summer and Lank went into the kitchen where Lank once again found himself marveling at how comfortable this all felt. For all his mistrust and suspicions about Summer, he was amazed, every day, at the turn their relationship had taken.

"A toast," her father offered at dinner. "To catching the kid who tormented Summer, and to Lank for his work on the case."

"To Lank," everyone said as they clinked glasses.

While Lank appreciated the gesture, a knot formed in the bottom of his stomach. No matter how content he felt each time he was with Summer, he had yet to be able to shake the feeling that they weren't out of the woods yet.

Sunday morning found Lank and Summer back at the top of the mountain, lying on a blanket, as the water flowed from the rock wall to the creek and rushed by on its way to the Lake Fork of the Gunnison River below. Summer had her head on Lank's chest as they told stories about their childhoods and the stark differences in their lives until recent events brought them together.

Lank was no longer sore from riding, and he guessed that, like anything in life, the more you did it, the easier it got.

After a while, Summer's chatter became slow and groggy, and she drifted off into a peaceful sleep. Lank enjoyed the feeling of her head on his chest, her rhythmic breathing, the soft way her hair fell across his shoulder and her leg curled lightly over his thigh. He sighed as he pulled his Orioles cap over his eyes to shield them from the bright sunlight and thought about the direction in which his life was now heading.

He guessed he'd have to invest in a cowboy hat instead of wearing this O's cap all the time, and the thought made him chuckle. If anyone had told him six months ago that he would be lying here planning his future with a woman as wonderful as Summer, on the top of a frigging mountain, with the horse he rode up on standing nearby, he would have laughed and told them they were crazy. If they had added that he would be seriously considering calling Deputy Santoyo and inquiring further about his job offer, he would've thought they were completely off their rocker.

After some time, he felt Summer stir.

"Did I fall asleep?" she asked as she sat up to look around.

"You did," Lank answered as he brushed her hair back with his hand.

"Why didn't you wake me? I didn't mean to do that to you?"

"What? I enjoyed every second of it. If I can't sleep with you, I'd rather have you sleep next to me."

She smirked. "Very funny." But as she looked around, he could tell that she was avoiding his gaze. "I've been thinking," she said. "Maybe it's time I level with you." Her mood had shifted, and instinctively he knew that what she was about to say would not be good.

"I lied," she said quietly, and Lank sat up. Summer, her back to him now, continued to look at the waterfall. "I lied to everyone. Megan and Johnny, my parents, the school, the police, everyone."

Lank's stomach clenched. Was this what he was dreading, the thing that had been bothering him? Were his instincts right all along? What was she saying? He swallowed and tried to squelch the multitude of thoughts and emotions that ran through him as he waited for her to resume.

Taking a deep breath, Summer turned toward him, and he saw the tears trailing down her cheeks. "Mr. Fields never came to my rescue the way that I said he did."

At first, Lank was confused. Who was Mr. Fields? What was she talking about? And then realization began to dawn.

"He did show up, and he did help me. He took me to the hospital, just like I said. But it was too late."

Lank closed his eyes and swallowed back the bile in his throat. He opened his eyes to look at Summer and nodded for her to go on, unable to speak himself.

"I made the doctors and nurses promise not to tell anyone. Of course, according to the law, they had no choice but to call the police, but I told them that my family was not to know. They were upset and disagreed. They tried to convince me to tell my parents at least, but what could they do? According to protocol, they alerted the state police SVU, but I wouldn't budge on my story, so there was nothing they could do about it."

Finally, Lank spoke. "Why?" he asked, his voice full of anguish. "Why hide it? Even from your family? Why not press charges?" Lank had seen a lot in his years on the force. He could easily picture the scene in her office and her emotional and physical state afterward. As a police officer, he was angry that she had lied. As a man, he was sickened at the thought of her being hurt like that. As the man who loved her, he was heartbroken that he hadn't been there for her.

"I couldn't," she said, adding quietly, "It was my fault."

It was all he could do to control his anger. "Your fault? The hell it was? What on earth did you do?"

"I'm a guidance counselor, trained to recognize when someone is about to go over the edge, that he has dangerous intentions. I was supposed to stop things like that from happening, but I didn't. I failed Jeremy, and I failed myself." Her voice was pleading as she looked to him for understanding.

"Are you listening to yourself? Is that what you really think? You're right. You're a trained professional. You should know that this wasn't your fault."

"Don't you see? I should have been able to stop it." She was crying as she tried to get him to understand. "I should have known better. I should have recommended that he see someone, somebody with more experience than I had. I should have alerted the principal, maybe even the police, that I suspected that he was a danger to himself or others. But I didn't. I didn't because I didn't see it. I didn't even recognize the one thing that should have been painfully obvious."

"Summer, no, you're wrong. I've seen this before. Some people are able to fool everyone, even those who should know better. Some people are beyond help." He reached for her, unsure how she would respond, but she let him pull her close to him as she cried.

"But now, how do I love you? How can I? I mean, like that?" She didn't elaborate, but he knew what she meant.

"You let me love you," he said quietly into her glowing hair. "When the time is right, you let me show you how it should be, how it will be. Forever."

Lank held Summer and let her cry until she finally pulled away.

"Do you, do you still feel the same way about me?"

Lank felt like his heart was tearing in two. He shared her pain and anguish.

Taking her face between his hands, he looked into her eyes.

"Summer, I love you. That will never change. Not today, not tomorrow, not ever. No matter what you do or say. I love you, and I will love and protect you for the rest of my life." He leaned in to kiss her, one small kiss, before hesitating and pulling back slightly to look at her. When she didn't pull away, he kissed her again. Then he pulled her to him and held her as tightly as he could for as long as she let him.

When Summer's breathing finally slowed, and he could feel her regain some of her composure, he let go.

"So, what's next?" he gently asked. "Please, tell me how to help you."

"Love me," she whispered. "Help me find my way back to trusting my instincts, to not be afraid, to let me give myself over to you without seeing him." Her lip trembled, and he nodded.

"I will," he promised. "I'll help you do all of those things. Most importantly, I'll help you find a way to forgive yourself."

She collapsed against him, crying once more. Only this time, Lank recognized the cries of relief.

"Are you sure you don't have it?" Lank asked after they had searched the entire house.

"I'm sure. It must have fallen off when we were at the waterfall. I'm going to go back up and look before it gets dark."

"It's just a necklace. I'll buy you a new one," Lank reasoned.

"No, it's more than that, and you know it. I can't lose it."

Lank knew what the necklace meant to her. As much as he hated it, he knew he had to let her go.

"I'll go with you," he decided.

"You're going to get on a horse twice in one day? I don't think so."

"Summer, come on. It's going to be getting dark soon."

"Then let me go. I'll be much faster if I go alone. I'll ride up there and find it before the sun even begins to sink behind the mountain. It's only seven. I have plenty of time."

Reluctantly, Lank agreed, but as he watched her from the front porch, ride out of the corral, he had a sinking feeling in his stomach that this was not a good idea.

CHAPTER NINETEEN

Restless and uneasy, Lank flipped channels on the television set, glancing at the clock on the wall every few minutes. Finding nothing to numb his mind and calm his fears, Lank turned off the TV just as the old hit TV show, *Murder She Wrote* flashed on the screen with Jessica Fletcher accusing someone of being a thief.

Thief.

The word hung in the air before Lank as if the writing on the Jeep was visible in the eerie glow of the summer evening. At the same moment that Lank realized they had never tied Luke to the actual painting of the word, he realized how dark it was getting. The word kept repeating in his mind over and over. Summer had never taken anything from Luke. There was no reason for him to paint it on her Jeep. A thought began forming in his mind but was pushed away by Lank's sudden anxiety that it was too dark.

He looked at the clock again and confirmed that it was just shortly before eight. Why was it suddenly so dark? A sense of déjà vu hit him, and he jumped up from the couch and headed to the glass doors that overlooked the deck and the mountains beyond.

Sure enough, the clouds over the mountains were dark and foreboding. Lightning split the sky in the distance, and the trees bent toward the earth. A sick feeling began to rise from his gut, but the sickness turned to fear and then a frenzied panic as the thing that, days ago, had been gnawing at his mind, was clearer than a Rocky Mountain morning. Summer had never stolen anything from Luke, but had she, in someone else's mind, taken something from an entire family?

His mind flashed to another scene, a black and white one that hung in a living room. As the lightning tore through the black clouds, and the trees bent sideways, Lank saw the exact same scene that was framed and hanging in Monty Begay's family home.

It is from my father's mountain. It was taken many years ago by my grandfather, before there were any houses built on these mountains but long after the government took the land. He had always hoped that the land would be given back to our people.

The photograph had been taken here. Right on this spot, and those were the mountains that Nibaw's grandfather had been looking at. He stood on this land, the land he had always hoped would be returned to his people.

Lank's heart skipped a beat as he grabbed his phone and ran for the door. Pausing only long enough to put on his shoes and grab his baseball cap, he headed for the barn. Suddenly, he remembered who he was and what he did and ran back inside. Reaching into the hall closet, he grabbed the rifle that Summer kept there. Stuffing cartridges into his pocket, he ran outside.

Once in the barn, he hit Johnny's number on his phone, put it on speaker, and threw it on the ground next to Beau's stall.

"Hey, Lank, what's up?"

"It's Monty," Lank yelled as he reached for a saddle.

"What?"

"It's Monty. He's the one after Summer. And he's going to go after her tonight."

"What the hell?" He heard Johnny move the phone from his mouth and call to Megan. "Are you sure?" he asked Lank.

"Hell, no, I'm not sure, but my gut tells me she's in trouble."

"Where is she?" Johnny was beginning to sound frantic.

"She lost her necklace and went back out to find it. She's up on the BLM."

"Lank, there's a squall coming," Johnny yelled.

"No kidding, Johnny!" Lank had the horse saddled and found himself praying that he had done it correctly. "I've got to go."

"Wait," he heard Johnny yell as he grabbed the phone, ended the call, and shoved the device in his pocket. Kicking the horse in the shanks, he held on as Beau, no doubt feeling the urgency, took off out of the barn. Just before they reached the gate, Lank thanked God that Summer, in her haste, had left it open. Lank wasn't sure he would be able to slow the horse down, and there was no way he'd know how to handle the horse if it jumped the fence.

The sound of thunder cracked the air, and a bolt of lightning lit up the sky. The wind almost knocked him off the horse as they headed into the trees. Luckily, Beau felt his urgency and ran into the trees without missing a beat.

☙

Summer reached for the shiny gold necklace just as she heard the twig snap behind her. A chill ran down her back, and she knew. She couldn't explain how she knew, but her body went on full alert, and she wasn't at all surprised to see the boy when she turned around. What did surprise her was who the boy was.

"Monty," she gasped. "What are you...why?" She was at a loss for words and tried to make sense of what she saw. Monty Begay stood at the edge of the trees, aiming a Winchester 30-30 rifle directly at Summer.

"I tried to scare you away," he said. "I tried to warn you, but you wouldn't leave. I didn't want it to come to this, but I'm running out of time. I waited all day for you to be alone, and I have to get home before they know I'm gone, so I need to be quick."

Summer watched him and knew that he was torn. He didn't want to hurt her. But he would. She could feel it.

"Monty, please, put the gun down. Let's talk about this. Why did you want to scare me away?"

"My grandfather is dying. He's dying, and you've taken the only thing that ever mattered to him."

Fear gave way to confusion and conviction as she realized he wanted to talk. He wanted her to know why he had done the things he did. The scene was all too familiar, but this time, she'd get it right. This time, she'd get him to talk rather than act.

"What have I taken, Monty? I'll give it back. Just tell me what it is."

"Don't lie to me," Monty yelled. "I know you're lying. You won't give it back."

The young man was crying now, and Summer tried to figure out what she could do or say to reason with him.

"I don't understand, Monty. Please, help me to understand."

"All my life, my grandfather told me stories about our ancestors, about how they cared for the land. He told me that nobody owns the land. The land owns us. *This* land owns us." He recklessly waved the gun around to show her that he literally meant *this land.*

"Monty, I still don't understand." Her heart raced in her chest, and she became acutely aware of the streaks of lightning on the mountain behind her.

"Our people take care of the land. Your people destroy it. Hundreds of years ago, these mountains were loved and cared for by my people. When my great-great-grandfather was young, he had a dream, a vision, in which a great carving of the Thunderbird was standing on a mountain. A child was playing by the Thunderbird, and my great-great-grandfather knew that the child would be his grandson, my grandfather. He knew that one day, our land would be given back to my family, and that my grandfather would live to see it happen. That spot stood empty for all those generations, and my grandfather knew that it belonged to him, that someday our family would have the land back, and that I would raise my family on that land."

Summer tried to follow his thoughts, but the wind escalated, and she felt the shift in the air, alerting her to the imminent arrival of the storm.

"But then you built on that spot," Monty screamed. "You built your filthy house on the place where my great-great-grandfather stood. He took a picture of the spot he saw in his dream. It took him years to find it. He walked every inch of these mountains, but just before he died, he found the spot. Just as in his dream, the Thunderbird appeared when he stood on that sacred ground. He took a photo of the Thunderbird as it neared." Tears streamed down Monty's face, and he shook the gun as he talked, moving closer and closer to Summer, who stood trapped at the edge of the creek. Thunder shook the ground as her mind raced over the options.

"My grandfather is dying! And all he ever wanted was to live on that sacred ground. But you stole it from him!"

Monty was less than ten feet away, and Summer knew that he was through talking.

"Monty, I didn't know. I didn't know that your grandfather wanted the land. I didn't know he was dying. You should have told me."

Monty laughed, the sound sending chills down Summer's spine.

"You wouldn't have listened. None of you listen. My father has spent his entire life trying to get your people to listen."

"Monty, please," she pleaded. "Give me the gun, and we'll go see your father and grandfather. We can work something out."

"It's too late," Monty told her. "My grandfather was taken to the hospital today. He's going to die without ever living on his land. But if he's going to die without ever being at peace on his land, so are you."

He leveled the gun at her, and took aim. As the gun went off, Summer dove to the ground. Pain ripped through her as she went down, and her world went black.

The sound rang out just before another crack of thunder reverberated through the night. At first, Lank wasn't sure it was a shot, but his gut told him it was. When he made it to the pine grove, he looked around for Black, but he was nowhere to be seen. He rode through the trees until a flash of lightning revealed the horse standing by the creek. Lank could tell Beau was skittish as he pawed at the ground and flared his nostrils. Another flash lit the night, and Lank leaped from his horse and scrambled to the figure that lay at Black's feet.

He rolled her over as the rain began to fall. There was blood on her head and on the rock beside her where she must have hit her head. It was a lot of blood, but she had a pulse, and Lank didn't see any other injuries. He reached for his phone to call for help, but he had no bars. He cursed the wilderness and hastily lifted Summer into his arms. He struggled to lift her onto the horse as the wind pushed at his back, and the rain relentlessly pelted them with such force that it felt as if buckets of marbles were being dumped from the heavens. As he laid her across the horse, Lank felt the golf-ball sized hail that the great Thunderbird hurled at them.

He struggled to tie Black's reins to Beau's saddle as his wet fingers slid on the smooth leather. Once he felt that Summer was secure, he climbed on Beau's back and urged him to move, gently but quickly. He was astounded to find that the horse seemed to understand what he wanted it to do.

When he reached the paddock, Johnny and Megan raced toward them from the barn.

"The police are on the way," Johnny told him as he watched helplessly while Lank and Megan gingerly removed Summer from the horse. "And an ambulance," Johnny's voice cracked. "I asked for one," he swallowed, "just in case."

The sound of thunder, rain, and hail all but drowned out what they were saying to each other, and they screamed to be heard.

"She hit her head," Megan yelled. "There's a lot of blood, but I think it's superficial."

Lank took Summer's hand in his and felt the necklace, still wrapped around her fingers. It was a miracle that it hadn't fallen off on the ride back. Remembering what Summer's grandfather had told her about the treasure on the cross, he closed his eyes and began to pray.

Lank, Johnny and Megan, Steve and Monica, Sheriff McCoy, and Deputy Santoyo gathered in the tiny waiting room at Gunnison General Hospital. Despite the number of people in the group, the room was silent. Megan sat between Lank and Johnny, holding each of their hands.

"She's starting to wake up," the nurse told them when she entered the room. "She's asking for someone named Abe."

Megan released his hand as Lank jumped up and followed the nurse.

When he entered her room, his heart lurched. She was hooked up to several machines, and the steady pumping and swishing played a melody that sounded too much like the one Lank heard when he said goodbye to his own father. Rushing to her side, he took her hand in his and kissed her knuckles. He wiped the hair from her brow and kissed her gently on her forehead.

"Hi, there," she whispered.

"Shh," Lank soothed. "Don't talk."

"I have to," she struggled to get out the words. "It was Monty."

"I know," Lank said.

"How?" She looked confused. "Did you catch him?"

Lank shook his head. "Not yet, but there's an APB out for him, and his father is cooperating. He had no idea. He really thought his son was innocent."

"My land, he—"

"Shh, I know. I figured it out after you left. There's a photograph in their house that was taken from the exact location of your deck. I recognized it when the storm came up."

"It was a squall," Summer said quietly.

"Yes, it was, Summer. Yes, it was."

Early the following morning, Nibaw Begay knocked on the door to Summer's room. He was surprised when the first thing she asked was, "How is Monty, and how is his grandfather?"

"My father left us last night. He has gone to be with the ancestors. He can now be at home on his mountain."

His words brought tears to her eyes. "Do not cry, Summer, for the dream was not meant to be. It was you that the Thunderbird protected last night. You are the right person to care for his mountain."

She sniffed and wiped the tears from her cheeks. "And Monty?"

Nibaw shook his head. "Monty was wrong. I would have stopped him if I had known. I am sorry."

"I know," Summer assured him. "So am I."

Nibaw nodded and turned to leave.

"Mr. Begay," Summer called. "Is Monty okay? Did they find him?"

He turned back to her. "Yes, he is okay. Thank you for your concern."

"Your father, would he like, I mean, would you like," She swallowed and took a deep breath. "I have a lot of beautiful places on my land. I would be honored to have your father at rest on one of them."

Nibaw's eyes misted over, and he nodded. "I think he would like that very much."

"So would I," Summer smiled. "And about Monty, please tell him that I will take care of his people's land."

"I will," the man said.

Lank watched, unnoticed in the hallway, the scene that unfolded in Summer's room. When Nibaw saw him on his way out, Lank nodded. The men didn't speak, but each understood what was unspoken. Summer was now safe.

"Hey," Lank said casually as he went to her side and bent down to give her a kiss.

"Hey, yourself," she answered back. "Did you get some rest?"

"Some," Lank told her. "I had a long meeting with Santoyo."

"Already? It's so early."

"That's the way it goes with this job sometimes."

Summer nodded, acknowledging that she understood and accepted that.

"Monty, where was he?" she asked.

Lank relayed to Summer the events of the past twelve hours. Mongwau Begay was arrested just after midnight. He hid in the woods until the storm passed and then headed home, assuming everyone in the house was either at the hospital or asleep. When he crept into the back of the house, Deputy Santoyo was waiting for him.

Monty confessed to buying the flowers weeks prior to giving them to Summer. He let them die and took them to the school once he found a box they would fit in. They were supposed to spook her into thinking someone meant to harm her, but she didn't show any signs of being scared. He killed the deer and left it on her step as a warning. He purposely broke the bird feeder in another attempt to frighten her off the mountain. He tried to break into the house, planning on leaving a dead marmot, but the security system scared him away. He never intended to harm her. He just wanted to frighten her enough to force her to move back home. He was certain that, once she was too frightened to return to her house, his family could find a way to buy the land.

When he heard about Lank, a big-city detective who had come to help her, he panicked. He knew how to make the snake tube. He'd helped the men, living on the Ute reservation near Mesa Verde, capture snakes when they were nesting too close to a house or barn. His intention was to make Summer realize that she wasn't safe on the mountain, but she had proven him wrong. Feeling he might have a better chance at scaring her if he could get rid of Lank, he took Luke's laptop and researched how to cut brake lines. He was a smart kid, and he knew that he had to find a way to cast blame on someone else. Knowing that Luke had been in trouble before, Monty thought he was the best scapegoat.

"He really intended to kill you?" Summer asked, clasping Lank's hand.

"Maybe, or maybe he just thought I'd leave. As far as he knew, I had no ties here, no reason to stay. Maybe he thought it would frighten me into giving up. Or maybe he really did aim to get me out of the picture for good. I guess it will all come out at some point."

"What about Luke?"

"Cleared. Monty was quick to tell the truth once he learned that you were still alive. Santoyo said it came as a relief to the boy. Once the realization hit him that he might have actually killed you, he was filled with regret. He never intended for it to go that far."

"I guess the thought of losing his grandfather pushed him over the edge."

"I guess," Lank said. "He spilled everything pretty quickly and easily once he was in custody. He said that he knew he had brought dishonor on his family."

They were silent for a few minutes. Summer closed her eyes, and Lank pulled up a chair, thinking she was going back to sleep.

"So, what are you going to do now?" she asked quietly, her eyes still closed.

"Well, for starters, you're looking at the newest Gunnison County Sheriff's Office detective." He smiled as he sat beside her bed, holding her hand.

"Really?" she asked, her eyes flying open. "You're staying?"

"Now that's about the dumbest question I've ever heard."

"I'd hoped you'd stay," Summer said through tears.

"I told you that I would be here to love and protect you, Summer, for the rest of my life. I meant it. Now close your eyes, and get some rest. I need you to get better. That house is too lonely without you in it."

"I know exactly what you mean." Summer smiled as she drifted off to sleep.

EPILOGUE

Lank stood on the sand and watched the sunrise over the ocean.

"It's not the same, is it?" Summer asked as she laid her head on his back and slipped her arms around his waist.

"Not even close," Lank said, taking her arms and pulling her around so that her back leaned against his chest.

"It's pretty, though. Different, but pretty." She looked out across the Atlantic Ocean. A sailboat drifted on the waves several hundred yards out to sea. Seabirds called to each other as they dove to and from the water looking for breakfast.

"Are you happy?" Lank asked.

Turning toward him, Summer smiled. "I've never been happier."

"Last night, I didn't, you weren't—"

"Abraham Lankton, last night was perfect. You were perfect."

He let out a sigh of relief. "Everything you hoped for and imagined in a wedding night?"

The rising sun cast a heavenly glow over her head, and Lank's heart tightened in his chest as he gazed into her eyes, so full of trust and love.

"Everything I hoped for and imagined in my life."

"I love you, Summer. I will always love you."

"I love you, Abe. Now, come back inside to bed. It's lonely without you."

"Lonely is one thing you'll never have to be again," Lank told his wife as he took her hand and led her back inside.

The End

If you enjoyed *Summer's Squall*, please leave a review on Amazon and on Goodreads. Thank you!

Amy

You may follow Amy at:
http://amyschislerauthor.com/
http://facebook.com/amyschislerauthor
https://twitter.com/AmySchislerAuth
https://www.goodreads.com/amyschisler

RESOURCES

Eric D. Zemper, PhD. *Injury Rates in a National Sample of College Football Teams: A 2-Year Prospective Study*. Journal. Eugene, Oregon: International Institute for Sport and Human Performance, 1989. 1 August 2017. <http://www.exra.org/FB89.htm>.

Lake City/Hinsdale County Marketing Committee. *Lake City*. 1 October 2017. 25 October 2017. <http://www.lakecity.com/>.

Native Languages of the Americas. *Legendary Native American Figures: Thunderbird (Thunder-Birds)*. 1 January 2015. 20 July 2017. <http://www.native-languages.org/thunderbird.htm>.

Southern Ute Indian Tribe. *Southern Ute NSN*. 1 January 2017. 20 July 2017. <https://www.southernute-nsn.gov/history/>.

SW Colorado Travel Region. *SW Colorado Travel Map*. 1 January 2017. 25 October 2017. <http://www.swcolotravel.org/page.cfm?pageid=15519>.

ABOUT THE AUTHOR

Amy began writing as a child and never stopped. She wrote articles for magazines and newspapers before writing children's books and adult fiction. A graduate of the University of Maryland with a Masters of Library and Information Science, Amy has resided on the Eastern Shore of Maryland for 23 years. She worked as a librarian for fifteen years and, in 2010, began writing full time.

Schisler's first children's book, *Crabbing With Granddad*, is an autobiographical work about spending a day harvesting the Maryland Blue Crab. Sarah Book Publishing released Schisler's novel, *A Place to Call Home*, in August of 2014. A revised second edition was released in March 2015. *Picture Me, A Mystery* was released in August of 2015 and won a 2016 Illumination Award as one of the top three ebooks of 2015 among Christian writers. Schisler followed up her success with the critically acclaimed, *Whispering Vines*, a 2017 Illumination Award winner as one of the best Christian romance novels of 2016.

Amy is the author of a weekly blog with followers around the world. Her topics range from current events to her daily life with her husband, three daughters, and two dogs.

Follow Amy at:

http://amyschislerauthor.com
https://amyschisler.wordpress.com
http://facebook.com/amyschislerauthor
https://twitter.com/AmySchislerAuth
https://www.goodreads.com/amyschisler

BOOK CLUB DISCUSSION QUESTIONS

1. Lank felt obligated to help his cousin, Megan, because she was by his side during one of the most difficult times in his life. How would you have felt if you were in his shoes?

2. Lank was suspicious of Summer very soon after meeting her. Did you ever suspect that Summer might have been involved, or did you believe her story from the start? Why or why not?

3. Lank was willing to give up his entire life back on the East Coast in order to be with Summer. Have you ever given up all or a part of your life for someone you loved? How did that work out?

4. Summer kept a large secret from her family and friends, being raped by her student. She blamed her inability to maintain a relationship on the mental and emotional scars she carried from the rape. Lank believed that it was the guilt of harboring the incident that was the problem. What do you think?

5. Monty was a confused teenager trying to stand up for his people, but he broke the law in order to do so. Did you feel sorry for Monty? For his tribe? Do you believe he was a dangerous criminal or a troubled young man?

6. The plight of the Native Americans is one that has only recently been brought to light in history classes and in the news. How do you feel about

the way they were and still are treated in our country?

7. If you were in Summer's shoes, how would you handle Monty's case? Would you press charges or try to get help for him? Would you, as Summer did, offer to allow his grandfather to be buried on your property?

8. Megan was a firm believer that all things happen the way God intends them to, and we just have to trust in Him to know what is best. Summer wanted to believe that as well, but she had a hard time accepting it. What are your thoughts about giving your fears, problems, and questions to God and letting Him take the reins?

9. Summer's necklace was very important to her. It tied her to her grandfather and reminded her of her faith. Do you have anything that you wear or hold onto that does this for you?

10. What was your favorite scene in Summer's Squall, and why?